TERMINAL COMBUSTION

ALSO BY JEN CRANE

DESCENDED OF DRAGONS SERIES

Rare Form

Origin Exposed

Betrayal Foretold

Descended of Dragons 3-Book Box Set

SUBTERRANEAN SERIES

Sunscorched

Terminal Combustion

TERMINAL COMBUSTION

SUBTERRANEAN SERIES, BOOK 2

JEN CRANE

CARPE NOCTEM PUBLISHING, LLC

<u>*Dedication*</u>
To Bebe and Gary
for unceasing support.

And to Marianne
for faith and generosity.

Published by Carpe Noctem Publishing LLC
Cover Design by Cary Smith
Terminal Combustion (Subterranean Series, Book 2)
Copyright © 2018 Jen Crane
All rights reserved.
First electronic publication: December 2018
First print publication: December 2018
Digital ISBN: 9780996575690
Print ISBN: 9781950032990

PROLOGUE

Council of Concerned Citizens World Headquarters
Sierra Papagayos Mountain Range
Free and Sovereign State of Nuevo Leon, Mexico
Latitude: 25° North

D r. Hugo Lindgren removed his glasses, let his hands fall from the keyboard, and leaned his head on the chair back. Some days he was so tired of it all. Of calculations and measurements. Of the same stale air circulating inside the facility. Of uniforms and fluorescent lights. Of hard-nosed, rigid superiors and disappointing underlings. And of destruction.

When they'd begun this mission, no one was certain it could actually be accomplished. They thought it could. They were willing to try. The fact was the world itself was at stake, and something had to be done.

Lindgren knew geochemistry like a first language, and the team of scientists, military leaders, and explosives experts at the Council of Concerned Citizens was the best in the world.

Armed with a noble cause—to stop overpopulation and save the world—the CCC had formed an unlikely alliance.

After the latest round of global climate talks failed, a group of environmental hardliners had had enough. They called themselves the Architects of Global Climate Governance, but really they were just a bunch of disgruntled climate scientists and policy wonks set on proving a point.

At first, the AGCG rallied for drastic steps to open the world's eyes to the devastating effects of pollution and over-consumption — a mission similar to that of the CCC.

The biggest environmental polluters were also the most overpopulated. A handful of countries were both destroying the Earth and gobbling up its waning resources.

They AGCG and CCC found a common cause in climate change. They resolved to do something so dramatic everyone would finally understand the apocalyptic future Earth faced if mankind continued down its disastrous path.

Together, the AGCG and CCC formed a bold plan. They would decimate Earth's ice sheets, both in Greenland and Antarctica, and scare the world into action.

Lindgren rolled his eyes as he recalled the final days before the weaklings at AGCG had backed out of the plan. "It's gone too far," they'd said. "This is too drastic a move. The world will never recover."

Oh, they had no idea. The CCC had never planned to stop at destroying the ice sheets. No, that was just the first step.

Decimating the ice sheets was how Lindgren had planned to release massive amounts of methane into the atmosphere, which he had— brilliantly, if he did say so himself— caused to combust. He had been the lead scientist on the effort. He was proud of his work, of the tangible solution to a worldwide problem.

His team had spent years calculating the effects of the plan, of the sunscorches. But the actual results had been beyond their wildest dreams. Besides the millions of people eliminated during the first sunscorch, sea levels had surged, devastating coastal cities across the globe. The entire eastern seaboard of the U.S. had flooded, and Florida had vanished.

Like a warped and bloated water balloon, the rapid rise in sea levels threw the Earth's axis from 23 degrees to over 40. The North Pole angled toward the sun. The southern-half of the world plunged into darkness and cold. Minnesota's climate became Hawaii's and the Northeast portion of the United States suffered frequent hurricanes.

Half the world became tropic, and the other half a tundra.

With ice sheets gone, the heat of the sun was no longer reflected, but absorbed, raising Earth's temperature even more. What few animals survived the scorch suffered mass extinction. Heat stress caused deaths and reduced fertility, and rising temperatures were prime breeding grounds for disease and bacteria. Not that they'd have had anything to eat anyway, Lindgren mused. Malnutrition quickly became rampant as the majority of edible plants' photosynthesis shut down at 113 degrees.

To what was left of the general public on the Surface, these catastrophes were unexpected, unexplained.

But Lindgren knew. His colleagues at the CCC, and the families they'd secreted away knew. Their drastic endeavor had worked. Sunscorches may have decimated the world, but they'd also saved it. Overpopulation was no longer an issue. Overconsumption? Gone.

Lindgren leaned forward to rub dry eyes, and returned the glasses to his nose. Recollections of the past brought him pride, sure, but also questions about the future. Was it time to allow Earth to recover? Had they done enough to guarantee its future?

After so many years spent underground, and considering the minimal amounts of methane his team had found over the last several months to ignite, maybe this should be the last sunscorch.

Perhaps it was time for the terminal combustion.

THE RIGHTEOUS HOLD THEIR TONGUE

Somewhere Beneath
Eastern Texas or Western Arkansas
Latitude: 33° North

Cooper swung a boot over the seat of the old motorcycle, giving the gas tank a pat as he dismounted. She had been his constant companion these long weeks on the road. The one he trusted, the one he could count on. In all their time together, she had never let him down.

He bent to touch his toes before straightening to work some of the soreness from his lower back. His body ached nearly as badly as his heart. Though it was the only home he had ever known, he would never go back to the Settlement. Not after they had ignored his requests and spurned his warnings. Not after he had begged them to intercede and save the lives of thousands. Not after they had stood by and done nothing.

His molars creaked a warning, and he worked his jaw to relax it. All the years he had spent working to defend the

Settlement. The training he had put in as a member of the Sixth Tier, their military's elite combat unit. The trauma of being sent undercover for nearly two years with Sarge's wretched crew. He had sacrificed most of his soul for the Settlement, a down payment for the day he would put a stop to the CCC.

Cooper laughed at the thought of the group's full name. Council of Concerned Citizens. Right. The only thing they were concerned with was ridding the world of poor people.

Cooper, and hundreds just like him, had searched for years for an opportunity just like the one he had found.

And what had the Settlement done when they had the chance to stop them?

What had their fearless leader done?

Nothing.

Nada.

When Cooper had called with information on the hidden entrance to the CCC's headquarters, Gisa Meier hadn't lifted a finger to help the world they had sworn to protect.

Zenon Franks, though, the slobbering imbecile, he had done something. He railed against Cooper's request to send the Sixth Tier to invade the CCC's headquarters. Hell, Franks had even opposed sending out a warning of the looming sunscorch.

And wasn't that always the way of it, Cooper thought. Those who do more harm than good always say a mouthful, while the righteous hold their tongues.

2

BIRTHDAY SURPRISE

Esperanza, Mexico
Free and Sovereign State of Durango
Latitude: 25° North

Nori smiled as she inhaled the warm night air. Life was better at the 25th Parallel. It was farther from the sun and cooler than it had been in Ralston, sure, but those weren't the only differences. Her new home thrummed with life. Music and laughter bounced from the streets up to her family's adobe-style home carved deep into the mountainside. Somewhere nearby rice simmered with dried chilis and onions. That it had all been grown hydroponically didn't diminish the aroma or quieten the growl in Nori's belly.

Though she was content at this new home, there was always something tugging at the back of her mind, as if a piece of her was missing. It had been a month since the last sunscorch. A month since she had sped through the Subterranean to find her parents. A month since she had last seen Sam Cooper.

7

"All right, spill." Kade slid onto the bench beside her and pinched the last crumb of flourless birthday cake from her plate. "What'd you wish for?"

As he popped the morsel into his mouth, Kade's chestnut eyes glinted with mischief. Or maybe it was joy. Since they had arrived at the 25th Parallel, he had transformed into someone else entirely. Someone playful, weightless, and very nearly happy.

"No way," Nori said and pushed against her friend's massive shoulder. "If I tell it won't come true."

"Sure it will. Birthday wishes always come true."

"Oh yeah? Whose wish have you seen come true?"

Kade's head fell to the side and candlelight caught his dark eyes as they slid in Grant's direction. "Mine."

Grant Corredor was the reason for Kade's newfound happiness. Until a month ago, though, he had also been the cause of his anguish. Kade had been a wreck when Nori first met him in a gritty Subterranean fighting syndicate called the Pit. Just days before she arrived, Grant had been presumed dead after jumping into a nearby ravine. No one at the Pit had known the depth of Kade and Grant's relationship, and he'd had to conceal his grief, to internalize it. It had nearly sent him over a cliff, too.

But on Nori's terrace, after her small but wonderful eighteenth birthday party, her friend was well on the road to recovery. Grant noticed Kade's attention, and his face lit.

Nori looked away, giving the two their moment, and caught sight of her mother standing at the edge of the terrace. The hard angles of her mother's face softened as she looked down on the lights of town, releasing some of the tension around her eyes. Since the accident that left her unable to walk, her health had steadily declined. Nori had watched for weeks as the pain and frustrations of being bound to a wheel-chair added years to her mother's face.

Pain and frustration were things Nori knew pretty well. Hypersensitivity to the sun in a sunscorched world meant being bound indoors except for a few blessed hours of darkness each night. Over the past 17 years, severe burns and infections had left her bedridden for weeks at a time.

The new patches of skin and old scars that marred her face had always made people uncomfortable, and she didn't have many friends. Before Kade, she hadn't really had any.

More familiar to Nori were loneliness and hopelessness, and as the old friends found their way back into her soul, her mood took a sharp, dark dive. She folded in on herself, fingers twisting in her lap. She was damaged; she knew that. She was also out of place here at the 25th Parallel, and too frequently out of sorts, though she did *try* to be happy. Her sorrow spiraled, and the fragments of joy she had collected from her birthday party began to wash away in a wave of despondency.

But then she caught sight of her sweet mother, who smiled down as something caught her eye. It was probably the smallest, simplest thing—something of beauty she found amidst the ruin. Her mother had always found joy even in the toughest times. Oh, to be more like her, Nori mused.

"You know what?" Nori shook the darkness from her mind like errant dust. "I think I'll keep this wish to myself."

"Like we don't know what you'd wish for anyway," Grant said, wagging sleek eyebrows as he made his way to the table.

"What?" Nori's father asked. Emerging from the house, he looked first to her, then to Grant. "What would she wish for?"

Nori's murderous glare in Grant's direction would've withered lesser men.

"An eclipse?" Grant bleated desperately.

Closing her eyes on another wish— that they would drop the subject— Nori stood and dusted the ever-present ash from her pants. "Well. Thanks, everyone, for a great birthday. I don't think a girl's ever had better parents… " She looked to her parents, whose faces beamed with adoration, before turning to Kade and Grant. "Or friends."

"Oh, no. Not yet." Kade's slow grin transformed his face. Every bit a powerful pit fighter, he had also been born with a killer bone structure. "Your night's not even close to over. There are three full hours of dark left, and we're gonna burn every last second."

"Oh yeah?" Nori perked. "A movie night?"

Kade and Grant shared a wicked look.

"Wait," she said, glancing between them. "What are you two up to?"

Kade's face still held a challenge as he crowded her space, daring her to disagree. "You, Nori Chisholm, are going to the club."

3

———

RAPTURE

"**B**ut I've never been to a club in my whole life," Nori said. "I don't even know how to dance."

Her protests did nothing to derail Kade and Grant's scheme, and before she knew it, she was mascaraed and lip-glossed and dressed to kill in a flared skirt and too-clingy top. And heels. *Heels.*

"Where are we going, anyway?" Nori slowed to a stop in the middle of the cobbled street and adjusted her push-up bra, which had transformed her own modest breasts into something from anime.

"My God," Grant growled as he threw his head back. "I have never heard someone complain so much about a good time in my entire life."

"A good time?" she argued. "Yeah, a lot of people are gonna have a *good time* when they catch sight of these bad boys." She crossed her arms, which only made the problem worse. "I cannot believe you let him buy this outfit, Kade."

"You look fantastic." Her friend shrugged. "And it's your birthday. Lighten up and have some fun for once in your life."

"Oh, I'm not fun?" Nori looked first to Kade and then Grant. Neither met her gaze. "You think I'm not fun," she said, and it wasn't a question. "Fine." She flipped her hair as she spun toward the door. "I'll *show you* fun."

The "club" was a metal prefab building with a warped and rusted roof and a hand-painted sign promising—or warning against—Rapture. Nori stumbled in the heels a third time, but gritted her teeth and kept walking. Though painfully misguided, Kade and Grant did have good intentions. They loved her, and were just trying to get her out of the house. And they were right— she needed a distraction. No sense sitting home with her parents again. Not tonight. Not on her birthday.

Sure, she was way out of her comfort zone, but that wasn't necessarily a bad thing. The last time she had taken a risk it had paid off big time. She had found the Subterranean, Sam Cooper, and these two exceptional friends. She could suck up her discomfort and smile to make them happy.

Straightening her back, then ducking again to hide her chest, Nori entered the rusty door to Rapture.

It hit her all at once. Deep, heavy bass gripped her around the middle, invading her body as if wrapping around her cellular makeup. Nori felt the beat in her feet, in her brain, in her blood. It was entrancing, and her shoulders moved in a shimmy that spread to her hips.

"Would you look at that." Grant's cat-like grin was smug. "She *can* dance."

"I can't help but move," Nori said as her mouth stretched into a wide smile. She yelled over the music, which was rhythmic and pulsing and infused with a smooth Latin voice. "What is this?"

"*Reggaeton*," Grant answered, his lip curling dramatically. In his growled accent, it came out *reh-geh-TONE*.

Nori shrugged and laughed as her body twisted. "I literally cannot keep still."

"*Eso, cariño*," Grant said, "*es el punto completo*."

She squealed when he grabbed her hand and led her to the dance floor. But she didn't resist. "Wait," she said with another laugh. "What did you say?"

"I said 'that's the whole point!'"

Grant was an exceptional dancer. It was true she didn't have a lot of experience, but his hips, as if on ball joints, swiveled in ways Nori's simply wouldn't. But that didn't stop her from trying.

Perhaps Grant's best talent was keeping Nori vertical as he spun her across the dance floor in the ridiculously spiky heels. She laughed and held on for dear life, waving to Kade each time they neared him.

Panting and parched after Grant's latest lesson on the finer points of salsa dancing, Nori dove for the drink Kade held out to her.

Her eyes shot wide as lime and liquor hit her tongue. "That is *not* water."

Kade shook his head. "No it is not, and you're welcome." He took a sip from his own salted glass and shrugged. "When in Rome — er — Mexico..."

"It *is* my birthday," Nori said proudly. She could not remember the last time she had so much fun. Maybe she never had. The music, the dancing, the clothes, the friends. A special night. Perfect.

She hoarded chunks of what she was feeling deep in her soul, which was how she got through the hard times. She saved happy memories for the long, torturous hours she knew were only a sun ray away.

Shaking her head—and the dark thoughts—away, something behind Kade caught Nori's eye.

Her smile melted. She managed a strangled, "It can't be" before her heart hit the floor.

Kade stepped protectively in front of her. "What's wrong?" he said. "What is it?"

Grant's hips skidded to a stop when he followed her gaze. "Is that..."

Nodding, Nori pushed her drink back in Kade's direction and stumbled toward the door.

Impossible. Impossible. Her mind supplied the word over and over.

And yet there he was.

The rest of the club fell away, the music silenced and the people gone in a blink. Every foot felt like a mile, and he was still thirty feet away. Would she ever reach him?

His eyes never left hers as she approached him, and her footsteps never faltered. Even in the vexing heels.

His hair was longer, she noticed, and dark curls turned up around his ears. He wore new clothes, though they were similar to the last. Jeans, a leather riding jacket, and boots were his uniform. She imagined him in nothing else, and she had imagined him a lot in the last month.

"*Ohmygod.*" Nori didn't hear the words over the music, but she could read Cooper's lips. His eyes flicked from the top of her head down to her peek-a-boo shoes and back again.

But when he met her gaze, weeks of pent-up uncertainty and longing hit Nori in a rush. Her heart was too big for her body, and it slammed against her ribs to escape. She had thought of him so many times since they'd parted that thinking of him, imagining what he was doing and wondering if he missed her, too, had become not just an obsession but a necessity. The alternative—admitting even for a moment that he might not have made it— wasn't an option. Not if she valued her sanity.

As she neared him, Nori imagined diving into Cooper's arms, holding on, and never letting go.

Reality was much different. Her mouth fell open and her face was hot. She could not move her arms or legs. Her ears worked, though, and suddenly she couldn't think past the music.

A weak "hey," was all she could manage.

Cooper's green-gold eyes had always been her favorite thing about his face. Clever and guarded, they were also kind. And sometimes sad. His every emotion could be found in them if one knew where to look, and Nori did. At that moment, Sam Cooper's eyes held relief and pleasure, and…interest.

Even submerged in rhythmic tones and thick bass, the silence between them stretched uncomfortably.

"So, you're not dead," Nori finally said.

Cooper shook his head, his mouth twisting to one side.

"That's good."

He nodded, eyes a little glazed.

"Cooper?" she asked.

He lifted his head, just once, a silent *what's up*.

"This conversation is a little one-sided. Can you speak?"

A slow smile pulled at his lips, and after a blink his eyes held such intensity Nori's breath caught in her throat.

"Not at the moment," he said. "But I can dance."

4

MIA

Nori closed her eyes, absorbing the singularly perfect moment of bliss as she and Cooper moved together on the dance floor. Sure, it was great to be reunited with her parents and to have Kade and Grant nearby. All things considered, her life was fine. She was fine.

But sometimes, okay, a lot of times, she hungered for a life of her own. A real life. Not this hiding in the basement and creeping around until the sun went down. She longed for the excitement and purpose she had found in the Subterranean with Cooper.

When his arm tightened across her back, pulling her closer, Nori didn't resist. He smelled just like she remembered, all leather and traces of the sun. Elemental somehow. She should have known he would be a good dancer. He moved like he did everything else, with confidence, and to his own intrinsic beat.

When Nori finally opened her eyes, the way Cooper looked down at her stole her breath. She flashed hot, and it wasn't the packed dance floor.

Being near Cooper again was the one thing she hoped for all those nights spent wondering if he was alive or dead. The nights spent alone. Memories of her time with Cooper were her most prized possessions. She replayed them over and over any time she thought of him, which was more often than she liked to admit. His warmth, the closeness, the thrill of clinging to him as they raced together through the Subterranean. The look he gave her when he said goodbye. *That kiss.*

And maybe those revered memories were why it stung so much. He had been gone for a month without sending even a word he was all right.

"Where have you been?" she demanded.

Cooper shook his head, frowning at her outburst. "What?"

"I've been worried sick." Nori put a hand over the heart that hammered against her chest and pulled away from him. "We've all been worried. I'm… God, Cooper." She covered her face, and her cheeks were damp beneath her fingers. "I'm glad you're here. I really am. But I can't just stand here dancing and smelling you like nothing happened."

"Smelling me? What are you talking about?"

Nori scoured her brain for a coherent thought. "Can we go outside? It's so loud in here I can't think."

Cooper nodded and glanced at his wristwatch, its brass face glinting in the overhead lights. "We've got maybe 35 minutes until the sun rises."

Breathing was easier for Nori outside, where there wasn't a fight for the same oxygen. Or maybe it was that the heat of Cooper's hands no longer burned through the fabric of her top. Balancing on one leg, she removed the heels and sighed when she finally stood on bare feet.

Cooper's low laugh was a sound she had dreamed about for a solid month. "Better?" he asked.

"Oh, God yeah." She fanned her face with her free hand. "What was I thinking with this outfit?" She looked down as she said it, and promptly pulled up the neck of her top. "Well, *I* wasn't thinking. Grant dressed me."

"I always knew I liked that guy." Cooper's words were mumbled, but his meaning was clear enough.

Nori didn't respond beyond clearing her throat. "Anyway, what I was trying to say before was… what happened to you? When the last scorch hit, we thought you must be dead, that you'd been caught or killed and didn't get word to your people to stop it."

Cooper nodded, his mouth tight. "I can see how you'd think that. No," he said. "I made the call. I have a friend —outside your old hometown of Ralston, actually—who has a sat-phone."

"'Course you do."

"I called the Settlement. When she denied my request I tried to convince her to send troops, to issue a warning. To do *something*." He shook his head. "But she stalled so long someone else got the warning out before she did."

"*She* who?" Nori asked.

"Gisa Meier, the Settlement leader."

"But," Nori crossed her arms, shoes dangling from one hand, "why did you have to convince her at all? Why would she not want to warn people? I mean, even if she doubted your intel, the worst that could happen is a false alarm." Nori shook her head. "I don't understand. All those people in danger and they did nothing?"

Cooper bowed his head, a thumb and finger to his temples. "She refused to show the Settlement's hand," he said. "She wouldn't risk revealing to the CCC we'd located its headquarters." When he looked up, his eyes were both pained and furious. "She gambled she wouldn't have to do anything. She hoped the Climate Research Center would detect the scorch and issue a warning on its own."

Nori balked, a spike of anger shooting up her spine. "People's lives are a hell of a thing to gamble with, don't you think? How ignorant and inhumane," she said. "What kind of leader makes that decision? This Gisa Meier better hope I never run into her." Nori's stomach turned at the thought of what would've happened if Climate Research hadn't issued a warning at all. As it was, thousands had died between the short hours of the warning and the scorch. "Word could've gotten out." Nori was on the verge of tears. "She could have saved so many lives."

"I know," Cooper said.

It wasn't what she wanted to hear. She forced herself to swallow, to breathe. "I thought you said the Settlement had been working to protect people, to take down the CCC," she said. "If this place is as organized as you say, why not send someone into that mountain headquarters to stop the scorch? Why not just blow the whole thing up?"

"They *have* been working," Cooper said and paced in front of the nightclub's entrance. "It *is* organized." He ran hands into his hair. "It was that dinosaur, Franks."

Nori lifted her palms in confusion, and Cooper slowed.

"Zenon Franks is second-in-command and holds a lot of sway over my— " Cooper closed his eyes, "— over Gisa. He should've retired— or been kicked out— years ago. He has his own agenda, and she doesn't see it. She never has. Franks and I have never been on good terms, and he belittles and disputes every piece of intel I submit."

"But all those people..." Some of Nori's anger receded and was replaced by horror. "I mean, no one really believed us here at the 25th when we tried to warn them, but we kept trying. We did what we could and got word out to the amateur radio community and it spread like crazy. I just…" Nori tossed her shoes to the ground and smoothed back her hair. She left her hands at her temples and turned to Cooper. "Help me understand, Cooper. Why wouldn't they try to stop the scorch or warn people if they could?"

He leaned against the metal building and let out a long breath, eyes on his dust-covered boots. "They weren't ready." He raised his gaze to hers only for a moment. "Or so they said. All these years, all the training and preparing, and when I find something they can move on, something concrete, they cowered in the safety of their own bunker."

Cooper's shoulders pressed toward the ground and his head hung between them. Nori had never seen him so defeated.

"So, what now?" She stepped forward, but he didn't look up.

"I don't know," he said. "I was so angry I couldn't go back to Chicago, to the Settlement. For a while I planned to take on that mountain myself."

Nori groaned. "I'm glad you abandoned that idea."

"I haven't spent all this time watching and waiting and selling my own soul just to throw it away," he said and the muscles of his jaws flexed. "But I wanted to."

Nori rubbed her chest, stress squeezing the breath from her.

"You asked where I've been," Cooper said. "I spent some time in Trogtown and a couple other places to see what I could learn about Sarge. I needed to see if he reported me to his superiors before pursuing us into Yahweh territory.

Someone is looking for me and knows my name. If Sarge didn't hire Stealth, then who?"

Nori took another step toward him. She was close enough he could touch her if he would just lift his hand. "And?"

"No one knew anything as best I can tell," he said. "No one really cared."

"What about whoever hired Sarge— and you? Will they notice he's gone? That you're gone?"

"Yeah, but it's the nature of the business," he said. "They choose people like Sarge and Jenks..." Cooper's eyes darkened and Nori wondered what he wasn't saying aloud, "who are vicious and vile. But expendable."

He was usually so strong, so determined. Sovereign. Something in Cooper was broken, and Nori's compulsion to fix it was nearly overwhelming. Silence stretched between them, and every cell in her body pulsed to hold him, to comfort him. But they weren't there yet.

"I hate to interrupt..." Kade's voice preceded the clang of the metal door shutting behind him and Grant. "But we'd better head back. Sun'll rise soon."

Despite the tension, Cooper's face lit when he saw them, and he hugged Kade outright.

Kade patted Cooper roughly on the back. "Glad to see you, too, buddy," he said. "But we've got to get Nori home. You staying in town?"

"I hadn't thought that far ahead," Cooper admitted.

"With us." Nori's tone was firm. Her parents would be okay with it. Probably. "You're staying with us."

5
———————

TO KEEP HER

Cooper had done a lot of thinking over the last few weeks. Probably too much. But, then, that's what he did. He researched, he planned, he prepared. Life was in the details, and he was a details man.

Drying his hair with a clean towel, he breathed in both detergent and the smell found only in sun-dried laundry. The second shower had been indulgent, but who knew when he would have the chance again.

Nori's house, and her little piece of the town, was great. He certainly saw the draw of the 25th Parallel. Well, he could see the draw for people used to living on the Surface. It was still creepy for someone like him, someone who'd spent his whole life underground. Life on the Surface was too exposed; attacks could come from any direction. There were fewer risks to be calculated in the Subterranean, and there was no question he preferred it.

He dusted a gray fleck from the towel, probably a piece of ash that found its way on board while the towel hung outside to dry. Ash made him think of sunscorches, which the people

22

on the Surface could plan for, sure. But scorches destroyed anything not made of metal or stone. How did these people find the strength to rebuild, to replant again and again?

He could hear them all upstairs, and when Nori's laughter drifted into the room, he smiled. She was happy here. And her parents were ecstatic to have her home, that was easy to see.

Before he had laid eyes on her, he had thought just seeing Nori again would be enough. He had thought to swoop in, make sure she was safe and happy, and move on.

He was starting over, after all. He was on the hunt for new allies, new resources. Hell, he needed a whole new plan since he couldn't count on the Settlement. It would take time, but he still had friends out there. He hadn't spent years undercover laying this groundwork for nothing.

The problem was, since the moment he saw Nori in that nightclub, every plan he made had Nori in it. Which was completely irrational. The Subterranean was too dangerous. She would slow him down, and she was another mouth to feed. Pee stops took twice as long when she was there.

And besides, even if he wanted her to go, there was no way she would leave this place, leave her parents, leave a shower and real bed to go back on the road with him.

Even if she *did* want to, she might not after he told her. God, she was going to be so pissed when he told her about the others. And he would tell her. Soon. He hadn't meant to keep it from her so long. He grimaced as he slipped his arms into his shirt. Okay, that wasn't true. He had meant to—at first. Giving her more motivation to run from Hank and the Pit would've been dangerous and stupid. And after she had left the Pit, well, he had never been able to find the right time. He shook his head as he pushed a foot into a boot. Oh, she was going to be so pissed when he told her.

Cooper wadded the towel in his hands and threw it into a corner. Who was he kidding? Despite dozens of reasons Nori shouldn't, and might choose not to go, he still wanted her. And not just because he had seen her in that tiny top and skirt, either. He had wanted her to ride tandem with him— forever if she wanted to— before he knew her body was as lovely and feminine as her face.

The girl had no idea how gorgeous she was. Her habits were formed from a lifetime of hiding scars. She probably didn't even realize how much she hid behind her hair or how often she looked to the ground. She avoided eye contact with everyone except her parents and Kade.

And him. He loved the way she looked at him. Intensely, deeply, like she could read his mind. There were times he thought maybe she could, but she would have run for the hills long ago if that were true. He should not want her this much. Not just to have her, but to keep her.

6

COME WITH ME

The yellow glow of candlelight flickered across Nori's mother's face, illuminating each new line. Had the lines been etched from pain, or stress? Probably a combination of the two.

"You wanna take a walk?" Cooper asked, his smooth voice cutting through Nori's thoughts.

It had been a great couple of days. Her parents had loved Cooper. Of course they had. He had been charming and respectful, laughing indulgently at her father's jokes and lovingly tending to her mother. Seeing Cooper with her parents had changed things. Shifted the two of them closer somehow.

"Sure," Nori answered. "Let's get out of here."

The night wind blew hair across her face and she snuck a look at him while twisting the bulk of it to one side. Away from the house, from everyone else, Cooper seemed more uneasy than ever. He had always let his guard down when they were alone. It was practically the only time he let the real

Cooper out. This nervousness was odd. But then, she could hardly keep dry palms around him, either.

"So, do you like living here?" he asked, shoving his hands into jean pockets, but quickly pulling them out again and crossing his arms.

"Living at the 25th, you mean, or back at home with my parents?"

He shrugged. "Both."

"The temperature's milder here," Nori replied. "There's more dark time, so I can be outside longer." She peeked at him as they walked. He nodded, but his mind was obviously elsewhere. "But, even so… "

Cooper turned, his fingers brushing hers. "What?" he asked.

"It's just… I'm stuck in the house a lot," she said. "With my parents." She shook her head, worried he would get the wrong idea. "I love them, I do. And my mom needs me right now. But after being on my own— well, with you, for so long — I feel smothered. Like there was more air underground, you know?"

Cooper's eyes closed on a long exhale. If Nori didn't know better, she would have thought him relieved.

"You've got Kade and Grant here, though," he said. "And you go out. You have a life."

"That was just for my birthday." She lifted one shoulder. "We spend most days at home. You being here has been the most excitement we've had in a month." Embarrassment heated her face. "I've liked having you here."

Cooper stepped so close his breath moved her hair. "I've liked being here," he said, gaze darting from her eyes to her mouth and back again.

His presence was so intense she backed away. "Grant's a

huge help with my mom," she said, "but he and Kade are pretty tight. They keep to themselves a lot." Nori straightened. "Anyway, it's fine. I'm safe. I have friends." She smiled up at Cooper. "What about you? What's next for you?"

"That's what I wanted to talk to you about," he said. "I came to see you, to tell you I'm all right." He kicked a loose stone. "But I can't stay. I'm leaving tomorrow."

Nori's heart abandoned its home in her chest and free-fell down the side of the mountain. "So soon?" she whispered.

"I've got a lot to do," he said. "If the Settlement won't do anything, I'll have to."

"What can you do?" she asked. "Will you go back and try to change their minds?"

His mouth twisted. "Not likely."

In the absence of words, Nori watched Cooper's eyes, searching for the emotions she had learned to read. They were there, though only flickers. Sadness and determination and fear.

"Where will you go, then," she asked, panic creeping into her voice. "What will you do?"

"There are other groups out there. Like the Settlement, but smaller. I'll have to start over, but hopefully someone will see the value in what I know. What I've done." Cooper's knuckles flexed as he spun the silver bracelet at his wrist. "Maybe it'll make a difference."

"Sure." Nori nodded. "Saving the world is important."

Leaving was the right thing for him to do. Wishing he would stay with her was selfish and unrealistic, she knew, but that did not make her wish it any less. And it did not diminish the pang she felt at knowing she would lose him again.

"Nori?"

"Hmm?" She looked up and found Cooper's gaze on hers, hard, like an attempt at telepathy.

"Come with me." The plea was desperate and pained, and Nori's errant heart found its way back up the mountainside and into her chest, where it pulsed and pumped to near-bursting.

I want this, Nori thought. I deserve this. She had not been truly happy, truly free, since she surfaced at the 25th Parallel. While the thought of going back underground might make someone else cringe, racing through the gritty Subterranean on the back of Sam Cooper's motorcycle was the best idea she had ever heard.

Yes, she thought, her cheeks aching from the stress of her wide grin. My God, yes.

Her dad would be a tough sell, but he had always been sensible and trusting. She had proved herself so many times, surely he knew she could handle this, too. It was he, after all, who had supported her going it alone with Barker that first time outside Ralston.

Her mother, though. That was a different story. She was over-protective — yeah, okay, in a completely normal maternal way. A nervous laugh escaped as Nori imagined the shocked and horrified look on her mother's face when she revealed the plan to go with Cooper.

But sensibility caught up to desire with a force, and Nori closed her eyes. A wave of regret and frustration washed over her, provoking tears, but she blinked them back. It was a nice thought. It had been wonderful to dream for a little while. But Nori couldn't leave her mother, whose health was too fragile by far. Every day she looked a little less substantial, as if the accident that took the use of her legs wasn't content until it took her last breath, too. Caring for her mother took more work than her dad could do alone. And anyway, Nori could never abandon her. Not when she had so little time left.

Cooper's gaze was warm on her face as she mentally ran the pros and cons— and the gamut of emotions. When she finally looked up at him, opening her mouth to turn him down, he stopped her.

"Wait," he said.

He stepped so close only clothes separated their bodies. His green-gold eyes shot back and forth between hers, as if he knew her answer, but might find a different one if he searched hard enough. Gone was the cool and confident Cooper she knew, and in his place was someone younger, someone vulnerable, someone nearly desperate. The look on his face said he wanted her to go with him as much as she wanted to leave.

"You don't have to answer right now," Cooper said in a rush. "Just think about it. Take the night and think about it."

Nori nodded against his chest, though she had the answer already. It wouldn't change. If the choice was between Cooper and her mother, there was really no decision. She swiped at her eyes with the back of her hand.

"Let's head back," he said, twisting his fingers into hers. His hand was warm and rough and right, and during the walk back to her house he squeezed so tightly at times she had to flex to loosen his grip.

"Nori?" Cooper asked once they were home. He looked at the old house's front door, at the blistered and disfigured roofline, at the cracked red clay and old stones at their feet— anywhere but at her.

"Yes?"

"Can I kiss you again?"

Stockpiled nerves exploded, and Nori's heart rate rose so

fast she was light-headed. Speech had apparently abandoned her, too, so she settled for nodding.

Cooper wasted no time in running a hand into her hair, pulling her gently toward him as he bent. As he neared, Nori watched his face, savoring every millisecond despite her raging anxiety. She absorbed a dozen tiny things in the moment before their lips touched— lashes so thick they fought for space, the smooth skin of his cheeks just above his short beard, the way his green-gold eyes stared straight into her soul.

The kiss was light, his lips gentle, almost unsure.

After a month spent wondering if Sam Cooper was even alive, Nori *was* sure. She pressed her mouth to his, seeking reassurance that he was real, accepting that fate had offered her this small happiness after a lifetime of thinking romance wasn't in the cards for her. She kissed him like she would never see him again. Because it was probably the truth.

Cooper pulled back at some point, his gaze drunk. "Well." He brushed his lips across hers one last time and nodded "Good night."

"Night." Nori smiled and closed the door between them.

Only later did she remember he was staying in the house, too.

"Nori?"

At Kade's call, Nori wiped her eyes and sniffed back any remaining tears. "I— " She cleared her throat. "In here."

Kade's body filled the door to her basement bedroom, one of three in the house with no windows. It's why they'd chosen the place. There was a den, a kitchen, and a bathroom, too—

all built into the side of the mountain. Their 25th Parallel home was perfectly safe from both sunscorches and the ever-increasing hours of sunlight, even for someone as deathly averse to it as Nori. She could live there with her parents for the rest of her days worry-free.

So why did she wish so desperately to abandon it? Why did the thought of watching Cooper leave without her rip her heart to shreds?

"Suns coming back up," Kade said and sat beside her. "Thought I'd find you in here."

She forced a smile. "What's up?"

"That's what I came to ask you. Everyone's in the den. Your mom handed Cooper his ass in a game of cribbage. He keeps looking to me for help, but it's no secret I'm scared of her, too."

Nori's smiled again. This time it was real.

"I finally saw through Cooper's act, though," Kade said. "He's really looking for you. Why are you holed up in here?" Kade held up a hand before she could speak. "And I know you've been crying, so don't even try to deny it."

"Oh, Kade," Nori hid her face in her hands before the tears and the story both flowed.

7

———————————

GRANT'S OFFER

Nori blinked, foggy, and confused. Something had woken her, but it wasn't the alarm. She lifted her head to see the clock, and time stopped. So did her heart. Someone stood motionless inside her bedroom door.

Finally, her brain made sense of her eyes' groggy assessment and her heart kicked back into gear. "What's wrong?" She shot up in bed and moved to stand.

"Nothing. It's okay." Grant raised his hands, probably to reassure her, but one held a flashlight which shined directly into her eyes. "Oh. Sorry," he said and positioned it downward.

Nori blinked through the white spots swimming in her vision. "Is everyone okay?" she asked. "Where's Mom?"

"She's fine," Grant said. "Everything's fine."

"What are you doing here, then?" Nori groaned and covered her eyes. "God, my head hurts."

"All that crying, I imagine."

Her head snapped up at that. "Kade told you?"

"Yeah." Grant hadn't moved, except to put a hand on the doorframe.

Nori patted the bed for him to sit and smoothed her covers, gearing up for whatever conversation he was so obviously ready to have. "What's on your mind?" she asked.

Gently sitting at the end of the bed, Grant aimed the flashlight away from them, which sent its luminary beam directly into her open closet. "I had an idea," he said.

"If this is about my clothes again, Grant, I swear to God."

He snorted a laugh. "It's not about your clothes. Though I am happy to offer my assistance at any time. Lord knows you need it."

"Can you please get to the point before my head explodes?"

"Fine," he said on a sigh. "Keep your olive khakis and work boots. Very coal miner chic."

"Grant." Grounding out his name did not improve the pounding of her head.

He shrugged playfully, but then pressed his hands between his knees. His face had grown serious. "I came to tell you I have a solution to your dilemma," he said. "You go with Cooper. I'll look after Ana. I'll care for her like she's mine."

Nori started to speak. Stopped. Tried again. After her emotional deluge the night before, she thought there were no more tears to be cried. She was wrong. A single tear slid down her face, past her lips, where her voice came out as a whisper. "Why would you do that?"

Grant fidgeted, visibly uncomfortable with her emotional response. He patted her leg awkwardly and looked away. "I already love her like she's my own. She and your dad took me and Kade in without question, when all either of us had ever known was rejection." He cleared his throat. "I can't tell you how meaningful something like that is. To be loved, accepted." Grant sniffed and shook his head. "Anyway." He cleared his throat. "You know my history as a medic, and I've got her schedule and meds down already."

"Oh, Grant." Nori found his hand and squeezed it. "It's too much." She squeezed again. "But thank you. Truly. It means so much."

Grant's eyes went comically wide. "Quit crying or your head'll never stop throbbing."

Nori laughed and shooed his concern away, but he wasn't finished.

"I mean it," he said. "Stop it right now. And you *can* accept my offer. You have to." Grant met her gaze, serious again. "Everyone's entitled to happiness, Nori. Everyone's entitled to choose how to live their life. If motorcycles and grunge are your thing, well, more power to ya. I'll stay here with your parents and the good air."

"You really would," Nori said. "You'd care for her in my place so I could go?"

"I'd do that and more, and you know it."

"I do know." She shook her head in wonder at the quirky, generous man who'd made her best friend so happy. "I promise to think about it."

Grant stood from the bed, shining the flashlight inside her closet again and frowning. "Don't blame me if half this stuff is mysteriously left outside during the next scorch."

"There's nothing wrong with my clothes," Nori yelled, and he chuckled all the way down the hall.

8

______

THE TALK

Sleep was impossible after Grant's early-morning visit. Nori's mind raced like Sarge was on its tail. She was desperate to go back to the Subterranean with Cooper, to have an adventure, to chase a dream. After years spent hiding from the sun, sheltered and secluded and thinking love would never be an option for her, she had finally found a way to be normal. And someone to be normal with. What if this was her only shot at a life of her own?

More than anything, though, she was desperate to pursue what might be her only way of making a real difference in the world.

Nori kicked at the covers and blew out an exasperated breath. Maybe Grant really could take care of her mother. He and Kade had made a home at the 25th Parallel. And as much as Nori loved her mother, Grant actually was better at caring for her. Besides his medical background, he found real joy in helping people. His offer had been sincere. She had seen first-hand his commitment and love for a month now.

And he was right. Everyone deserved a shot at happiness. This was hers.

After another round of tossing and turning, a failed attempt to chase down sleep, Nori threw off the offending covers and got out of bed, determined to be selfish for once in her life.

THE KITCHEN WAS ALREADY OCCUPIED. Her mother sat in an old armchair they'd hauled near the table, and her father held a percolator in one hand and a ceramic cup in the other.

"Coffee?" he asked.

"You know I don't drink that stuff, Dad."

"Aw, come on," he said. "It'll put hair on your butt."

Nori laughed as she scoured the pantry for breakfast. "'Chest,' Dad. The saying is 'it'll put hair on your chest.'"

"Nonsense." His top lip curled. "No girl wants hair on her chest."

Nori laughed again and watched her father's eyes dance. He was so happy to have her home. She knew because he had told her a thousand times. Her heart nose-dived to her stomach at the thought of what she was about to do.

"I love you, girl," her father said. "Hairy butt or no."

"I love you, too, Dad-o."

"Hey, now." Her mother's voice was soft but clear. Nori turned from the pantry and found her looking better than she had in days. "Am I invisible over here or what?"

Nori kissed her mother's hair with a too-loud *mwah*, and passed her a cup of coffee.

"What's on the agenda today, Ana?" Her father asked, raising his eyebrows as he lifted the cup to his lips.

"Oh, I thought the three of us could make a little breakfast for our troops," she answered. "Then later I might finally let someone win at cards."

"You *are* feeling good today," he said.

"I'm on the mend," she said. "You just wait."

Nori dared to hope. The conditions for her proposal couldn't be better. The morning's banter proved both her parents were feeling chipper. But the words still didn't come easy. Scratching an imaginary itch on her nose, Nori straightened and steeled her nerves.

"Hey, ah, guys?" When her parents' gazes swung in her direction she cleared her throat and nervously touched her nose again. "I've been thinking."

"They told us this would happen if we let her read," her father said, shaking his head in mock disappointment.

Nori's smile was tight. Spit it out, she told herself. Just power through. She licked dry lips and took a breath, her gaze nailed to the floor. "Cooper asked me to go with him," she said in a rush. "Back to the Subterranean." She didn't dare look up yet. "And… I want to go."

"Not a chance in hell." Her father's reaction was both immediate and adamant. It wasn't the words themselves, but the calm way they oozed from his mouth that frightened her. No discussion, no argument. Just… no.

Nori dared a peek at her mother, whose mouth hung open. The lively movement of her hands and head normally made up for the stasis of her legs, but after Nori's announcement, she stared straight ahead, completely still.

She's in shock. Guilt sent waves of nausea through Nori's middle. Saliva pooled at the back of her throat and she closed her eyes, working to get a grip. She would not let guilt derail the discussion. She couldn't. Be selfish, Nori. She gritted her teeth and scolded herself. You've got to be ruthless and selfish.

She stepped toward her father, whose eyes were steeled, determined. "Dad, this is something I have to do—"

"Nonsense." He cut her off. "You don't have to do anything except stay here in the safety of our home."

"I *want* to do this," Nori argued.

He opened his mouth, but it was her mother's words that came next. "You can't possibly want to go back underground into all that darkness and filth," she said. "Into the danger and violence and unknown."

Nori's shoulders crept toward her ears in an apologetic shrug. "But I do. And that's not how I see it. I feel safe there. Free. This is the right path for me, Mom. I know it."

"You don't know anything yet," her father said. "You're just seventeen years old." The condescension in his words stung, but also made her angry. She used it to steel herself for the fight ahead.

"I'm eighteen now, actually."

He rolled his eyes, but Nori forged ahead. "Did you really expect me to stay here with you forever?" she asked. "Running from the sun and hiding in the basement for the rest of my life?"

Neither of her parents spoke. It was obvious that was exactly what they'd thought.

"Can't you see that's no kind of life at all?" Nori pleaded.

"But you'd *be* alive," her father argued.

"No." Nori's voice was a whisper. "I wouldn't. Not really."

Her father ran a hand over the top of his head. "This house… this place. We made this life for us— all of us. I can't protect you if you're not here," he said.

Nori moved closer to him and clasped his arm with

shaking fingers. "That's what I'm asking for, Dad. I'm asking you to let me go."

"Don't you want to be here? Don't you want to be with us?" Her mother's frail voice broke on the last word, breaking Nori's heart, too.

Blinking back the tears that stung her weary eyelids, Nori rushed to her mother and sank to her knees. "Of course I do. You know I do."

"Please, Nori." Her mother's body trembled with deep sobs. "I need you. I need you to be here."

Nori's resolve shattered, and the slivers of it fell to the floor, bloodying her knees. "All right." Nori smoothed her mother's hair over and over. "It's all right. I'll stay."

9

———

NO-GO

Cooper was tuning the short wave radio when he heard Nori enter the room.

"I'm so sorry," she whispered. He didn't turn. Couldn't turn. Not until he knew her answer.

"I can't leave her," she said. "It comes down to that."

He nodded, hands still occupied with the radio and his face turned from her. "I understand," he said. And he did. It wasn't the answer he wanted to hear, but he had known it was likely. He would survive. He always did.

His flesh erupted in goosebumps as Nori stepped beside him and ran the tips of her fingers along his cheekbones. He turned first his head, then his body, toward her.

"Oh, Cooper," she whispered, her sharp blue eyes reading the disappointment in his face.

For a moment, he considered letting her feel it, giving her a taste of the loneliness he felt day after day out on that road. He wanted to show her how it felt to lay your heart on the line and be rejected. For a moment, resentment and anger and fear reared their ugly heads and threatened to tell Nori where to shove her sympathy.

But his feelings for her ran deeper than this one wound.

"Really," he said. "I get it." She was so close he could feel the heat of her lean body. "Am I disappointed?" he asked and touched the corner of her mouth with a thumb. "Very." Her head fell to the side and he gave her a sad smile. "Am I heartbroken?" he asked, twisting his mouth into a wry smile to make light of the words he meant more than he wanted her to know. "Very nearly."

Looking down into the face of the girl he had hoped would take the first step toward a life with him, he was consumed with regret. Coming here had been a mistake. He knew she had a family and friends who loved her. A sick feeling twisted his guts. He was stupid to hope for so much. He knew it the moment he found himself slowly making his way back to the 25th Parallel. And yet he made the trip and hoped she would say yes all the same.

Cooper cleared his throat and ran his fingers across Nori's cheekbone. The light scarring did nothing to detract from her beauty. It was only the canvas on which some god had painted too-big eyes and a smart, perfect mouth.

Maybe it was just his imagination, but he could almost see the thoughts speeding through her mind. He would swear that as they stood there she considered running away with him despite her parents. For a brief, glorious moment, he thought she believed the lie, that she would actually do it. Her lips pulled into a grin as she looked up at him, ridiculously happy. He smiled in response. It was reflex. But it faded just as quickly. She would never choose him over her parents. He avoided her face after that, hugging her tightly to him instead.

"God, I wish things were different," she murmured against his chest.

He gripped her tighter. "Me too."

They stood there a small eternity. He knew what came next, but refused to separate, holding on while he could.

"What is that music?" Nori asked after a while.

"Someone's transmitting nearby and still has old vinyl records," he said.

"Are they good?"

A chilly void swept across Cooper's chest when he separated from her to turn a knob on the old radio. A man's tortured voice drifted into the small room, lonely and yearning for his beloved's arms. The irony wasn't lost on Cooper, who wasted no time in resuming his hold. "You wanna dance?"

Nori's head snapped up. "What, here?"

"We didn't get it right the first time," he said, his voice cracking only a little from nerves. "Let's try again."

He moved before she could answer, leading her across the room in a sway as poignant and desperate as the old song.

10

DANCING

For once in her life, Nori Chisholm relinquished herself to the moment. These were their last, after all. Clinging to Cooper's wide shoulders and following his lead, she closed her eyes and let her body move with the music. The thrill of being near Cooper sent blood pulsing from her heart all the way to her toes. She smiled, welcoming the feelings, and laughed at the near-lightheaded joy of simply dancing with him in the unremarkable room.

Nori had always prided herself on self-reliance. She didn't need anybody to be happy; certainly not a guy. And she didn't *need* Sam Cooper. Oh, but she *wanted* him.

Her blood ran cold as the thoughts of a future without him surfaced. She would be relegated indoors again, playing the third wheel to Kade and Grant, or hanging with her parents.

No. She pushed the thoughts from her mind before they could suck her down, squashing the dread as Cooper spun her around the room again.

"I knew that first night in the foyer." Cooper's words glided through the silence.

Nori looked up, and was quickly snared. "Knew what?" she asked.

"This. That we could have this."

Her throat had seized, but a response eluded her anyway.

"Even later," he went on, "when you busted my nose and kicked my ass. I knew." Thick black lashes lay against his cheekbones when he blinked. "Who wouldn't want to stand next to your light?" His lips pulled into a sad smile. "I needed the warmth. I saw so many things when I was undercover. I *did* so many things that eroded my soul bit by bit and left me cold. I never thought I'd do good— feel good— again, but when I met you, for the first time, I hoped I might."

Cooper's emotional admission both thrilled and frightened her. What on earth had he done? Being undercover with Sarge and his crew couldn't have been easy. Had he watched their violent sprees? Participated? A dark shiver ran through her at the thought.

"If you don't mind." Cooper cleared his throat and his gaze slid sideways. "I'd like to hold onto that hope just a little bit longer. I know I'm fooling myself, but, well, I need something to look forward to."

Nori nodded, not even sure what she was agreeing to. It was the first time she had ever known Cooper to show vulnerability. He was broken, and she had no idea.

The song stopped abruptly, and static filled the air. Cooper stepped away from her, switching off the radio with one hand and squeezing her trembling hand with the other.

"There are some things I have to tell you before I go." His voice was so quiet. So sad. "I'd saved it until the last because, well, you're going to resent me for not telling you sooner."

Cooper dropped her hand and began to pace the small den. "I'd hoped to show you, but..."

"Cooper," Nori pleaded, begging him to understand. "I can't go."

"No." He shook his head. "I know. I'm not trying to make you feel guilty about your decision. I understand." He stopped, crossed his arms, but then dropped them to resume pacing.

Nervous was a new look. The Cooper she knew was confident, controlled, cool.

"What is it?" she asked. "You're scaring me."

"God, Nori." He looked up at the crumbling concrete ceiling as if seeking divine intervention. "You're going to be furious I've kept this to myself for so long, but... well... you're not the first girl I've known like this."

Shock and embarrassment sent Nori's spine straight. It took several beats before she could reply.

"I... ah... well, I assumed as much," she said. "I mean, not everyone's spent their entire life under a rock— and their parents' supervision— like I have."

Her chest was tight, and she could actually feel the heat slinking up her face. Did she really have to come right out and admit her innocence? Is that what he wanted?

"I assumed you'd had girlfriends," she said. "I mean, I know there aren't a lot of Subterranean women, but you're... ah... well, you grew up in a commune, right?"

She was babbling. She knew it. And yet she couldn't stop.

"I haven't..." She looked away from him. "Known anyone like this... If that's what you're asking."

The sound of Cooper's laughter put a stop to her renegade mouth. Her gaze snapped up to his, and she watched him struggle to breathe. He was nearly wheezing, eyes squinted and white teeth gleaming in an open-mouthed guffaw.

Humiliated tears pricked at Nori's eyes, and a white-hot

shot of rage scorched her insides. He was laughing. *At* her. And not just a snicker. She jerked away, stomping for the door without a word.

Cooper's laughter cut off, and she could feel him behind her. He caught the hand at her side and held it, forcing her to stop. Stepping in front of her, he slipped his other hand behind her neck, rubbing gently at her nape.

Too much. Too intimate, Nori thought, and shrugged away from him. He shook his head, his face contrite. "I'm sorry. Don't leave. I... that's not where I was going. That's not what I meant."

"What did you mean?" Nori ground through her teeth.

"I meant I've known other people like you, who can see in the dark, who burn in the sun."

Nori's head snapped back. "I don't understand. What are you saying?"

"There are more," he said. "People who got the Lumin vax."

11

———

LUMIN

Cooper's throat seized and he worked to breathe. He hadn't been this nervous in years.

"What's a 'Lumin vax?'" Nori asked, her dark, slender brows drawn together.

Forcing out a breath and hoping to buy some time, he led her to the sofa. "Let's sit down. I'll... I'll start at the beginning."

Eyes narrowed, she sat at the end of the dark leather sofa and pulled a pillow into her lap.

What if I didn't tell her? The thought shot through Cooper's mind like a stray bullet. I don't really *have* to leave. No one knows I'm here. I could stay, get to know her family. I could lay my head on that pillow in her lap and let the whole world go to hell.

As quickly as the idea was born, though, Cooper put it down. He knew himself too well. He would be happy for a few days. Around Nori, it might last weeks. But the itch to go would find its way to the top of his skin. He would have to scratch. He would have to leave her eventually.

Anyway, he could not keep what he knew about the Lumin vax from her any longer. He had already kept the secret too long.

Cooper closed his eyes and resigned himself to telling her the truth. To leaving. "Has your mother ever talked about getting a shot when she was pregnant with you?"

Nori, who'd been watching his face so closely, frowned. "Nothing specific. I know she took a lot of vitamins. Every woman does."

"There was a specific one, a clinical trial. Not everyone got it. Your mother's doctor must've been selected." At her impressed look, he couldn't help but add, "These doctors were paid a lot to participate. Or, I should say, for their *patients* to participate."

"O-kay," was her slow reply.

"It was billed as an immunization," he said. "A way to prevent DNA damage after the nuclear strike at Barksdale."

She perked. "I remember hearing about that. It was in Louisiana a year or so before I was born."

"Right." He nodded and took her hands, which had gone cold. "Well, the medicine wasn't what they told the doctors — or the public." Rubbing his thumbs over the tops of her soft hands, he dropped the first bomb. "In truth, the CCC developed the vaccine at their R&D facility at Cheyenne Mountain."

Nori's face wrinkled. "'R and D?'"

"Research and development. Anyway, it wasn't a immunization against radiation at all, but a way to *alter* DNA." He risked a look up and found her mouth slightly open, her head turned quizzically. He forged ahead. "Of... of a fetus."

The blood drained from Nori's face and she stared at him so long he slumped in his seat to escape her glare. That's when he realized she wasn't looking at him at all. She looked through him, lost in thought, fitting all the puzzle pieces together.

I've just shaken her world like a snow globe, he thought, still stroking the back of her hand.

It was several moments before she spoke. "You're saying my mom got a shot when she was pregnant that… changed me somehow?"

He nodded, inching closer to her. What he really wanted was to hold her, but she hadn't moved since he started talking.

Her head lifted and tilted, doubt and suspicion warping her normally-serene features. "Changed me… how… exactly?" she asked.

Chewing at the inside of his jaws, Cooper proceeded as gently as he could. "The, ah, point in developing the drug was to create a line of people who could see in the dark, who didn't need sunlight to survive. A race designed to live underground."

Nori snorted, then sobered when she noticed he wasn't smiling.

"You're serious?" she asked.

He nodded.

"I'm a member of a superior race?"

Cooper shrugged, but nodded again.

"I knew it!" Nori's face lit with mock conceit. "And I don't even have to drink blood." She lost the smile and lowered her voice as she leaned forward conspiratorially. "Or do I?"

She thinks I'm making this up, Cooper thought, forcing the next words past his lips. "The problem was, since it was developed and tested inside a mountain, no one knew about the side effects until it was too late. Until an entire population of children had received death sentences."

Nori's face melted to a frown. "My reaction to the sun, you mean?"

"Yes."

"Well, why aren't there more?" She pulled her hands from his. "If doctors gave women like my mother these shots, why haven't I met others my same age?"

"Because of the scorches," he said, and the statement hung heavy as smog. "The first scorch happened when you were, what, four or five? The Lumin-vaccinated kids that weren't taken by infection or a weakened immune system after what would've been fairly harmless sunburns, well, they didn't survive the scorch."

"But I did," she said and the color that had risen to her cheeks drained again. "Lucky." Her voice was barely a whisper. "I was just lucky. I was inside." Tears formed in the corner of her eyes, magnifying the blue swirls. "I was young," she said. "But I remember." When she squeezed her eyes shut, a tear fell from each one.

"I'm sorry," Cooper said, and his heart squeezed painfully as her knee trembled beneath his touch. "I'm so sorry."

They stayed like that for a while, silent and still. Nori was lost in her memories, and Cooper was at a loss of what to do for her.

When she finally looked up at him, not just her face, but her entire aura had changed. She sat up straight, her face wiped clean of emotion. She dusted off his pity like ash on a sleeve.

"So, what?" she asked, her voice cautious, curious. "You think I'm the only one on the Surface who survived?"

"I don't know." He reached for her hand, but pulled back when she looked down suspiciously. "Possibly," he said. "You haven't met another, and neither have I."

"But there are others like me living Subterranean? They're surviving?"

"No. I mean yes." Cooper fumbled for words. "They're not just surviving, Nori, they're thriving."

One corner of her mouth ticked up in a half smile. Neither of them spoke again for what seemed an eternity, but Cooper watched her clever eyes as they narrowed, deep in thought. It was obvious when she reached some conclusion because, without another word, she stood and marched for the door. Still frozen to the sofa, he watched her every determined stride.

"Well, come on." Nori threw the words carelessly behind her.

"Where are you going?"

She held the door open, motioning for him to hurry through. "To tell my parents I'm leaving. This changes everything."

Cooper's heart stuttered to a stop. "That wasn't my intent," he said. "I just wanted you to know everything… about yourself… that I knew."

"I know that."

"But. Your mother…"

"Will simply have to understand." Nori shrugged, but Cooper saw the flicker of emotion in her eyes. "If I have a chance to stop the monsters who did this to me and killed so many others… " Her delicate nostrils flared, and his stalled heart roared back to life. "I'm going with you, Sam Cooper, and there's nothing you can do to stop me."

God help him, but he didn't even want to try.

12

A SHORT GOODBYE

"But," Nori's mother said around a sob, "where will you live?"

Nori didn't have a good answer.

"Where will you sleep? How will you eat?" Her mother's head shook furiously. "These are all basic necessities, Nori. And the dangers underground… You're just a child. And with your condition— " She didn't finish.

It was all true, but the doubt still stung, and Nori stiffened, slowly withdrawing from her mother's arms.

"I think what we're not considering, Ana," her father said softly, "is that she's no longer a child. And that the Subterranean may very well be her home."

Nori closed her eyes, grateful for her father's unexpected support.

Her mother, though, finally lost the fight against her emotions and moaned like she was in mortal pain. Her father clasped her pale hand and rubbed it over and over. He was comforting himself, Nori suspected, as much he comforted her mother. It was the final breaking blow to Nori's fractured heart.

The two had stood silent as Cooper recounted what he knew of the Lumin vaccine. Their shocked silence, though, had been quickly replaced with the filthy shadow of guilt. When her mother put together that a prenatal inoculation had caused Nori's life of agony, she had become physically ill. Nori, her father, and even Cooper had scrambled to clean up and help her through the nausea, but once the ordeal was over, only the truth remained. Tension had gripped the room and didn't let go.

"I don't want to hurt you." Nori's voice was thick with emotion. "But I have to do this. They created me. Don't you see? They did this to me— to us— and now I have a chance to stop them." Nori bent to her knees beside her mother's wheelchair. "I'm going, Mom. I hope someday you can understand."

Her trembling hand was cold against Nori's cheek. "I understand," she said. "I do. And I'm so proud." Nori leaned into her cool palm as her mother whispered, "I'm just so scared."

Clearing his throat, her father stalked toward Cooper, who had faded into a corner. "I think it goes without saying that I'm counting on you to protect my daughter's life with yours," he said.

Cooper nodded, his face serious. "She does pretty well on her own," he began, but at her father's rising finger quickly added, "but yes. I'll protect her like she's my own."

Nori's heart stuttered at his words, and even more so when she snuck a look at his face. His gaze raked over her possessively and... lovingly? She rose, but kept her mother's hand. "We really need to get going if we're going to get underground before daylight. Where are Kade and Grant?"

"Here," came Grant's confident call from the other room. "Just giving you some privacy."

"Well, if you're listening," she said, "you might as well hear it all. Come in here." Nori rolled her eyes and grinned at her parents, whose answering smiles didn't quite reach their eyes.

"I got you this," Kade said shyly and handed her a box. "It's just supplies. Food and things you'll need in the Subterranean."

"Like mascara," Grant threw in playfully.

"Uhm." Her father's steps were tentative. "Your mother and I got you something, too."

It wasn't wrapped, and when he pulled it from his pocket, it gleamed in the overhead light.

"Dad?" Nori looked from him to her mother, certain the latter had no real role in the gift.

"Well," he grumbled, "the one you had was pitiful. So dull you could barely cut through peanut butter."

"It's a knife," Nori said dumbly.

"Yes, *that's* a knife." He nodded pridefully at the huge steel switchblade in her hand. "It's for protection." He cleared his throat. "Or peanut butter."

By the time goodbye hugs were completed, both Nori's arms and tear ducts were spent. It was raining when they stepped into the darkness, and she was glad for the weather. The slow trek away from her house and family would have been hard on them all. Instead, with a last quick wave, the two ran to Cooper's bike, resumed the tandem riding position she had grown to love, and sped into the storm.

13

ON THE ROAD AGAIN

With the force of their speed whipping damp hair behind her, Nori relaxed— really relaxed— for the first time in a month, and rested her forehead to Cooper's back.

They'd made it back underground without incident, but were soaked to the bone. Nori clenched her teeth to keep them from clattering. It was the only drawback of a Subterranean life— the permanent chill, a constant 55 degrees even as the world burned above them. Shivering, she tucked in close to Cooper for warmth, pressing the front of her body to his. He tensed at first, but then ran his hand on top of hers and squeezed before laying on the throttle and propelling them ever faster.

Though warmth radiated everywhere she and Cooper touched, there was plenty left unsheltered. *I can't stand these wet pants a minute longer.* The thought had no sooner crossed Nori's mind than Cooper slowed to a stop and dismounted. He stood beside her, hand outstretched.

"I should've done this sooner," he said, his gaze too intense. "Let's get you out of those clothes."

Nori's brain, accustomed to the monotony of gray and gritty tunnels, short-circuited. "Wh-what?"

"I'm still wet, and freezing. You've got to be, too. I'll start a fire if you want to change first."

Nori shook herself, laughed at herself, then rifled through the bike's saddlebags for dry clothes. By the time she returned, Cooper's fire blazed and the warm air stretched out to meet her.

"My turn," he said, tucking a stack of clothes beneath his arm. "Your mom sent dinner. We're back to Vitabars and MRE's after that."

They ate mostly in silence, Nori with her feet so close to the fire they stung. With a full belly and dry clothes, they had no real reason to linger. And yet they did.

Each time Nori looked up at Cooper she found his eyes on her. And each time she caught him he looked quickly away. She ran a hand inconspicuously across her mouth and cheeks in search of stray food, and when she turned to put her back to the fire, she caught him looking again.

"What?" she asked.

"What?" he said.

"Is there something you want to say?"

"Why?" he asked.

"Well," Nori said, "you keep looking at me. It's making me nervous."

"Sorry."

"So, is there?" she asked again.

"What?"

"Something you want to say?"

Cooper's mouth pulled into a shy grin as he stared into the

fire. His gaze flicked to hers and back to the flames. "I just missed you is all."

Warmth oozed from Nori's heart and poured down her limbs until even her frigid toes were toasty. She couldn't fight her own smile. "I missed you, too." She cleared her throat. "Who'd have thought that day I saved you in the alley we'd end up here?"

Cooper mumbled something and she angled her head toward him. She couldn't have heard right. "What?"

"Nothing."

She watched his face, red even in the firelight. Cooper, who held his cards so close to his chest, who'd been no more emotionally available than his motorcycle, had said, "I hoped."

"Cooper, I've been thinking," Nori said as she packed the last of her things onto the bike.

"Dear God." He closed his eyes dramatically, and she swatted his arm.

"I'm serious," she said. "I know we're going to find allies—your friends. But, well, we could go right by the CCC headquarters on the way. Don't you think... don't you think we should swing by and see what they're up to before we leave the area?"

"You think we should risk spying on a secret military installation again to 'see what they're up to'?" Cooper threw his leg over the bike and settled in. "No. Our plan is to rally our allies, pool our information, and formulate a plan to take out those murderous bigots." He stood to kick-start the engine and landed roughly down onto the seat. "No side-trips. No risks."

"No fun," Nori said under her breath.

"The CCC's no joke, Nori. We got lucky last time. If they'd caught us… " The muscles of his jaw worked. "There's a reason their secrets are so well-kept. That place is operated with an iron fist, and if you're not part of the hand, it'll smash you flat."

Nori swallowed, nodding, and scooted in behind him.

14

RECON

"I cannot believe I let you talk me into this," Cooper said, irritated at himself more than at Nori. She hustled to keep up, so he walked even faster.

"You know it's a good idea, Cooper."

He knew no such thing. In fact, he thought it was a terrible idea. And yet, there they were.

"We might learn something to help us when it's time to attack," she said.

"*If* we decide to attack."

"You know we will. We have to." Nori took several quick steps to get in his line of sight. "You said it yourself. Going undercover is what you do best. Well, we're here. We know the way in…"

Her eyes were bright with excitement, which, he realized with a groan, is why he had agreed to come in the first place. Seeing her happy was a rare and beautiful thing. How could he deny her? How could he dull that shine?

"Let's infiltrate the enemy and conduct some recon," she said. "We'll report the terrain and obstacles to our allies."

Cooper stopped walking and turned, but in her enthusiasm and strategizing, Nori didn't notice. She smashed into his chest and looked up with a grunt. Cooper pressed his lips together to keep from smiling and his chest shook at the effort of repressing laughter. As she searched his face, her expression was excited, naive. Nori Chisholm laid herself bare when she looked at him, and the gratitude Cooper felt for her was sobering. Suddenly, he had no idea which he wanted to do more — laugh at her or kiss her.

His face must've revealed the internal battle because she noticed the change in him and squatted into a defensive position, squinting at the area around them. "What is it?" she asked, nearly breathless. "Did you hear something?"

That was it. The over-the-top military jargon, her ninja-like crouch — it was too much, and Cooper couldn't take it in anymore. He released the howl of laughter he had been holding.

Nori's head whipped toward him. Her face went from confused to shocked to furious in a fraction of a second, and her glittering gaze turned to stone. Her little lips tucked to an angry pucker and she threw her hands to her hips, which really just made the whole thing that much funnier.

"Where did you learn to talk like that?" Cooper asked, wiping a tear from one eye. "One of your books?"

Her nostrils flared, but Nori didn't say another word. She flung angrily around and marched from the main road in the direction of the *cenote* they'd found weeks ago with Kade.

"Nori," he called behind her, sloshing through the knee-deep water. "Nori, wait." He worked to wipe the smile from his face. "I'm sorry."

The look she shot him could freeze time. She didn't speak,

only stared him down as she ducked through a smooth hole in the tunnel wall.

"Oh, come on. Wait up," he said and chased after her. "You know I can't see in here."

She had stopped just inside the opening, but not to let him catch up. Her head craned upward, her mouth open as she gazed at the collapsed limestone sinkhole. What little Cooper could glimpse in the dark was amazing. To someone like Nori, who could see the entire thing, it must be majestic.

Cooper touched her elbow, and when she didn't flinch, closed his fingers around her arm and turned her toward him. She wouldn't meet his gaze.

"I'm sorry," he said again, and meant it. "You have to admit that was pretty funny, though." He shook his head again. "'Infiltrate the enemy.'"

Nori wasn't smiling. He should probably let it go.

Nah.

"All right, soldier," he said and stood to attention. "Let's conduct some recon."

Nori's eyes were like two tiny flamethrowers but her voice was syrupy sweet. "Oh, after you," she said.

Laughter died in Cooper's throat. If she thought he would back down from leading them through the inky cavern, she was way off. He patted his pockets for a flashlight and could feel her eyes on him, dissecting him in the dark. With the flashlight nowhere to be found and his pride at serious risk, he sniffed and straightened. Then he stepped into the unknown.

It didn't take long. He was essentially blind, and lost his footing less than thirty seconds after he began fumbling through the blackness. The toe of his boot caught on a rock, and there was nothing to hold on to as he pitched forward. It all happened in a heartbeat.

Stumble.

Plummet.

Splash.

The water was freezing, and Cooper gasped, swallowing a mouthful of mineral-rich water. On hands and knees he coughed and sputtered, finally rising back to his feet. He was soaked to the bone, his body stiff with cold.

Nori's satisfied giggle said she had enjoyed her little revenge, and humiliation quickly warmed him from the inside out. She brushed her leg against his arm spitefully as she passed.

Cooper was still wringing out his shirt when he caught up to her.

"There's the entrance." Nori nodded to a faded symbol near the door, and Cooper clicked on his light. "How do you think we get in?" she asked.

"Get in? We aren't getting in," Cooper scoffed. "Are you insane?"

"Well, I didn't come all this way just to sneak around *outside* the headquarters." She said it like he was the ridiculous one.

Cooper rubbed his arms, still wet and covered in goosebumps. "Actually," he said, "that's exactly what we came all this way to do. We're evaluating the viability of a future attack—"

"Oh, it's okay when you use big words?" Nori asked.

Most of his patience was at the bottom of a frigid pool. He worked to keep his voice low, and since that wasn't possible, at least a rough whisper. "We're here to see if the opening is still accessible from the tunnel." He shined his light up up dramatically, then back down to her face. "It is. Let's go."

Nori's eyes lit eerily, sending the reflection of his flashlight back at him. "What could it hurt to poke around a little bit?" she pouted. Her extraordinary eyes were wide with innocent pleading. And it was totally feigned.

He shook his head, shivering as a drop of water fell from his hair to his neck. "No way, Nori. I—"

Whirring gears stopped Cooper mid-sentence, and he turned toward the noise. Without conscious thought, he reached for Nori, gripping the front of her shirt and pulling her with him against the wall. Her body was warm. *Dry.*

"Cooper, what…" Nori's objection died at the press of his fingers to her lips. He released her shirt, but held onto her arm and kept her close at his side.

After a series of clicks and a slow grinding, the thick metal door into the CCC opened as if they had willed it to happen. Nori elbowed him in the ribs. She was grinning, her face beaming with excitement.

It wasn't excitement Cooper felt, but dread, and her face melted to match his when two men in uniform shined lights in their direction— lights attached to impossibly large gun barrels.

Nori's body jerked as if she would bolt through the water and out of the cavern. She might've done just that if he hadn't been holding her arm. Panic surged through him. Running was Cooper's first instinct, too. But it was followed almost immediately with the urge to fight. Instead he forced himself to breathe, to think. *Rational. Judicious. Concise.* He repeated the mantra under his breath until his racing heart slowed.

Nori had pressed her body against his, her breaths so short they were more like pants. Well, if she had wanted to get an idea of what they were up against, she had gotten it. They'd been discovered by professional, mercenary-style soldiers with big guns.

Rational. Judicious. Concise. What in God's name was he going to do to get them out of this? When the idea struck, Cooper closed his eyes. It was a risk. A big risk. But in the absence of any other ideas it would have to do.

Cooper jerked Nori's arm so hard her teeth clacked together. She whipped around, and the look in her eyes almost cost him his nerve. Her eyes were wide again, terrified, and her little pink lips trembled. But he couldn't think about her feelings. Not now. Instead he narrowed his eyes to something cold and cruel and didn't meet her gaze again. He couldn't, even as she murmured a nearly-imperceptible "Cooper?"

"Found this one snooping around," he said and motioned to the water-worn hole they'd entered together only moments before. "I was bringing her in to see if she's one of yours."

The brawnier of the two men stepped forward, but didn't lower his gun. Nori, thank God, had bowed her head and closed her eyes so they wouldn't reflect the light.

"Who are you?" the man asked. "And what are you doing out here? Give me one reason not to put a hole in your skull right now."

Here's where it got tricky, Cooper knew. If he was going to pull this off, he had to appear confident. Unafraid. In charge. He shrugged away his fear, threw on a grin, and spoke slowly. "I'm employed here," he said. "It's my job to find sneaks and freaks, though I admit they're not usually this..." Cooper cleared his throat obnoxiously, "well put-together."

The big soldier exchanged a look with the other one, who shrugged. They were thinking about buying his story. Some of the strain eased from Cooper's neck.

This version of himself always disarmed people. Throwing men off-balance and warming them up with a good-ole boy facade was the oldest trick in the book. It endured because it always worked. *We have something in common*, Cooper's words and movements said. *We're just alike and, really, don't all manly men like us have a weakness for pretty girls.*

He risked a look at Nori, who was shaking. She didn't think they'd buy it. But her mouth fell open as the big soldier lowered his gun and the other followed his lead.

"I'm gonna need to see some identification or something," the big soldier said.

Cooper used his free hand to pat his pockets. "Musta left it on the bike. Don't worry. I'm one of Sarge's."

"Sarge?" The soldier's brows lifted. "We thought he was dead. Hasn't reported in at least a month." He slung his gun onto his back. "They'll want to debrief you."

"Happy to help, Lieutenant," Cooper said. Flattery. Another tool in his toolbox. The stripes on the man's uniform said all Cooper needed to know. Not high up enough to count, but above someone, somewhere.

The man's pleasure at the acknowledgment of his rank didn't escape Cooper's attention— or Nori's. She rolled her eyes before returning them meekly to the floor.

"I'll take this one," the Lieutenant announced, reaching for Nori. She jerked from his grasp, though, and tucked herself behind Cooper. One fist closed around the back of his shirt as she hid her face at his back.

A mix of fear and regret rippled through Cooper's body. He closed his eyes, working harder than ever to remain calm after Nori's mistake. Before the soldiers could question why she would duck behind a man who'd captured her, Cooper shook Nori, hard. He felt less guilty about it than the first time, hoping it warned her not to do something so stupid again. To remind her how much trouble they were in. She would have to do better on the fly to make it through this. *If we make it through this*, he thought, wishing he had never let her talk him into getting so close to the headquarters.

"That's all right," Cooper told the Lieutenant, not bothering to hide the frustration in his voice. "I've got a good hold on her."

"Not so fast," the Lieutenant said and then turned to his partner. "Simms, why don't you pat 'em down first?"

"Both, sir?"

"Yes, both." The Lieutenant's sandy hair was trimmed above his ears, the back a clean, straight line. He rubbed a palm over the gun at his hip and licked too-thick, almost feminine lips. "I'm sure Mr..."

"Cooper, sir. Sam Cooper."

"I'm sure Mr. Cooper is telling the truth, that he's one of Sarge's and loyal to the cause." He directed his comments to Cooper. "But, you'll have to forgive me for not taking a stranger's word for it. No offense meant, I'm sure."

"None taken." Cooper flexed his hands, forcing his fingers, his whole body, to relax.

Simms patted Cooper's legs with determined efficiency, so it was obvious when he found the gun tucked into the small of his back. After an accusing glance at Cooper, Simms held the gun out to his superior.

"You don't mind if I hold on to this until we confirm your story, do you?"

Cooper cleared his face of the storm of emotion raging in his brain and shook his head. "Sure don't."

"Good." The Lieutenant nodded to Nori. "Check her, too."

Simms performed the same quick sweep of her arms and legs, and when he got to the pocket of her jeans and slowed, Nori closed her eyes.

"Found something." Simms was quick, professional, as he pushed the contents of her pocket upward and drew out a knife.

"What did you plan to do with that?" the Lieutenant asked.

"Can't a girl carry a good knife without having some kind of intentions?" she asked.

"Not when she's snooping around a top-secret military installation, no," he said. "She cannot."

"I wasn't snooping," she lied. "I didn't even know what this place was until you started talking. You may very well have a security problem, but it's not me."

Cooper stared straight ahead, but squeezed her arm, a clear signal to shut up. She did.

"Well, if that's true," the Lieutenant said, "you're having a very unlucky day."

"My specialty," Nori mumbled too low for the Lieutenant to hear.

Cooper heard her, though, and put the full force of his scalding warning in his eyes. She was only digging herself deeper, and as impulsive as she was, she would bury the both of them.

Despite his glare, Nori shrugged and looked away. "I'm gonna want that back," she said to the lieutenant.

Cooper inhaled through his nostrils, clenching his jaws shut not to tear into her.

"Excuse me?" One of the man's sandy eyebrows rose toward his hairline.

"My knife," she said. "It was a gift. I expect to get it back once I'm cleared and out of here."

The smug, sinister look on the Lieutenant's face said either she would never see it again, or that she would never get out.

He didn't address her demand. "Simms," he said. "Lead on to External Command." Then he swept his hand out dramatically. "If you please, Mr. Cooper."

With Nori's arm still in his grasp, Cooper prodded her forward.

And just like that, they were whisked inside the top-secret headquarters of the Council of Concerned Citizens, the military-style bureaucratic group long considered responsible for the destruction of the modern world.

All in a day's undercover work, Cooper thought, shaking his head at either the best— or worst— thing that could possibly have happened.

15

COOPER CHECKS OUT

The wide halls of the facility were stark but clean. Meticulously so. Walls were noticeably free of grime. Floors were clear of grit and debris. The overhead lights flickered and buzzed, but there were no burned-out bulbs.

Nori's head, in contrast, was a roaring mess of fear and confusion as Cooper pushed her down the hall. The Lieutenant hadn't said much since they'd entered the facility, and she was glad for that. She used the time to study her surroundings, though there wasn't much to learn. The corridors they passed were marked, but not with anything that made sense to her, and they all looked the same. She was lost in a maze of concrete and metal, and she held little hope of finding her way out on her own.

Cooper was taking the ruse a little too far, in her opinion. Though he made the manhandling look rougher than it actually was, she had bitten her tongue the last time he jerked her.

"You're hurting me," she ground through clenched teeth. The lieutenant, Iberville, she thought his name was, smirked, and it took all of her resolve not to kick him in the kneecap.

Cooper pulled her to him with a menacing grin and leaned in close. Besides their echoed footsteps, the only sound in the too-bright hall was the dramatic buzzing of the overhead lights.

"We're in this together now," he said, his mouth so close to her ear she shivered. The smirky soldier watched, so she was sure to keep her face appropriately fearful as Cooper mock-harassed her— which, at that moment, wasn't terribly difficult.

"If we want to get out of this alive," he said so low she could barely hear him, "I've got to play the part. It's not going to be pleasant, but I'll try to protect you."

"Wait, what?" Nori pulled back to see Cooper's face. The gold flecks of his eyes spun and reflected under the artificial light, but it didn't obscure the sobriety of his glare. He was afraid.

The soldier laughed again as the color drained from her face. "What's going to happen to me?" Nori asked, and this time the tremor in her voice was real.

At the end of a hall marked "G2" in bold, black letters, the soldiers stopped. The Lieutenant waved a card attached to his belt in front of an electrical box, which beeped, then pushed open the door into a room of desks and private offices.

Simms took off after a quick nod from the Lieutenant, who ushered Nori and Cooper into a sterile interrogation room and left without another word.

In the room alone, Cooper stood so close she could hear the breath rushing past his lips, his hand still on her shoulder. She scanned the room, turning to face him, but he held his grip— and her in place.

"Have a seat." Cooper's tone wasn't gentle. "We'll get this all sorted out soon."

The irritation she felt came out in a coarse, "What's wrong with you?" as she tried to pull from his grasp again. Cooper shook his head ever-so-slightly, ducking and flicking his eyes to a tiny box beside the overhead light.

When comprehension dawned, Nori closed her eyes. It was a camera or surveillance of some sort. They weren't alone.

It didn't take long for someone with authority to join them. A fit man in his fifties with utilitarian glasses whisked into the room and stood opposite Cooper. He didn't sit, and he didn't ask Cooper to, either. The polished black handle of his gun gleamed in its holster at his side.

"Lieutenant Iberville said you're one of Sarge's..." His lip curled in distaste as he searched for a word. "Associates."

Cooper straightened. "That's right."

"Sarge reports to me, but I haven't heard from him in some time." He eyed Cooper suspiciously. "Which is highly unusual. Sarge is many things, but unreliable isn't one of them."

"Actually, sir," Cooper said, "that's why I'm here."

The man's fine dark brows drew together, but not in confusion. "Oh?"

"Yes." Cooper's throat bobbed as he swallowed. "I didn't catch your name, sir."

Nori knew Cooper well enough to see the gears grinding in Cooper's head, but she doubted the interrogator saw anything besides cool confidence.

"Mathers," the man answered. "Captain Charles Mathers."

"Captain Mathers, I'm Sam Cooper. I've worked with Sarge for two years now." His gaze around the room was exaggerated, and he moved in close to the Captain and lowered his voice. "Sarge sent me in his stead."

Again with the eyebrows. "Is that right?" Mathers said.

"Sarge…" Cooper said slowly. "Well… he has reason to believe we have a mole, or a tail— or both. Either way, he wouldn't risk coming here himself."

"Cooper, was it?" Mathers asked, lifting his head dubiously.

"Yes, sir."

"Well, Cooper, we have systems in place for this type of thing. Why would Sarge send you instead of using standard protocols?"

Cooper cleared his throat. "Sarge suspects his communications are being intercepted, too."

Captain Mathers' head lifted and some of the tension left his face, as if Cooper's answer was acceptable. "And the key phrase?"

Panic slid across Cooper's eyes, sending them wide as Nori watched in horror. "The key phrase," Cooper repeated.

"Mmm," Mathers grunted. "If Sarge sent you, he would have given you the key phrase."

Cooper's grip tightened on her shoulder.

Mathers' eyes grew more narrow with each passing millisecond, and his hand tensed, as if it ached to touch the pistol at his hip.

"Stand by to pop smoke." The words flew from Cooper's mouth with force, like he had been slapped in the back.

Mathers' hand, which had inched toward the gun, relaxed.

The moment was tense and ridiculous, and a nervous scream bubbled just under Nori's breath. She pressed her lips together to keep it where it belonged.

When she finally risked a look at Cooper again, his eyes were heavy lidded—to hide his relief, she guessed.

Nori shot him a look that screamed disbelief. "*Where did you pull that from?*" she mouthed.

Cooper shook his head. He was still under scrutiny.

Mathers, though, appeared satisfied. "All right, Cooper. We can discuss Sarge momentarily. What's pressing right now is the intruder you found at the southern access."

"Yes, sir," Cooper answered without hesitation. "As I approached the southern access tunnel, I saw someone wading through the water. I trailed her to determine if she was lost, an escapee, or trying to find a way inside."

Nori felt like she had left her own body, as if she was a puff of air above them all watching Cooper lie and manipulate. He was so *good* at it. It was second nature to him. To her horror, she began to believe the story.

Cooper didn't look at her as he spoke, and she was glad because he might've spotted her disappointment. He was an expert liar. Brilliant, even. With a sadness more profound than she understood, she remembered the lie of omission he had told her, how he had kept what he knew of the Lumin vax from her for so long. How could she trust him now, after knowing he withheld such important information from her?

"... witness her entering the rotunda?" Mathers was asking.

"I did not," Cooper said. "She was already there when I discovered her, though I did not see a mode of transportation on my own way in. She could have arrived alone from either the tunnel or the false ceiling. Or she could be working with someone we haven't yet discovered."

Mathers scoffed. "Nobody's entered from the false ceiling. That area's heavily surveilled. The cameras from the tunnel, though, weren't pointed to that new hole in the wall. We only caught sight of you two once you approached the door."

Mathers stopped, sucked air through his front teeth, marched to the door, and stuck his head out. "Iberville," he yelled into the hall. "Get a team on that hole in the rotunda A-S-A-P." He enunciated each letter with a gruff clip before slamming the door shut.

"Well?" Mathers said and turned a pointed glare to Nori. "You working with anybody?"

Her heart flew into her throat, and she swallowed to clear it. She looked to Cooper, who nodded encouragingly. The problem was she had no idea what he wanted her to say. Sure, lying came easy to him, but she lacked his experience.

"Best tell us the truth now," Cooper said. "We'll find out eventually, and we'll go easier on you if you don't give us much trouble."

A slow croak escaped her gaping mouth when she tried to force words from it. "I... I don't know what you're talking about," she shook her head frantically. "I just saw that hole in the wall and went exploring."

She looked to Mathers, whose face was grandpa-like, nearly sympathetic. Maybe he believed her. Maybe they'd let her go.

"What were you doing out there in the first place, hon?" he asked. "Were you lost?"

When Nori didn't answer, Mathers stepped closer. She realized with a jolt that the look in his eyes wasn't sympathetic. It was predatory. She was a thin-winged fly, and he had spread honey, waiting for her to land in the sweet trap.

She could hardly breathe. Her entire body, including her lungs, had frozen in fear and panic. "I was lost." Her voice was hoarse, barely a whisper. "I was supposed to meet up with a friend from Bannera, but he never showed."

"And you were traveling alone? Out there?" Mathers

shook his head ruefully. "I don't think so. Where's your family, girl?"

Her mouth was so dry she couldn't form words. She shook her head, helpless to say anything else.

"She's lying, obviously," Cooper said.

Nori's ponytail whipped as she swung her head to see Cooper's face. He didn't flinch, and she could see no regret in his eyes at all.

"Nobody in their right mind would travel those tunnels alone," he said. "Certainly not this one. Look at her. Sheltered and naive… She's shaking hard enough to break a tooth."

Humiliation, betrayal, and undiluted anger roared beneath Nori's fear with such ferocity that if Cooper had been close enough, she would have bitten his ear off, broken tooth or not.

Mathers, who had lost the sympathetic facade, laughed and nodded. "Maybe she just needs time to think." He marched to the door again. "Iberville." His grating voice echoed down the sparse hall. "Lock her down."

16

ON LOCK DOWN

"No." Nori scraped for purchase on the slick floors as Simms and Iberville ran their arms under her shoulders and forcibly dragged her from the room. From Cooper.

"No!" Heart thundering in her chest, her voice rose with each foot that separated them. "Don't touch me!" she howled, her body twisting as she tried escape. "Take me back. Please! Take me back!"

The soldiers ignored her frantic pleas, dragging her farther down the hall. She lost sight of Cooper when they rounded a corner, and a new surge of panic filled her lungs. Pulling with all her strength, she fought to free her arms from their grasps, but they only held on tighter.

She kicked wildly, finally landing a blow on the smaller soldier's knee. He grunted, but didn't slow. Bypassing panic and embracing full-on hysteria, she careened her neck to bite the other man's arm. He saw what she intended before she reached his sleeve, though, and snapped her shoulder up into her own chin.

Her shoulders were still in iron grips as Iberville and

76

Simms shoved her into an elevator. Letting the men hold her weight, she lifted her legs and pushed off the side of the elevator, twisting in another attempt to free herself. Iberville was knocked off balance, but all it did was make him angry. He twisted her arm in its socket until she thought it would pop out like an old Barbie doll. After that, Nori quit resisting. Pain and the taste of a bloodied tongue cleared some of the fog of panic, but that only made way for hopelessness.

Simms punched a button on the wall, and her stomach lurched when the elevator didn't go up, but down. Way down. When it finally stopped, they ushered her into another desolate hall, but not before she caught the numbers on the elevator frame. "8." They were eight floors down. How big was this place? Bigger than she had ever imagined, she realized, as she passed ten metal doors then twenty.

At some point Nori gave up the fight and let her body go limp. Her feet dangled behind as they dragged her, but it was her shoulders that paid the price. Satisfaction from the strain on their faces overrode any discomfort she felt, though, and she gritted her teeth in grim determination against the pain.

"Put your feet down or we'll let you fall." Iberville's eyes cut in her direction. "Be a shame to bust up that face."

If Nori had learned anything in the last half-hour, it was that these people didn't make idle threats. She stood, struggling to keep up with their clipped pace… to where, she had no idea. That is, until the soldiers stopped in front of a metal door with a narrow window just above her line of sight. A jail cell.

"In ya go," Iberville said after fumbling through a wad of keys to open the door. "Maybe a little time alone'll jog your memory."

Nori raised her chin but kept her mouth shut. And her feet

in place. She didn't voluntarily enter the cell. She couldn't. The thought of confinement caused deep waves of alarm that began at her chest and flowed through her arms and legs. One look into the tiny room had frozen her entire body.

When she went weak in the knees, Simms caught her and stood her upright.

"I'da beat the intel out of her." Iberville said it as if she wasn't standing right next to him.

"And what if she's telling the truth?" asked Simms, his thin voice sharp with reproach. "What if she's just some girl at the wrong place at the wrong time?"

Iberville grunted and shoved her into the room, and then down onto the small, thin cot. "Then we'd know for sure."

"That's why you're not in charge," Simms retorted.

"His daddy probably bought him that rank," Nori said. Her smart mouth was all she had left.

The look Iberville gave her as he backed out of the cell was pure evil. "Enjoy your company," he taunted, flipping off the light switch. "Vermin and bugs love the dark. And soft little girls."

Soft? Little girl? Nori thought to lunge for him, but a defiant surge of satisfaction rippled up her spine. They didn't know about her... abilities. She released an evil smile of her own.

"The only thing soft around here is your enormous gut." Nori looked at him meaningfully. "Or maybe not."

Iberville surged into the cell, fist raised, and Nori scrambled backward. Luckily, Simms caught him around the shoulders before his fist connected. He hauled Iberville out and slammed the door.

It had been several long moments, but the roar of blood pounding through her head hadn't quietened. She thought the men were gone, that she was safe, and just as she let down her guard, Iberville banged on the door and said something horribly raunchy. She backed away until her legs hit the rickety cot. Dropping onto it, she pulled her knees to her chest and listened for a long time. They never came back.

Nori's nerve evaporated once the threat was gone, and she rocked back and forth on the unforgiving cot, eyes open but unseeing. She shivered, alone in the frigid room, though her mind had taken her somewhere else. A place where she burned with fever, her sweat soaking the sheets.

Though confinement had been as constant a companion as her pain, she had never learned to live with it. Being stuck in her bedroom sick and alone for much of her childhood had left as many scars as the sun had.

Trapped once again, the knowledge she couldn't escape, that she was bound by the four narrow walls, Nori was wild with fear. She threw her arms out to stop the room from spinning, to keep them from closing in on her. Leaning back against the wall with her eyes squeezed shut, she couldn't contain the agonized groan that left her lips.

Though she sobbed, tears did not fall. And though she fought to breathe through the paralyzing claustrophobia, it did not abate. Not for hours.

***

NORI'S EYES SNAPPED OPEN. She didn't remember falling asleep; didn't know where she was. When she sat up, awareness flooded back and her heart sank to the cold, concrete floor. She was oblivious to how much time had passed. Had she slept through the night? Had anyone opened the door to her cell? No. She would have heard that.

Her movements were as sluggish as her brain, but she couldn't find the energy to care. Besides crippling claustrophobia, she felt a soul-deep sense of betrayal. Making matters worse was how stupid she felt for feeling that way. Cooper was playing a role. He was going along with the facade to gain the trust of Mathers and get in with the CCC. She knew that. And yet her gut churned as she replayed the chain of events that led to her imprisonment.

The night before she and Cooper had reached the *cenote*, in a solemn, fire-lit conversation, she had confessed her secret fears. Cooper had, too. It was a defining moment in their relationship. Flames had reflected in his eyes, giving their golden flecks an ethereal cast. She laid open her soul, telling him about the miserable weeks of her life spent bedridden and lonely. Cooper had not said a word as she told him of the dreamless nightmare that was much of her life, when pain was only interrupted by flashes of the faces of her parents.

She felt guilty even as the words tumbled from her mouth. Self pity was a weakness she never allowed herself to wallow in. He hadn't judged her, though. Instead, he slid his arms around her and held her, even when she tried to pull away. They stayed like that forever, her back warmed by the fire, and her soul soothed by Cooper's acceptance. She had fallen asleep in his arms, and they had slept that way until the fire died to embers.

Nori shivered as the memory snapped, colder and more alone in the cell than she had been before.

She stood and banged on the metal door. "Hey." She hit it with her palms again when no one answered. "I want to talk to someone," she yelled.

Silence. No footsteps. No murmurings. Nothing.

"Helloooooo." But her calls met only silence.

What if I was really ready to talk, she wondered. Who'd even know?

Too agitated to sit again, she paced the small space.

"All the banging and yelling in the world won't get you out of here." A woman's muted voice drifted into her cell. "Believe me, I've tried."

Nori's head whipped in the direction of the sound. "Hello?" She put her palms to the concrete wall. "Are you — are you talking to me?"

"You see anybody else?"

"No," Nori answered with reluctance. "*Is* there anybody else?"

"Not nearby, best I can tell. Hasn't been anybody. Not till you showed up."

"Are — are you in a cell, too?"

"Right next door. Howdy neighbor. Sorry I didn't bake any muffins." The woman's tone was thick with irony.

"Who are you?" Nori asked, and when the woman didn't answer right away she added, "I'm Nori."

"Pleasure." The detachment in her voice said it was anything but.

"When will someone come by, you think?" Nori asked. "I need out of here. And maybe some food."

The woman laughed. "They'll feed you, though you'll wish they hadn't."

Nori wasn't sure about that. Any food was better than starving. Her stomach growled in agreement. "How long have you been here?"

"Couple weeks. Maybe a month." The woman paused. "I think. Time runs together."

Nori nodded, but stopped since there was no one to see her head move. The woman's voice was so familiar. That was impossible, though. She didn't know many people underground. Any women, anyway.

"What are you in for?" the woman asked.

"I dunno," Nori answered. "I got lost and wandered where I shouldn't have. They accused me of spying and when I didn't admit to it, they brought me in here."

"Oh, come on, now," the woman scoffed, her voice leading. "You weren't snooping? Not even a little bit?"

An alarm sounded in Nori's head. The woman could be a plant, just another tactic the CCC was using to get information. "Not even a little bit," she said, her tone leaving no room for interpretation. And that was the end of the conversation.

Abandoned.

After endless hours spent alone in the cell, the word was stuck on repeat in Nori's head. Abandoned. Abandoned. Abandoned. It bounced and mocked over and over until she ached to scream, to throw something, to hit something— or someone.

Where *was* Cooper? Was he even trying to get her out? Could he, when he was the reason she was down here in the first place?

He was. He had a plan. She nodded in an attempt to reassure herself. Surely, Cooper had a plan.

I mean, it wasn't like she would be held captive indefinitely. *Someone* would notice she was gone. *Someone* would come to help her. But when she thought it through, panic worked to a lather within her chest. The only person she knew who had any idea where she was... was Cooper.

She stood and hammered on the steel door with the sides of her fists until they throbbed and swelled. Though she screamed for someone to let her out, to come speak to her, at least, they never did.

"You'd be better off saving that energy." It was the woman next-door again. "You'll wish those fists were fresh when you get your first late night visitor."

Nori's rage plummeted, replaced by a slow, sick dread. "What do you mean?"

"I think you know what I mean," the woman said, her voice laced with something. Not malice. Not fear. It was something stronger: loathing.

Nori swallowed. "Was it one of the guards?" she asked. "Did— did someone hurt you?"

"Not as much as I hurt them."

17

THE LAY OF THE LAND

"And this, Mr. Cooper," Mathers said as he nodded to a set of double-doors that opened to a cafeteria, "is the mess hall. You hungry?"

Cooper pushed everything from his mind. He tamped down the fear— and the guilt— that boiled just below the surface. He ignored the urge to search every square inch of the facility until he found Nori, breaking her free of the prison he knew must be tearing her apart. Hiding his emotions beneath an aloof outer layer was a craft he had honed for years. He pushed himself out and let the other Cooper in.

"I could eat."

Like the rest of the high-tech bunker, galvanized steel conduits carried electrical wires across the ceiling and down the gray walls to narrow boxes housing light switches or power outlets. Male and female soldiers chatted across formica-topped tables, and the smell of cooked food filled the place with a warmth Cooper hadn't expected.

"Pasta bar's my favorite," the Captain said in a tone that indicated Cooper would be having it, too.

Taking a hard plastic tray and a thin silver fork from the end of a buffet, Cooper fell in behind Mathers. "I'm not used to facilities this big," Cooper said as he took in the rest of the room. "Or so nice. About how many can it hold?"

Mathers' chest inflated at the compliment. "This main mess can hold about 500 at a time."

Cooper hoped his expression said *impressive*. "Have to stagger chow times, then, I gues. You must house, what, about 2500?"

Mathers opened his mouth to answer, but his eyes narrowed and he closed it again, lips pressed to a thin line.

Cooper cursed himself. He knew better than to dig too deep too soon. Mathers was obviously still on the fence about him, despite the fact he passed the key phrase test.

And hadn't he gotten lucky with that! When Mathers had asked for it, Cooper knew he and Nori were dead. Key phrase? What key phrase? But just as he was thinking of wrestling the old man's gun and taking him hostage, the words Sarge had so often yelled like an anthem before kicking his motorcycle to a start smacked Cooper in the face. "Stand by to pop smoke." Sarge had said it nearly every day Cooper rode with him. If it was a top-secret key phrase, he certainly hadn't kept a tight lid on it. But nobody had ever accused Sarge of being a genius.

Cooper motioned toward the sea of tables in the mess hall, forcing a wide smile and abandoning his line of questioning. "After you, Captain," he said.

Mathers didn't move right away, but probed Cooper's face with shrewd speculation. If a look could shred a man's skin and reveal what lay underneath, Mathers had it down. Cooper felt like a bug beneath a magnifying glass with the sun's roasting ray just centimeters away. Should he run? He wouldn't get ten feet, surrounded as he was by soldiers. He had no choice but to stand there, his face plastered with an open, expectant smile.

After an eternity, Mathers lifted his tray and turned without another word. He took an empty seat surrounded by uniformed soldiers. Cooper followed and sat his food onto the table, though he was suddenly uncertain if he was still invited.

"How long were you under Sarge's command?" Mathers asked as he lay a napkin neatly in his lap.

"About two years," Cooper answered. "Long enough to be glad I was on his side. Now there's one man you don't want to cross. I once saw him beat a mine worker in a bar for looking at him the wrong way." Air whistled through Cooper's teeth on a grimace. "Turned out the man had a bum eye, but he never used the good one to look in Sarge's direction again." Nerves had Cooper jumpy, and when he leaned back to laugh, he hit the chair behind him.

"Sorry," Cooper mumbled to the back of a close-clipped head.

When the soldier turned, Cooper froze. He couldn't breathe, couldn't move, couldn't think.

The soldier's eyes went wide. "Coop?" he said and dropped a thin fork, which clanged as it hit the tray. Only then did the soldier notice Mathers, his gaze flicking from Mathers to Cooper and back again.

This could go either way, Cooper thought, fighting the tremor in his hands. Either I'm dead or I'm cleared. He wiped sweaty palms on his pants and scanned the mess hall for exits.

A grin split the soldier's tight features. "It is you," he said, hand stretched across his body toward Cooper. "I knew that girly head of hair couldn't belong to anyone else." He shook Cooper's hand, gripping too tightly and holding on two seconds too long. "Don't worry," he went on, "I've seen one or two blow-dryers in this place, so you're good."

Mathers shocked them both by barking a laugh. "Now, how do you know Standridge?" he asked Cooper.

Cooper's synapses were not firing. The hardwiring of his brain short-circuited as he tried to rationalize Cal's presence. A hundred thoughts crowded his brain, but no good answers. When he didn't respond to Mathers' question, Cal thumped him on the back good-naturedly, if a bit too hard. "What're you doing here, man?"

Cooper shook himself, clearing his mind of doubt and fear, arranging his mouth in the non-threatening smile he had perfected over the years. "Oh, just passing through," he said.

'What the hell are *you* doing here?' is what Cooper wanted to ask. Breathing through the uncertainty, he quieted his mind and steadied his pulse, sorting through his next steps. Would being known as Cal's friend help win Mathers' trust? The way Mathers eyed him, Cooper thought maybe not. With no real way to know, he opted to play it safe.

"Good to see you... man," Cooper said. Adding the pause before dismissing the soldier insinuated he had forgotten Cal's name, which of course he never could. Turning from Cal, Cooper resumed his conversation with a wary and watchful Captain Mathers.

"I'll never forget it," Cooper said. "Sarge has always been mean as a snake, but this was vicious even for him. He bent to pick up the glass eye, polished it on his sleeve, and pocketed it like a coin."

"Mr. Cooper?" Mathers said his name with a cool confidence that did not correspond with the story Cooper had just finished. He had expected another barked laugh, a guffaw, even, as the story often earned. Mathers offered neither.

"Sir?" Cooper replied.

"Would you like to see the stockade?"

"Sir?" Cooper asked again.

"I thought you might like to look in on your friend before our debriefing."

Nervous energy, hot and sharp, sped through Cooper's veins, but he kept it clear of his face. "The girl, you mean?" Cooper shrugged. "I trust you're handling the situation appropriately." Mathers inclined his head, and Cooper added, "But since it's my first time at your facility, I'm interested in whatever you'll show me. This level of organization — of excellence — is new to me and I'm fascinated."

The flattery did not have the effect Cooper intended. Mathers' keen gaze remained sharp, his posture rigid and straight. He was one tough mother. "Stockade's a good place to start, then," he said.

Normally, Cooper's long stride was hard for others to match. He had learned to slow when someone walked beside him, but Mathers didn't need the help. The man's clipped steps were efficient and brisk. As they walked, Cooper took mental snapshots of the facility's layout. There were elevators, but Mathers led him down several flights of stairs.

When they finally arrived at the stockade, Cooper was stunned. He hadn't expected a dungeon, but certainly wasn't prepared for the opposite. The smell hit him first. A mixture of bleach and piss, the searing fumes cleared his sinuses so thoroughly he took short, shallow breaths through his nostrils as his eyes took in the white. The concrete walls surrounding the jail cells were painted a bright alabaster, and beams of stark light shone down from bulbs protected by metal cages.

Cooper sensed something behind the thick metal doors, but no one stirred or called out as they passed. He felt an odd urge to duck as he walked by, to hurry and apologize for the disturbance.

"We do have some long-term residents here," Mathers said with a smirk. "But most are temporary—a private who had one too many and knifed his buddy— that sort of thing."

The Captain stopped midway down another long hallway, his eyes trained on Cooper's face. "And here we have the girl you brought in." He motioned to a metal door with a sliver of a window near the top and a small slot at the bottom for food trays. "Want to pay her a visit?"

"Not especially," Cooper said, though all he wanted in the world was to see Nori Chisholm's face, to make sure she hadn't been hurt. Did she have food? Was she strong enough to make it through another isolation? Pain twisted his chest at the image of her cowered in a corner with a fist in her mouth so she didn't scream. Too much, Cooper thought suddenly. I can't do this. I can't take it. He closed his eyes, breathing through the frighteningly primal need to keep her safe.

"No?" Mathers lifted an eyebrow. "I'll have Iberville look in on her later, then," he said. "He has a reputation of being good with the ladies."

A wave of revulsion and rage swept over Cooper so quickly it almost knocked him down. He imagined himself taking the gun from the holster at Mathers' side and pistol-whipping him. He would find a key to Nori's cell on the Captain's unconscious body, pull her out, and throw him in. They'd find a way out of the facility together and run for Chicago or Mexico— anywhere. For the briefest charged moment, Cooper let himself believe it could work. But as Mathers' hawk-like gaze came back into focus, he knew it couldn't. This was a test, and probably a trap.

"No." Cooper shook his head and oozed boredom. "On to the bunkhouse?"

"Certainly." Mathers words were appropriate enough, but the tilt of his head, the squint of his eye, the angle of his posture told Cooper he was still very much a suspect.

Cooper channeled his training as he toured the headquarters of the CCC. He played dumb when appropriate; he was unassuming and friendly. Outwardly, he was a model of mild interest and superficial conversation.

But inside, his allegiances were split like a canyon. One part of him paid meticulous attention to building structure, personnel, weaponry and shift changes. But despite his efforts to reclaim it, the other half of his heart was inside a cell with Nori.

"Believe it or not, I've got more to do than play tour guide all day," Mathers said. The abrupt shift in tone caught Cooper off guard.

"Oh." Cooper stood to attention. "Yes. Yes, sir, I imagine so. I appreciate the time spent showing me your fine facility."

"Lot of men gather in the bar when they're off duty." Mathers adjusted his collar, though it didn't need straightening. "Not something I indulge in," he said. "But a lot of men do." Without another word, the Captain turned and clipped down the hall.

"Guess I'm dismissed," Cooper said under his breath.

18

SECRETS AND LIES

The bar looked like any other. Rows of glass bottles framed a mirrored wall behind a long oak counter. It was the only place in the facility that wasn't oversaturated with artificial light, the architect's obvious efforts to make residents forget they were underground. The place had a soft, almost yellow glow. A familiar rock anthem played low in the background, and it smelled faintly of booze and fried food. Cooper felt right at home.

Only a few stools were taken, so Cooper made his way toward a free one. He was just about to order something when the bartender's attention snagged on something behind him.

"Plenty of tables in the back."

When Cooper heard the familiar voice behind him, he pressed his hands onto the bar and took a deep breath. He rose from the barstool and turned, and Cal tackled him, nearly knocking the breath from his lungs. He squeezed back the best friend he'd ever had, the best friend he thought was dead.

When they finally separated, he couldn't stop staring at Cal. How was his friend standing in front of him? Why was he here, of all places? They stood like that for so long, not moving and not saying anything, that the bartender cleared his throat uncomfortably.

"You got a problem?" Cal asked, his voice sharp. The old man shook his head and quickly found somewhere else to be.

Cooper followed Cal to a booth in the back near a row of pool tables with nearly-threadbare felt. He had a hundred questions for his friend, who'd disappeared in the middle of the night over two years ago. Where had he been all this time? Why hadn't he come home, or at least contacted someone? Why was he wearing a CCC soldier's uniform? And how did he get in with the band of murderous zealots.

Oh God, Cooper thought, his heart in his boots. Cal hadn't really joined them, had he?

"What are you doing here, Cal?" he finally asked, his whisper rough. It was both odd and wonderful to see him again, and it was all Cooper could do to keep from hugging his friend's neck again. Or wringing it.

"I thought you were dead," Cooper said. "Everyone did. You disappeared without a word to any of us-- to Meggie or my mother or me..." His temper surged as he recalled the months of slow-spreading grief that infected the Settlement. "It's been years, and not a word?" Cooper gritted his teeth, his knuckles creaking under the grip of his fists.

"What are you talking about?" Cal said. "Franks knew I was leaving." He leaned across the table. His face, for once, was serious. "He ordered me to go. He said he'd tell you." Cal's forehead wrinkled in confusion. "You saying he didn't?"

Cooper glared at his friend, but he shook his head.

"Did anyone tell Meg?" Cal asked. "Or Gisa?"

"Not that I know of," Cooper said. "No. Franks couldn't have told Gisa. She'd have said something to me."

"I should've known better than to trust him." Cal's lip curled in disgust. "He's hated me—hated us both—since the day we made the Sixth Tier."

"Way before that," Cooper said. "He hated you the moment you stepped foot on the training floor. Remember how he would make you spar the biggest guys, give you the most push-ups? Franks never thought you were serious enough."

"He never thought I was *good* enough," Cal corrected.

"That, too." Cooper said. "He couldn't stand to watch you win. Hated it when you did."

"And I loved to watch him boil," Cal said, his teeth peeking through an evil grin. "You know, sometimes I think I'd never have stuck with it if I wasn't trying to prove that old goat wrong."

When Cal leaned across the table, the pendant light gave his sandy head an odd yellow glow. "I never knew why he hated you so much, though," he said. "You took the program seriously. Overly so, if you ask me. If Franks hated that I was such a jackass, why didn't he love you? Why didn't he take you under his wing?"

The question made Cooper uncomfortable. He had wasted years wondering the same thing. He had spent far too much time feeling inadequate and aimless, and ultimately ashamed for putting so much value behind the approval of the one man who'd never give it.

Cooper sniffed and changed the subject. "You nearly got me killed today," he said. "We could've worked together if you'd acted like you didn't know me. We trained for this, Cal. For *any* surprise. And you blurt my name? Rookie mistake. What were you thinking?"

A muscle in Cal's thick neck twitched. "I'm sorry," he said.

"You're right. But you were the last person I expected to see here, and my mouth kicked in before my brain did."

"Not a new problem for you." Cooper's tone was matter-of-fact. "Which is why I never thought you'd finish the program."

"Luckily, you were wrong," Cal said with a pointed glare.

This back and forth was familiar to Cooper, and comforting. Cal had lived two floors below him for most of their lives. They'd been best friends as kids and trained together for the Sixth Tier as they grew older. They were inseparable.

Everyone— except Zenon Franks— loved Cal. Witty and fun, people were drawn to him. Especially women. Hell, Cal was better at women than anything else. And the baffling part for Cooper had always been that they knew it, but didn't care. Cal had declared himself unattainable, and once that was established, women were satisfied to simply occupy some of his time. It was the most confounding thing Cooper had ever seen— and one of their defining differences. Compared to Cal, Cooper had been clumsy and awkward. He had tripped over too-long legs, too shy to approach girls who giggled at him but couldn't look away.

Cooper smiled and pushed the old thoughts away. It was a long time and another life ago. Now, he was just as cool as Cal. In fact, wearing Cal's persona was his best trick. Stepping out of his own skin and into Cal's had gotten him past social awkwardness and uncertainty. When working undercover, he pretended to *be* Cal, and confidence oozed from his pores. Lies did too, which came in handy.

"So," Cal said slowly, "if you didn't know I was here, why are *you* here?"

Cooper relayed as quickly as possible the saga of meeting Nori and their chance discovery that the CCC was responsible for the world-burning sunscorches. He waited for Cal's shock, for outrage. It did not surface, though his face had gone pale near the end of the story.

"We already knew that, Coop," Cal said. "I gave Franks that intel six months ago."

As the implications of Cal's words sunk in, blind, murderous fury sent blood rushing past Cooper's ears, drowning out the rock anthem playing on an old jukebox.

"What?" he finally managed.

For the first time, it occurred to Cooper that Zenon Franks wasn't just an obtuse old fart. If what Cal said was true, he was pure evil, and maybe even working his own angle from inside the Settlement all along.

"What are you saying?" Cooper asked again.

"Franks sent me down here over two years ago," Cal said. "I've said all the right things, made the right friends, and was stationed as a grunt in command. That's where I met Lindgren."

Cooper's mind, set on a roller coaster at the new information, suddenly derailed. Thoughts and theories sprinted to win the race to the front— until he processed Cal's last words. "Wait," Cooper said. "Who's Lindgren?"

Cal cocked his head to the side like Cooper was slow. "Right," he nodded. "I guess you wouldn't know if Franks didn't tell you. Lindgren is the lead scientist behind the scorches, and I think I can turn him."

19

AN INTERROGATION

Nori woke to the rustle and clink of keys. Someone was opening her door. She had no idea what time it was, and no way to tell.

After the woman next door's warning, Nori had searched the cell for some way to make a weapon, but the old military-issue cot was useless. She hadn't been able to separate any of the metal from the canvas.

Taking a breath, she stretched her neck, thankful for the weeks she had trained with Kade. It was knees and knuckles, then. She might not be able to fend off more than one attacker, but she could take out an eyeball in the process.

Light shot into the cell when the door swung open, and Nori shielded her eyes, blinking to adjust. When she could finally see well enough to work out their forms, her heart plummeted. Simms and Iberville were back. Without a word, the two men grabbed her by the shoulders again and pulled her from the room.

"No," Nori said, her voice hoarse from lack of use. "I want

to go back," she said. It wasn't entirely true. She wanted out of the jail cell, just not with them.

"Where are you taking me?" she asked, looking first to Iberville, whose thick jowls thrummed as he walked, and then to Simms. "Where are we going?"

Neither answered as they dragged her to the end of the hall, her arms screaming until the men finally stopped in front of a windowed room. Nori tried to peek inside, but the view was obstructed by cheap horizontal blinds. Simms opened the door and pushed her inside without ceremony, but Iberville gave a weasel-like smirk before closing the door behind her.

She was alone, at least. Two chairs flanked a metal table, but otherwise the room was empty. Dread coiled in the pit of her stomach at the thought of being interrogated, and she paced the length of the room. When no one came, Nori sat in one of the chairs, but rose almost immediately to resume pacing.

Left on her own so long, she jumped when the door finally opened. Captain Mathers ignored her, stalking inside and pulling out one of the chairs. And hot on the Captain's heels was none other than Sam Cooper. Nori's nostrils flared on a sharp intake of air. Relief and longing hit her just moments before resentment and fury.

Mathers motioned for her to sit in the chair opposite him without so much as looking at her. Nori refused to give him the satisfaction and stood, knees locked and arms crossed.

Cooper positioned himself to stand with his back to the window— behind Mathers. Nori watched him with thinly-veiled rage.

"Has anyone hurt you?" Cooper's abrupt question drew a scowl from Captain Mathers, who shrugged after a beat.

"Well," Mathers said when she didn't answer. He looked at her for the first time. "Have they?"

She considered lying, if only to hurt Cooper, to scare him because she had been so scared. Obviously, he had not spent his nights shivering in a concrete cell. But the look in his eyes stopped her short. Normally cutting and clever, Cooper's eyes were tired. The deep bruising beneath them made her think he'd had little sleep... and a lot of worry. And that he was afraid enough already.

"No," she finally answered. Her tone was surly, but Cooper's eyes closed in obvious relief.

Mathers stood from the table and clipped across the room until he stood mere inches from her. Nori didn't look up at him, and instead focused on the gleam of his black military boots.

"Now," Mathers said, his intimidating presence so close chill bumps erupted on her skin. "Let's get right to it," he said. "What series of events led you to be at the south entrance, where Mr. Cooper apprehended you?"

Nori flicked her eyes to Cooper. What am I supposed to say here, she wondered. Any suggestions?

Cooper was silent, but leaned toward her expectantly, as if he couldn't wait to hear her answer.

Nori's mind raced to come up with a plausible story, but everything she considered was nonsense. What reason did she have to be outside the hidden entrance to a top-secret facility? Something pulled at her mind, something Cooper had said one of the rare times he had opened up about his undercover work. 'When making up a story,' he said, 'stick as close to the truth as possible so there's less to remember.'

Mathers was so close Nori could see the stubble of his

beard. When she finally met his gaze, it took all her nerve not to flinch.

"Best tell us the truth, hon" he said. "We have ways of getting to it eventually. There's a whole team, in fact, who specialize in truth…" He showed his teeth, but it wasn't a smile. "…extraction."

Nori swallowed. An organization as big as theirs would naturally need to excel both at keeping their own secrets and intercepting others. Her mouth was so dry she could barely move her tongue.

"Spit it out," Cooper said, yanking her attention back to him.

Nori leaned around Mathers' too-close body and caught the slightest nod of Cooper's head. Whatever that meant.

Tears stung her eyes. She sniffed and shook her head and went for it.

"I…" Nori paused. Cleared her throat. She was going to be terrible at this. Lying was Cooper's great skill, not hers. "My family just doesn't get it," she said in a rush. "They don't get me. I'm nearly grown, but they try to keep me locked up all the time. I want to live." It was as close to the truth as she could get. She stood up straighter. "So I left."

Mathers' steel gaze scrutinized her face. One side of his mouth lifted in a mocking grin. "You're telling me you ran away from your mommy and daddy and ended up here?" he asked.

Nori gave a reluctant nod.

"You expect me to believe that you left home— alone— and travelled tunnels known for their treachery, and stumbled onto our facility?" Mathers crept even closer. "That you were lost and wandered up to our secret back entrance?"

"Well," Nori said and stalled, searching for confidence. "When you say it like that, sure, it sounds suspicious."

"Indeed," Mathers smirked and rotated his head to look behind him. "Eh, Cooper?"

Cooper's scowl and menacing nod was spot-on, and Nori wanted to roll her eyes. Or scream. Or hit someone.

"All right, now." Mathers stepped away from her and rounded the small table, taking a seat in the chair. "Story time's over," he said. "Tell me what really happened, huh?"

Nori held out her arms, feigning exasperated innocence. "I did."

"Come on." Mathers gave an encouraging nod. "Let's talk this out sensibly. You seem like a smart girl. Surely you can see we're not buying this load of malarky. Time to come clean and see how we can move forward."

"I don't know what you mean," Nori answered, throwing her eyes wide. "It's the truth. I'm unlucky, sir, not underhanded."

Mathers' thin lips pointed at his earlobes. "You're not as smart as I thought you were," he said. "And I'll tell you something else. You're not as smart as you think you are, either." He stood in one swift movement and flung open the door, barking at the two men waiting outside. "Get in here and take her," he said.

Nori risked another look at Cooper, whose veins protruded from his neck.

Iberville entered first. "Where to, sir?"

"Put her back until I authorize enhanced interrogation," Mathers said. Nori's stomach bottomed out. That sounded an awful lot like torture. "Regs require I get the go-ahead from Mills first." Mathers threw the words behind him and strode down the hall.

Nori let out a shaky breath and looked to Cooper expecting a nod of approval for her story, or some kind of encouragement that everything would be all right. But the look on his face sucked the breath from her lungs.

"What?" She stepped closer, but Cooper shook his head.

His eyes were wide. Scared. "I know that name," was all he said before leaving the room, too.

20

OF A PRIVATE NATURE

One-hundred and twenty-one. That's how many concrete blocks made up each of the three full walls of Nori's cell. The wall with the door had only ninety-five. She hadn't yet counted the grains of sand in the mortar holding the blocks together, but that was next. Rolling her neck, she closed her eyes and wished for a pillow.

How long she had been been inside the cell, she didn't know. Her neighbor had been right. Time ran together in the clink. Nori shook her head and huffed a laugh at herself. 'Clink,' she repeated.

The jangle of keys outside her cell saved Nori from the rabbit hole of solitary confinement. She rose from her cot and backed away from the door, fists clenched and knee at the ready. The door opened only long enough for someone to slip inside before closing again. She would know those thick jowls anywhere. Iberville stood just inside her cell, a nervous grin on his waxy lips. She backed into the corner, but it wasn't far enough to avoid the stench of his sweat. Revulsion rose in the back of her throat and she breathed through her mouth not to vomit.

"I thought you might could use some company." Iberville's words slithered through the room and he took a step, which in a ten by ten room put him far too close for Nori's comfort. She swallowed convulsively.

"I brought you something from the kitchen," he said and when she didn't move, lay a plate with two oblong white things on her cot. With his hands empty, he wrung them nervously. "Most people outside of here've never had eggs before." He stretched his big lips into a smile, and the acrid taste of fear coated Nori's tongue. "They're a delicacy."

He's trying to seduce me, Nori thought in horror. He has brought me gifts. Realization struck as his eyes slid down her body, and a disgusted shiver snaked down her spine. She wouldn't be able to fight him off. He outweighed her by at least one-hundred pounds. He could force her into anything he wanted. A pistol flashed at his hip like a threat.

The only way to keep him away, Nori realized as her heart pounded within her chest, was be to convince him he didn't want her. She closed her eyes and put every watt of brainpower she had into a solution. When the idea struck, she winced. It wasn't great, but it would do in a pinch.

"I'm glad you're here," she said, using her fear to sound uncertain and embarrassed.

Iberville didn't smile. He wasn't stupid; just dumb. His head tilted to the side. "Is that right?"

"Yes," Nori said. "I've been needing to talk to someone."

"What about?" Iberville's eyes narrowed.

She scratched her upper thigh and scissored her legs, bouncing as if she was at the same time uncomfortable and ashamed. "You have a doctor here, right?" she asked.

Iberville's eyes reduced to slits. "We do."

"Good," Nori gushed. "I—I need to speak with him. Or her." She looked up through her eyelashes and grimaced. "Preferably a *her*, actually."

"You sick?" he asked.

Nori nodded, eyes downcast.

Iberville cleared his throat. "What... ah. What's the nature of your illness?"

"Private," Nori whispered. "It's of a private nature." She pulled air through her teeth and scratched again, though a bit higher than her thigh.

Iberville's eyes widened as understanding dawned, and his demeanor changed. He backed toward the door and opened it without a word. "I... ah... I'll see about having the doctor sent down," he said, and slammed the thick metal door between them.

A slow, wicked smile crossed Nori's face, and she nodded Iberville good riddance. She didn't know how long her little trick would work, but it was good enough for now.

No sense letting good food go to waste, she thought, and took a closer look at the plate. The man really had brought eggs. She picked up the oddly-shaped thing, inspecting it from every side. If there were eggs, that must mean... *chickens*. She would never seen a chicken. No one she knew had ever seen a chicken, though someone had told her eggs came from chickens' butts. She had never believed it. If I get out of here alive, Nori thought, I'm going to find out for myself.

"Clever, clever girl." A woman's laugh, wicked and amused, crept into Nori's cell. "Or have you really caught something?" she asked. "Either way, your little plan worked, didn't it?"

Nori closed her eyes and let out a hopeful breath. "Time will tell."

21

FRAMEWORK AND MINUTIAE

Though Cooper had always been good with details, the floorpan of the CCC facility had begun to run together. Cal had learned to navigate the place over time, though, and swiftly led him to narrow hallways and hidden stairwells he never would have found on his own.

"So, there's this girl," Cal said, looking over his shoulder at Cooper as they ascended a set of stairs.

"There always is," Cooper groaned.

"Hey, she was hot, man. And smart. A Lieutenant, so she wasn't supposed to be fraternizing with me, right? So we needed somewhere to meet up. Somewhere private. Somewhere we could be sure no one would wander in."

"Is there a point to this story," Cooper asked, "or are you just bragging?"

"Anyway," Cal said, ignoring him, "she was on track for a post at the primary command center. Her dad is some big shot and she's following in his footsteps. Whatever. She had been training for a while, getting ready for the day she could operate the real thing, you know? And she practiced at something they called 'secondary control.'" Cal cracked a door leading to another floor, peeking his head through to make sure they were alone before exiting completely.

"So she starts sneaking me in to secondary control, maybe to impress me a little, but mostly because nobody ever interrupts us there. Ever. This place is a well-kept secret, right, and nobody has a key except the big shots— who never use the place— and her. And me, because she gave me one. Because it's *our place*."

"Still feels like you're bragging," Cooper said as the two hustled down a sparsely-lit hall.

"One night, we got a little carried away and she bumped something. The entire control panel lit up, turning our skin in green and blue. I was kinda digging it, but she started freaking out," he said and laughed. "I was like, 'what's the big deal? It's not real.' And she was like, 'You don't understand. Secondary control is operational, too. It's just saved for emergencies.'"

Cooper smiled as he grasped the point of Cal's story. "You still have it?" he asked.

His friend grinned and opened a fist to reveal the tiny silver key.

"So, I've got a plan," Cal said as he swung open the door to the secondary control room.

This was no surprise to Cooper. Over the course of their childhood, Cal was always coming up with a new plan, which usually got them both into trouble, but was always enough fun to make the punishment worth it. A brilliant team, Cal was the idea man and Cooper filled in the details. But the people at the

Settlement had never fully appreciated their talents, so naturally they were forced to display them. Often.

One of Cal's most ambitious plans had been to show the Settlement Elders the facility's vulnerabilities— in case of attack. Cooper had thought the idea ingenious, and set in motion a three-pronged plan to rearrange the ammunitions store, stall the sub-to-surface ventilation system, and jam the exits.

Looking back, Cooper could certainly see the naivety behind the plan. The stupidity, even. They never imagined the Elders would think it was an *actual* attack. And they hadn't accounted for the considerable wrath they'd face for scaring the bejesus out of the entire community. The shenanigan had been the first stop on an epic journey toward the mutual hatred Cooper shared with Zenon Franks.

Ultimately, Cooper and Cal had been caught at the electric panel as they attempted to restore power to the exits. Their captor? None other than Franks himself. The rancorous old man wasn't just any Elder, but second in command of the entire Settlement. He had yanked them into his office by their collars, his cheeks ruddy with fury as he shoved them onto a stiff black leather couch.

"It's up to me whether you boys stay or go," Franks had said, straight to the point as usual. "You went too far with this last stunt, and there'll be a big contingent that'll want you kicked out of the Settlement. Our safety here relies on our ability to trust each other, and you've eviscerated that trust. You've left me no choice." Cooper remembered the words like it was yesterday, not years before. "I'm forced to take a decisive action that fits the severity of your crime," he had said.

"'Crime?'" Cal had attempted to wave the seriousness away. "Sir, it was just a prank. Our intentions were pure—"

Franks had stalked forward until he stood over Cal, who melted into the couch. "You call trying to asphyxiate an entire population a prank?" he asked. "There was such a run on the east exit Darby Holderness was nearly trampled to death. She's in medical now with a set of broken ribs."

"I didn't know that." Cal's pained grimace summarized Cooper's feelings, too.

"Just what did you think would happen when you stole our weapons and shut down the air filtration system?" Franks demanded.

Cooper had shut his eyes, regret and shame souring his stomach. "I guess that's just it. We weren't thinking."

"In our defense," Cal said, his tone inappropriately chipper, "we didn't steal the weapons. We just moved them." Cooper kicked his friend's leg, but Cal didn't take the hint. "We thought to show you and the other Elders our vulnerabilities. We thought it would help. And that maybe you'd let us into the Sixth Tier early."

Franks had barked a cruel laugh. "Well, you've screwed yourself there, Standridge. There's no chance you'll even get into the program now. Either of you. Too risky. Too stupid."

Cal had gone into shock, his face ashen as he stared at the wall of Franks' office, unblinking and uncharacteristically quiet. It had always been Cal's dream to join the Sixth Tier, the Settlement's elite military team. Cooper's, too. Everyone in the Settlement knew the members of the Sixth Tier. Children would stop, open-mouthed to watch as they passed. Cooper's own mother had been a founding member, and since he had shown so much promise in both fighting and strategy, it was always assumed he would be invited to join them.

Cal had no such connections. His mother worked in the laundry, and not much was known about his father. Cal was clever and charming and strong, but he wouldn't weather a blow like this. Not with Franks set against him.

But considering his mother's status, Cooper just might.

Zenon Franks had always been the one thing Cal was afraid of. Cooper would never forget the way Franks had turned a cold gray eye on Cal that day. "This was all your idea, I'm sure, Standridge," he had said.

It was so slight, Cooper might've missed it if he hadn't known his friend so well. The corner of Cal's right eye twitched. A muscle spasm, nothing more. But for Cal, who was always as cool as copper, the sign of his fear was another man's pants full of piss.

"It was my idea."

The impulsive claim came out louder than Cooper had intended, but it got Franks' attention. The stiff gray hair on the man's head barely moved when he whipped around. A silent standoff lasted for several long moments as Franks eyeballed Cooper, who lifted his chin in defiance.

From the corner of his eye, Cooper caught Cal's mouth open, ready to dispute their roles. But Cooper sliced his head to the side, just once, and Cal shut his mouth. His friend's face contorted, his jaws working like mad. But he stayed silent.

Cooper had stood and lowered his head, giving his best impersonation of contrite. "We've made a terrible, serious mistake, sir, that put the people we love in danger," Cooper said, meeting the man's furious gaze. "Cal and I are, truly, very sorry, and swear not to do anything so stupid again."

"Damn right you won't," Franks had spat. "And since it was your idea, you'll have plenty of time to think about your ignorant and dangerous actions when you're in the hole."

"How long?" Cal croaked.

"Two weeks seems reasonable," Franks said.

The sentence had been a punch to the gut, and while Cooper struggled to breathe, Cal shot up.

"Mr. Franks, sir, please," Cal said. "Two weeks in the hole will drive him insane." Cal grabbed the sleeve of Franks' coat, but released it under the man's murderous glare. "Please," Cal begged again. "It was all my idea. We didn't mean it, sir. We're just kids."

That last bit would've made Cooper laugh under any other circumstances. Cal hadn't considered himself a kid… ever.

Franks didn't even acknowledged Cal had spoken. "As for you, Standridge," he said, "you'll report to sanitation for the two weeks Cooper's in the hole. Clean up some of the crap you've caused." Franks opened the office door, the end of the conversation painfully clear. "Cooper, follow me."

"Yo, Coop," Cal said, jarring him from the painful recollection. "Where'd you go, man? You wanna hear this plan, or what?"

Cooper shivered, cold to his marrow at the memory of the deep, dark, solitary confinement that loomed just beyond. He thought of Nori, who'd so quickly become his anchor, his touchstone to what was right and good. Her light had warmed his wintered soul. She had no idea how much they had in common. And she had no idea how much he had come to need her. Yes, he needed a plan. A good one. A plan to stop the scorches, take out the CCC, and make it out of this god-awful place alive to cobble some kind of life together where neither of them felt confined.

Cooper paced the length of the small room, seeing everything and nothing. Cal knew the drill. They'd been here before, and after laying the framework, he was silent while Cooper worked out the minutiae.

"What we need," Cooper said after a while, "is a dry run."

"A dry run?" Cal repeated.

"If we knew how this place would react, if we knew their emergency procedures, we could use it to our advantage." Cooper locked his hands behind his head and turned to Cal. "How could we set this place to high alert without getting caught?"

"You leave that to me," Cal said, his face beaming at the prospect of stirring up trouble.

22

ANOTHER VISITOR

Footsteps outside her cell door sent the hairs of Nori's neck on end. Was it Iberville again? Had he actually sent for a doctor? Or was it a different guard? The place was crawling with them.

Backing against the wall, Nori waited, her chest rising with each breath.

The door opened in a rush, and only mid-way, before closing just as quickly.

Someone was inside the cell.

"Cooper?" Nori whispered.

He was crouching, and squinting to see in the darkness, but it was definitely him. When she spoke his name, his wide shoulders relaxed and he took a tentative step toward her, reaching out in the dark. "Nori?"

She clasped his outstretched hand, grunting with surprise when he pulled her to him. She tried to pull away. It wasn't a conscious decision, just her first instinct. Panic rose in her chest and made it hard to breathe. But Cooper didn't release his hold. He held her, resting his chin on her head and rubbing her back until the panic subsided and her breathing slowed.

A lifetime later, he backed away, eyes roaming over her face in the low light. "God, I didn't think I'd ever find you," he said. "Are you all right?"

Nori moved out of his reach and really did try to fight her growing anger. "I'm fine," she said and crossed her arms across her chest. "No thanks to you."

Cooper's eyes snapped to hers. "What do you mean? What's happened?"

"Nothing's happened," she scoffed. "Everything's just perfect. I mean, what could possibly be wrong?"

"You're angry," Cooper said.

"You're right." Nori balled her fists at her sides, but what she wanted to do was to beat Cooper with them. "Where have you been, Cooper? You left me down here to rot!"

He stepped toward her, his arms out as if to hold her again, but she dodged him. "Has someone hurt you?"

"Besides you?" When Cooper flinched, Nori felt only minimally guilty. "No," she finally said. "No one's hurt me. Yet. But I've been locked up in here for days, freezing and alone. I've been scared to death, Cooper." Her voice quavered, but she pressed on. "I had no idea if you were dead or alive, or if you would come and get me out of here. The last thing Mathers said was something about torture." She heaved a breath, holding back a sob. "It's the not knowing that's so hard."

Cooper closed his eyes and let out a long breath. "That," he nodded, holding his arms out but not approaching her again, "and being isolated again, I'm sure." Nori could see his eyes even in the darkness, filled with regret and worry. "I'm so sorry, Nori. I came as soon as I could."

Despite her better judgement, she fell into his arms and stayed there, fighting the stupid tears that begged for release. Someday she was going to get control of her tears, and when she did, they'd never fall again.

"I can't stay long," Cooper said after a while.

"Good." Nori sniffed and cleared her throat. "Let's get out of here."

A crevice formed between his dark eyebrows and he looked away. "I didn't come to get you out." Before she could even put words to her fury, he said in a rush, "Not yet. I will. I promise. Just… not yet."

"What do you mean 'not yet'? I can't stand being down here, Cooper. I'm going crazy." She swiped a chunk of hair from her face and scrubbed her eyes. "The isolation is getting to me. I want to help you stop these maniacs, and then find a way out of here. Now."

"That's not how it works," he said. "I need you to stay here, to be patient for just a little while."

Nori's face heated as her blood boiled. She wondered if steam would rise from her hair in the cold, damp room. Cooper dared leave her alone— again— in a jail cell while he… what? She crossed her arms again.

"Tell me where you've been all this time." She lifted her head defiantly. "Tell me what you've been doing while I've been rotting in here."

"I'm working from the inside," he answered. "I've been gaining their trust and gathering intel. Learning my way around this place so I can get you out."

"Get me out now," she pushed. "Take me with you now. I can help. You know I can." As she spoke, the look in Cooper's downcast eyes was so pitying that her anger stirred again.

"I know you want to take these guys down as badly as I

do, Nori. That's why I'm begging you to just stay put for a little while longer. Please. It's important. I'm working on a plan."

Some of the fight left her. How was she supposed to respond? She hated for him to think she was weak. But if she said okay, he would close the door and abandon her again. "This sucks," she finally said.

"It does." Cooper nodded. "It sucks—" He froze and turned his head more fully toward the plate of food on her cot. "Are those eggs?"

Revulsion warred with hunger within her stomach, which growled from one or both.

Cooper looked at her middle and then back up. "Why haven't you eaten them?"

"Because Iberville brought them," she answered.

"Iberville?" Cooper's head tilted and his nostrils flared. "Why would Iberville bring you food?"

Nori raised her eyebrows.

She could almost hear the bones of his hands grinding together in fists. "Did he—" Cooper cleared his throat. "Did he hurt you?"

"No," she said. "I got rid of him."

"How?"

"Doesn't matter." Nori shrugged. "I'm okay. For now. But you have to get me out of here, Cooper, and soon."

23

DRY RUN

Cooper followed Cal down a series of stark white identical halls and up several flights of concrete stairs. So far, no one they passed had suspected them of anything—just two guys doing their jobs like everybody else. But no way that wouldn't last.

"You ready for this?" Cal asked and pushed open a heavy metal door. Cooper nodded. He was as ready as he would ever be.

The open door revealed a new landscape. Concrete halls were no more. Cooper's mouth fell open as they entered an enormous tunnel rough-cut into the mountainside. Silver electrical conduits ran down the middle of the high ceiling, concealing the wires that carried currents from the facility's generators. Caged LED lights were spaced every eight or ten feet, their flicker and buzz the only disturbance to an unsettling silence.

"Where are we?" Cooper asked, feeling insubstantial compared to the facility that seemed to have no end. "This place is huge."

"I've done my share of exploring over the past two years," Cal said, "but there are places even I haven't seen." He pointed to another big metal door with a complicated-looking keypad to the left of its levered handle. "The western entrance is just through there, though we can't get past that door without top clearance."

"What's on the other side of that door?" Cooper asked. Nothing drove his curiosity like a boundary.

"A garage," Cal's eyebrows lifted on a cat-like grin. "Huge. Full of military vehicles."

"You've seen it?" Cooper wanted to go beyond the door so badly he could practically feel the cool metal of a Humvee beneath his fingertips.

"Yep. Once. I volunteered to join Mechanical just so I could check it out. I lasted two weeks before they figured out I was *not* cut out for heavy equipment."

"Can we get in there?" Cooper had inched toward the door, greedy for the treasures parked on the other side.

"Don't need to," Cal said. He hadn't moved past a red box attached to the wall. "Not today. All we need to know is what happens when I break this glass and pull the alarm."

"What do you think's gonna happen?" Cooper asked.

"Not sure." Cal shrugged. "The guys in Mechanical said it was designed for external threats. It's a manual alarm in case something goes bad wrong beyond that door. You asked for a dry run, well, here goes."

Cal smashed the glass and pulled down the metal lever. Within seconds the tunnel's white lights flashed red, and a deafening, howling horn blared through the facility.

Cooper's first instinct was to hide, but that wasn't the plan. Instead, he and Cal hid in plain sight, pretending to have their own assignments, pretending to be a part of the response, but all the while watching the emergency plan came together. Except, no one treated it like an emergency. Soldiers who'd trained for years to defend the bunker jogged leisurely to what they thought was just another drill. Once at their pre-set stations, soldiers chatted and laughed. One took apart his gun and cleaned it. The response was a joke. A complete and utter joke.

"Well, did you get what you needed?" Cal asked Cooper as they left the area along with two dozen soldiers. The warning had been cleared, the emergency alert declared a glitch or human error.

"Yeah," Cooper answered. "I mean, the response was unimpressive, but the information was exactly what I was looking for. Instead of storming the entrances to fend off attack, the priority was protecting assets. They guarded the arsenal, the food stores, the reservoir, the air filtration system."

"A few were stationed at the entrances," Cal argued.

"Yeah, but not too many for us to take out if we had to."

"So, we're good?" Cal asked again once they made it back to the secondary control room to regroup. "You've got what you need?"

"Well, we can't use that alarm again now they've disabled it."

"Yeah," Cal grimaced. "I didn't anticipate that. It's all right, though. I've got another plan."

"Here we go," Cooper mumbled as he leaned back in the rolling chair and lifted his boots onto the desk beside a row of keyboards and buttons.

"So I mentioned about the Lady Lieutenant who's got it bad for me, right? She'll do anything I ask. This is our place. I'll bring her back up here. I'll talk her into proving that primary control can be bypassed. I'll watch how she does it, and when the time is right, I'll steal her ID badge."

"There are a lot of moving parts in that plan," Cooper said. "I don't love it. I mean, what if she doesn't take the bait when you ask her to show you how to bypass primary? What if she does, but you don't understand it? What if you need more than her ID badge?" Cooper's gut churned nauseously. Apparently it agreed this was not Cal's best idea.

"Have I ever let you down before?" Cal's voice was wounded, but he backed off at Cooper's expression.

"Is that a joke?" Cooper laughed. "You've had a lot of ideas, sure. But half of them have landed us in trouble!"

"Oh, and that's my fault? You're in charge of the details, man. You don't like my ideas, you shouldn't implement them."

"You cannot be— "

Cooper didn't finish the sentence. Someone was at the door.

He and Cal had left the lights off, relying only on the headlamps they wore, but Cal switched off his headlamp.

"Quick. Over there," Cal said, and Cooper followed him into a tiny supply closet.

Outside the door, lips and low laughter mingled to make the sounds of two people meeting less for business than for pleasure.

Cooper hadn't needed to see Cal's face to know he recognized his Lady Lieutenant.

"Well, that was not something I ever wanted to do," Cal said, which might've been the understatement of the century.

The Lady Lieutenant and her friend had eventually left secondary control, allowing Cooper and Cal to escape the cramped supply closet. Since their secret meeting place was not such a secret after all, they had landed back at the bar. It was not ideal, Cooper thought, considering they were making clandestine plans to implode the place.

"I have no idea how you've stayed alive this long," Cooper told his friend. "I have half a mind to murder you myself."

"You don't have to be so cranky," Cal said. "I'm the one who should be upset."

"Yeah. You should." Cooper's jaws ached from the pressure of grinding them. "Your Lieutenant nearly got us thrown in the brig today. Or worse if we'd been found."

"Well how was I supposed to know she'd show up there?" Cal's new frown formed a line between his eyebrows.

"'*This is our place*' you said." Cooper mocked. "'*She'll do anything I ask*' you said. '*Lady Lieutenant's got it bad*' you said." Cooper's laugh held no humor. "Looked to me like Lieutenant's got it bad for any able body.'"

Cal didn't respond to the jab, which was uncharacteristic. Maybe he really liked the girl. Or maybe humiliation had finally gotten to him. Cooper had known Cal for a long time, and been around for a lot of girls. *A lot.*

He put his money on the latter.

24

COOPER'S CONNECTION

If Cal said "don't sweat the small stuff" one more time, Cooper was going to go off the rails.

"It's just you can't get hung up on what this guy might say, all right?" Cal had been warning him about Dr. Hugo Lindgren for the last eight minutes. "I mean, he's definitely psychotic. One of those mad scientist types, you know? But the fact is, he's our way into the system. And probably our way out of here. So—"

"I get it, Cal," Cooper snapped. "I can't kill him."

"No matter what he says." Cal shook his head and his face, for once, was serious. "Keep your eyes on the prize, right? Just don't sw—"

"Say it again and I'll punch you in the throat."

Cal didn't say another word, which spoke volumes about their desperation. They needed Lindgren now more than ever, considering the Lady Lieutenant was no longer an asset.

"This place gives me the creeps," Cooper finally said.

"It's just a chapel, Coop. Least scary place in the mountain."

Cooper shivered at the memory of his time spent with the Sword of Yahweh. "You haven't seen what I've seen."

"How did you come to know this Lindgren, anyway," Cooper asked. "And what makes you think he's turnable?" He stood and began to pace. "Someone committed to a cause like this guy doesn't just suddenly have a change of heart. Someone so integral to an operation doesn't just leave. How do you know this isn't all a trap?"

"You know I love chess, right?" Cal leaned on the pew in front of him, resting his chin on crossed arms.

"Yeah."

"I'd been here maybe a full year when I found my way into a regular game," Cal said. "These guys meet up week after week, rotating partners. I do all right, but I'm not there to improve my game. Not really. And I notice this one guy. People react to this guy. Whisper about him. 'Architect of the sunscorch,' somebody said. 'Brains behind the whole thing.'" Cal leaned back in the pew and rubbed his chin. "I mean, I don't believe for a second one guy is behind it all, but the more I research, the more I listen, I think maybe he's the real deal."

Cooper, who had stopped pacing, stood in front of his friend. "Go on," he said.

"Anyway, this guy's a master at chess, and I work my way up, earning his attention as a worthwhile opponent."

"You remember who taught you to play, right?" Cooper cut in.

"Yeah, and you remember who defeated his teacher, right?"

"I remember." Cooper grinned. "You were always so aggressive."

"You always played too defensively. At any rate," Cal

continued, "I play this guy, and he beats me, of course. But he's impressed, I can tell. Next week we play again. And again after that. We start to have deep conversations. Now, this guy is such a brain he talks in riddles. And I think, okay, I can do that, and so I start talking philosophically about women and the world—anything he wants to talk about. I totally b.s. my way through it. Maybe he knows; maybe he doesn't. But he's entertained, and that's valuable to him."

"So he considers you a friend?" Cooper asked.

"Yeah," Cal said. "I think he does."

"Does he trust you?"

Cal's mouth twisted as he shook his head. "Doubt it. A man like that couldn't trust if he tried. But he needs a friend, this guy. Something's weighing on his mind. So he starts telling me how he's tired of destroying things. He wants to build something, to plant something, and to watch it grow. He wants to see an alder again before he dies. Whatever that is."

"It's a tree, I think," Cooper says.

"I mention the growing lights and hydro gardens on the seventh floor, and how last month they'd grown these tender, delicious things called peaches. But Lindgren wants more. To plant a seed in real sunlight, like his ancestors, he says. Maybe it'll happen, I tell him. It's been a while since the last scorch. Maybe they've stopped. And then he gets real sad. Super melancholy.

"And, sure," Cal went on, "I know who he is. I know he's responsible for the destruction. 'But what if there were no more sunscorches,' I ask him, in line with our philosophical discussions. 'Would the world pick up where it left off? Would trees grow again? Would babies ever be able to walk on soft grass? Are birds gone forever? Can a lush, green Earth only be found in the past? Has it been ruined forever?'"

"Well?" Cooper finally asked when his friend didn't finish the story. "What did he say?"

"Nothing." Cal shrugged. "He stood and left. I haven't seen him since."

"Are you freaking kidding me?" Cooper's voice came out too loud, too angry, and he whispered, though it was still heated. "That conversation is what you're basing this whole thing on? That's what makes you think you can turn him?" Cooper ground his jaws and looked to the ceiling, faux stained glass tableaus hand-painted in crisp blues, deep reds and vivid greens. "You've lost your mind, Cal Standridge. And you're going to get us both killed."

"Jesus Christ," Cooper said and gripped the hair at the top of his head. "You've invited him here, to the chapel, haven't you? This is a trap, and we really are headed to the brig."

"Calm down," Cal said. "If there's one thing I know, it's people. You know it's true," he retorted to Cooper's derisive snort. "I'm right about this guy. You'll see."

"Either you're right, or we're dead," Cooper said. "I'd never have bet on those odds."

"Yeah, well you always play too defensively."

A small eternity later, when Lindgren still hadn't shown, Cooper watched as Cal absently rubbed the foot of a statue of the Virgin Mary, worn smooth with time and touch.

"Where's your guy?" Cooper finally asked. "Or are mad scientist types not confined to the constructs of time?"

"Hilarious," Cal mumbled just as the door to the chapel swung open with a sinful creak.

"Dr. Lindgren, hello," Cal called too eagerly. The man's head, covered in white hair that fell in messy clumps around his ears, whipped toward him. "I haven't seen you since I played the Slav Defense to your Queen's Gambit," Cal said, his tone oozing good-buddy charm. "Thought maybe you'd resigned for good."

"Nah, just busy," Lindgren replied, though his gaze flicked around the room curiously. "Don't vorry. I'll be back to defeat you again." He leaned his head to the side. "Vhat are ve meeting here for?"

Before Cal could reply, the scientist caught sight of Cooper. "Who is zhis?" he asked, his face hardening. "Vhat is zhis?"

Cal gave the smile he was so good at—the disarming one Cooper had imitated until he got it right. Cal's was still better. He motioned to Cooper. "This is my longtime associate, Sam Cooper. Cooper," Cal nodded what was obviously meant to be encouragement. "Dr. Hugo Lindgren."

It took every ounce of strength Cooper could find when Lindgren extended a long, thin arm. He shook the murderer's hand, though he hated himself for it. What he wanted was to break it, to rip it from the socket, and use it to beat him until he was unconscious.

No. Cooper reigned himself in. Exhaled. 'Don't sweat the small stuff,' he recited beneath his breath.

"Vhat's going on, Cal?" Lindgren asked cautiously. "Vhat can I do for Mr. Cooper?"

"Actually," Cal replied, "it's what Mr. Cooper can do for you."

Lindgren's shrewd eyes narrowed behind his glasses. "Meaning?"

"You and I have become relatively close friends over the course of these last few months, wouldn't you say?" Lindgren didn't answer, but Cal proceeded anyway. "I know you're tired of this place," he said. "Tired of these people. I know you dream of seeing the outside world healthy again. You dream of going home."

Cooper felt like a voyeur watching Cal and Lindgren's exchange. As Cal spoke, the scientist's face changed. Longing softened his severe features for the briefest moment before he pushed his glasses higher on his nose and it disappeared.

"Dreams and reality are two vastly different zhings," Lindgren said, his cheeks reddening with anger, and his voice tight with what Cooper suspected was fear. His slight accent held a Nordic tint. Was he Danish? Swedish? "I cannot believe you had zhe nerve to set zhis meeting," he seethed. "I'll have you arrested for treason."

"No, you won't." Cal's tone was untroubled.

"I vill," Lindgren said. "I don't know who you zhink you are. Talking to me like zhis. You little ferret. You little turd."

His eyes fell to the side as he mumbled something about cowards and commitment and consecration. Cooper looked to Cal, who shrugged slightly.

"You're not going to have me arrested, Lindgren," Cal said. "You're not going to do anything. You want to know why?"

"Oh yeah? Vhy?" the scientist asked with a laugh.

"Because you actually said those things about a new life to me. Because you believe them."

"No one will believe you," Lindgren retorted. "Not over me. I'm a hero here. A legend."

"Yeah, but people have seen us together plenty of times," Cal said. "They've probably overheard at least some of our discussion. And you met me here tonight, alone, at a very inconspicuous and private place."

"Vhat?" Lindgren scoffed. "Are you threatening to claim we're lovers?"

"I hadn't thought of that, no." Cal's grin took an evil slant. "But I might use it later. I'm saying if you accuse me of treason, you indict yourself. And I'm willing to bet I'm not the only person in this facility you've said some unpopular things to. I'm willing to bet somebody, somewhere has seen this other side of you, too."

Cooper watched as Lindgren's mouth tightened. Cal had him. He was right.

"Vhat do you vant?" the man spat.

"I want to help you get out of here," Cal said. "We both do."

"Vhy would you help me? Vhy do you care?"

"Oh, I don't," Cal said, his eyes wide. "Not really. I just want to blow this place to hell and stop the scorches. And I think you do, too."

"All right, so vhat," Lindgren admitted. "I have been zhinking I'd like to start a life somewhere. And it would suit me fine if Orval Mills got what was coming to him." Lindgren stopped, his gaze hardening as it shot to Cooper and then to Cal. "But I need assurances. I want safe passage out of here. And money."

"Why the hell would we pay you, you murderous pig?" The words scrambled from Cooper's mouth before he could catch them and from the corner of his eye he caught a glimpse of Cal's head snapping back in surprise.

Lindgren blinked several times. "Because I have information on zhe terminal combustion," he finally said. "And only I can stop it."

25

NEWS OF LINDGREN

W ho'd have thought it'd be the smell of my own hair that finally sent me over the edge, Nori thought. 'Poor Nori,' they'll say. 'Couldn't handle the isolation.' Ha. If only they knew it was the fetid stench of my own head that finally did me in.

Her neighbor had been silent since before Cooper's visit. Not a peep despite Nori's repeated calls. Was she still there? Was anyone there? Was there another human being anywhere nearby, or was she rotting away completely alone in this godforsaken concrete prison?

Isolation had given her a lot of time to think. *A lot* of time. At first she had thought about how she would like to strangle Sam Cooper the next time she laid eyes on him. If she ever laid eyes on him again. Oh, how she would like to lay eyes on him. She would give anything to be on the back of his motorcycle, wild and free with an entire underground world to explore. She missed not knowing where life would take her from one day to the next. Inside the tiny cell her day was always the same. Same walls, same floor, same door. Every.

Day. Wake up cold, stare at the walls until someone delivered cold bland, mushy food, try to occupy her mind by remembering old songs and stories, go to bed cold. Start all over again.

Those times she thought of her mother, though, she pounded the cell door with her fists and screamed at the loss, at the time wasted. Time her mother didn't have.

She longed to laugh with her dad and Kade. She even missed Grant's sass. Oh, wouldn't he love to see her hair and wardrobe right about now.

Sometimes, when she let her mind wander about others like her, the ones Cooper told her were thriving underground, a warm ribbon of hope swirled inside her. Could she live among them? Would Cooper be there?

And just as quickly as hope had snuck in, it would whisk away again, taking little pieces of her soul with it. She was sick and tired of the hellhole they'd put her in. She was scared and lonely and angry. And foul.

God, I stink like the dead was her last thought before she fell asleep on the filthy cot.

"Hey."

Nori moaned and rolled toward Cooper's voice, floating in the space between waking and dreaming.

"I've got news," he whispered.

"Mm?" She raised her eyebrows, though her lids remained closed.

"Nori, wake up." Cooper's hushed voice was rushed. Excited. "I don't have long. Sit up and talk to me."

One of her eyes popped open, revealing only parts of

Cooper's too-close features. She sat up and scrubbed her face. "Are," Nori cleared her throat, hoarse and tight from screaming. "Are you really here?"

"Of course," Cooper said and shook his head. "What kind of question is that? There's something important I have to tell you."

"Okay, what?" Her brain was foggy, but she tried to focus.

"I've met someone," he said, and he was pleased with himself. Proud, even.

Her brain really was misfiring. What did that have to do with anything? Why would he say that? To her of all people? "Congratulations?" she said slowly as anger began to burn the tops of her ears.

"No. Nori, listen. There's a man named Lindgren— a scientist here. He wants out, and we've got a plan. I just need you to be patient."

She blinked several times before she could speak. "Patient?" she repeated. "I'm in this freezing jail surviving on scraps and funky gray water while you're off playing spy, and you want me to be *patient*?"

"No," he started. "I mean yes. I… " Cooper's top lip curled and he sat up straight. "God, Nori, you stink."

For several bewildered seconds she could not speak.

"I stink?" She whispered the words over chapped and pealing lips, barely able to hear herself over the blood roaring in her ears. "I wonder why that is. Look around," she said. "Do you see a shower? Soap?" Cooper's shoulders tensed, but she didn't slow. "There's not even a washcloth, Cooper. The toilet flushes about half the time and the cot is closer to concrete than cushion."

"I stink?" she repeated, then huffed a laugh, though she wasn't amused. She was humiliated. Horrified. Mad as hell.

"*You* haven't gone without, though, have you?" She looked Cooper up and down, taking in a set of new clothes and a freshly-shaved face. He had eaten recently; she could smell it.

"I'm sorry," he said. "I didn't think before I said that. But I swear to you I'm working as hard as I can. I'm sorry you're here; sorry this happened. You're safe, though, I made sure — " A proud grin slid across his mouth. "Well, I tried to make sure you were safe, but you took care of that yourself, didn't you?"

He grinned, but after a look at her face quickly schooled his features. "The whole facility thinks you've got a VD," he said and rubbed her arm. "It's quick thinking like that that'll keep us alive. Good work."

Nori was pleased with his praise, though she hated herself a little for it. "Yes, it worked," she said, "but now I wonder what they've done to the little food they shove through the slot in the door."

"I really am sorry, Nori," Cooper said. "I hate this as much as you — "

She cut him off with a murderous stare.

"I hate this, too," he said instead.

Rolling her neck to release some of the pent-up hostility raring to jump out and strangle Sam Cooper, she finally said, "Tell me more about this Lindgren."

26

SOMEPLACE MORE COMFORTABLE

"Raising again?" Cooper glanced down at his hand, but the cards hadn't changed. "You make a pair of jacks from that flop?"

Cal's only response was to lift an eyebrow until it pointed at his hairline.

"You boys want any food?" The bartender, an old man whose cheeks were in a race with his mouth to the bottom of his face, held up a menu.

"No thanks," Cal called and motioned to Cooper. "I'm about to eat this guy's lunch."

Cooper smirked. "You remember the last time we played?"

"I remember you crying about something," Cal said as he slid three blue chips toward the center of the table.

"Call." Cooper pushed his own stack of chips into the pot. "And no. The whining was all you." He lifted his wrist and twisted the silver bracelet ever-so-slightly. It was enough. Cal's gaze shot from the thin metal band to Cooper's face before resting somewhere above his head.

"I never meant to lose that," Cal gritted. If glares could

start fires, the place would have been aflame. "You know how much it meant to me."

"Then you shouldn't have thrown it in the pot."

Cal lifted his head in a single provocative nod. "Play you for it now."

Without conscious thought, Cooper touched the cool metal at his wrist. It was a reminder of what he had endured these last two years. Of who he'd had to become. Like sliding on a mask, when he wore Cal's bracelet, he could morph into someone else. Not Cal, exactly, but close. Sometimes he imagined his alter ego slipping from the metal and enveloping his body like a hard outer layer. An exoskeleton to protect the softer stuff inside.

"Not a chance," Cooper said, and meant it.

As he watched, Cal's expression changed from irritated to strained to a fabricated friendly in a matter of seconds. His gaze snagged on something—or someone— behind him. Cooper straightened in his chair, on high-alert as he scrutinized Cal's every nonverbal cue.

"I do love a good game of hold 'em," Captain Mathers said in tone at once too sharp and too casual.

Cooper considered what he and Cal had been discussing. Had Mathers overheard them? Probably not. Anyway, it didn't matter; they hadn't mentioned Lindgren or their scheme since the last hand.

"You know," Mathers said as he slid into a seat directly across from Cooper. "Poker is so much more than a card game."

The man's mouth was a hard, thin line. It held neither a smile nor a scowl, but his mood was evident enough.

"People like to pretend it's a friendly match between buddies," he said cooly. "But make no mistake. Poker is war.

And in war, like poker, the most common mistake is underestimating your opponent.

"Take you, for example, Mr. Cooper," Mathers continued. "I hadn't thought I'd underestimated you. When you first arrived, I observed you. I took your measure. I thought I had you pegged. I admit I was suspicious at first." He popped a crunchy snack from a bowl on the table into his mouth. "When you just happened to appear out of nowhere with that girl, I mean. But then you knew Standridge, here, and the key phrase. So I sat back and I watched. I took a risk. I played my game. And you know what?" He looked first to Cal, but soon the weight of his attention landed on Cooper again. "I'm calling your bet."

Cooper's mouth was so dry his tongue felt enormous, useless. But he had no words to form with it anyway.

"But what am I doing?" Mathers asked, and his tone was back to overly-casual. Or maybe sarcastically at-ease was a better term. "This isn't a conversation to be had here. Let's go someplace we can talk. Someplace more… comfortable."

———

THE INTERROGATION ROOM inspired neither conversation nor comfort. Cooper's leg cramped, and he bent to rub his calf. Sitting back up in the hard chair next to the hard table in the cold, hard little room, Cooper worked to release the muscles he had been holding so tense. He worked to relax —or at least *appear* relaxed— by first flexing and loosening his toes before working his way up to his legs and back. He worked the tension from his fingers, his arms, his shoulders, and he rolled his neck. Even his jaw and forehead muscles were tight, and as he released those last holds on nervous tension, he wondered again what was taking Mathers so long.

After dumping Cooper in the stark interrogation room, Mathers had announced he would return shortly. It had been at least 10 minutes since then. Hell, Cooper thought, Mathers was probably standing outside the window just beyond his line of sight. Watching. Waiting. Inflicting what he thought was mental pressure on a guilty suspect.

Truthfully, Cooper *was* tense. He *was* feeling the heat. Had Lindgren come forward and blown the whole thing? Had Cooper and Cal been overheard? Seen? Mathers had dismissed Cal before leading Cooper to the row of interrogation rooms, but he saw the way Mathers watched his friend. Was releasing Cal a trap to watch his next move?

Cooper heaved a heavy breath and wished to God he was on the other side of the door and not trapped inside the tiny room. Then, something moved beyond the blinds at the window, attracting his attention. It was just a glimpse, but he would swear he had seen the black frames of Mathers' military-issue glasses just seconds before the man whisked into the room.

"Sorry for your wait," Mathers said, but his tone held no regret. "Now, where were we?"

He rounded the small rectangular table and sat in the chair opposite Cooper oozing menace and confidence. "Oh, yes," he said and leaned across the table, his forearms at rest on the hard surface. "We were discussing how you've been sneaking around the facility when you thought no one was watching."

Who's standing outside the door? The question played over and again in Cooper's mind. There hadn't been anyone but him and Mathers when they'd entered, but that could've changed. Maybe Mathers was assembling support while Cooper waited inside. Maybe not. But was it worth the risk?

If I take Mathers to the ground, he thought, I can grab the gun from his belt. I'll knock him out with it and leave this godforsaken room. But who's standing outside the door? One or two guards, I could take. Any more than that, though, and they'll gun me down before I get halfway down the hall.

"Now there's a look I've seen before," Mathers said cheerfully. "That," he nodded to Cooper, "is the face of a man about to run. I would advise against that particular course of action, though." He rubbed the hilt of his pistol to punctuate the next point. "It's been far too long since I've taken her out, and she's restless."

Cooper's leg bounced beneath the table, and he flexed his thigh to stop it. "I think you've misread me," Cooper said, leaning toward Mathers and contorting his face to skew innocent and misunderstood. "I'm not sure what's going on, but I'm sure if you tell me what I'm accused of, I can clear it all up pretty quickly."

"Oh, I have no doubt you'll come up with some excuse," Mathers agreed. "But it won't work this time. I'm on to you, son. We've seen you going into that girl's cell. You know, the one you said you didn't know. The one you said you'd *happened* to catch sneaking around at the same time you *happened* to arrive."

Some of the tension eased, and Cooper blinked in relief. So they didn't know about Lindgren. It was the best news he could hope for, given current circumstances.

"Oh, that." Cooper waved the accusation away. "Yeah, I've been down there a couple of times."

Mathers' intended response died on his tongue, and he

sputtered to come up with another. "You admit you've been communicating with a prisoner?"

"Well, yeah," Cooper said and shrugged. "She's cute, and there aren't a lot of women in this facility. I suspected she had a thing for me after that first night. She saw me as a protector, someone to defend her." He leaned his head from side to side. "I may have led her to believe that was true in order to," he paused dramatically, "get to know her better."

Mathers' thin lips disappeared entirely. "Do you expect me to believe you've been visiting this girl late at night not to conspire with her, but to, to…"

Cooper gave a wolf-like grin and Mathers stared for several beats, the gears of his brain obviously grinding to determine whether Cooper told the truth or not.

"You don't have to worry about me going back, though." Cooper's tone was matter of fact.

"No?" Mathers looked angrier with every passing minute. "Why not?"

"I guess I wasn't the only one she had a connection with. Word is she's caught something." He glanced meaningfully at Mathers. "If you know what I mean. And honestly, I'm not surprised." He shook himself and made a disgusted noise. "Did you know prisoners in your facility aren't allowed to bathe?"

27

INDIGO'S PROPOSITION

Nori didn't know the specifics, but Cooper had somehow arranged for her to bathe. At least she assumed it was Cooper. Two guards she had never seen before announced a trip to the showers and escorted her from the cell. They didn't speak; they barely looked at her.

She didn't care, because they left after ushering her into a huge, empty room where simple but functional shower heads stuck out of concrete walls. There were no shower curtains, just waist-high concrete dividers. Definitely designed for men. If the guards walked in while she showered, they would surely get a waist-high eyeful.

At first, Nori covered herself with one arm and bathed with the other, but soon enough she forgot about modesty. She forgot where she was, and how she had gotten there, and that there was little hope of escape. She forgot everything and simply enjoyed the pleasure of a shower, which was hot and long and glorious.

Too soon, the guards yelled for her to finish, so she turned off the shower and braided her thick hair while it was still wet. Someone had laid clean clothes out for her— a set of dark green uniform pants and a gray t-shirt.

"Think you boys could scrounge up a coat and some socks?" Nori asked, though she knew the answer. No one was going to be doing her any favors. They could, however, be counted on to protect themselves. "It gets so cold down in my cell I'm afraid I'll catch cold. Sneezing and coughing." She shook her head. "I'd hate to be the one to escort me next time."

After a long, irritated look at her, the shorter guard nodded toward a closed door, and the other returned with a too-big sweatshirt, a pair of socks, and a blanket. She hated to thank them since it was only when it was in their own interest they finally granted her a common courtesy.

She hated it, but she did it. Neither guard acknowledged her before resuming their hold on her arms and hauling her back down the hall toward her own personal hell.

When a thundering Iberville surged around the corner, Nori stopped so quickly she lost her balance. Anticipating the crash, Iberville threw out his hands to steady himself. His eyes widened when he recognized Nori, and he jerked his hands back as if he had bathed in lighter fluid and she was on fire. Nori was thrilled at his revulsion, and her grin in his direction was sickly sweet.

Iberville snarled, which did nothing to improve his looks. Neither did the swollen and angry purple of his right eye.

"I'll take this grime off your hands," he said and gripped Nori above the elbow. The two guards didn't argue. Iberville dragged her alongside him, forcing her to keep up.

Dread settled deep in the pit of Nori's stomach, but was soon replaced with irritation. He was hurrying her to her cell, where she would sit on a hard bed, cold and alone. For days.

"I am so *sick*," she said and pulled her elbow back to her middle, "of being jerked around by my arm."

Iberville was too strong for her to be a real threat, even though he did have a new limp.

"You know," she mumbled, letting go of any fight she had left, "if you treated me like a guest, instead of a prisoner, you might get more cooperation."

"You're not a guest, you filthy twat. You're a prisoner."

Not for long, Nori thought, remembering Cooper's promise and finding her fight— and her evil grin— again. Not. For. Long. "Where'd ya get that shiner," she asked. "Chicken coop?"

Iberville had a particular talent for twisting and lifting a shoulder almost to the point of dislocation. Nori teetered over the line of consciousness as he displayed his talent, but he pulled her back just before she could abandon the pain. And then, with one final twist that sent stars shooting behind her eyes, he threw her into the cell.

"Hope you enjoyed your shower." He ground out the words. "You won't get out of this cell again anytime soon."

Nori tilted her head as she rubbed her shoulder. "To tell you the truth, Lieutenant, I'm shocked by all this attitude." She shook her head in mock disbelief. "I seriously doubt rejection is new for you."

Fury flashed behind the man's eyes and his pudgy jaw clenched shut. "You can rot in this cell, for all I care," he said. "You won't see me back down here again."

Nori turned from him so he couldn't read her face. So he couldn't see her satisfied smile.

That, she thought, is exactly what I was going for.

Struggling to remember the words of a song she had known by heart since childhood, Nori hummed the tune and sang the chorus. The second verse, though, was as elusive as her escape. Boredom had replaced the sun as her great enemy. Well, boredom and loneliness. Cooper had not been back. She'd had no word from him at all. Guards were the only other people she saw, but when they brought food, they didn't hang around, and they sure didn't speak. The female neighbor whose reassuring presence she had taken for granted at first was still silent.

Nori's thoughts turned to her parents. Was her mom okay? She closed her eyes and imagined her mother's face, which had grown even more hollow the days before she left. Was she still in pain? If she thought hard enough, she could still smell the sweet mix of her mother's skin and shampoo, could still hear her voice. If only she had never left she would still be safe at home with her parents. A loving daughter would never have abandoned her mother in her last days. Fat tears slid down Nori's clenched jaw. Guilt chewed at her conscience, and she chewed at her nails until they were gone. Her conscience didn't go anywhere though. It hung heavy like a weight around her neck, weary and troubled.

Where was Cooper, anyway? Had he been discovered? Had he been jailed? Worse? Anxiety clawed beneath the skin of her arms, over her shoulders and down her back. It wanted out. If she wasn't careful, it would destroy her in the process.

On hands and knees on the cold concrete, Nori extended her legs behind her and lowered to the floor, pushing herself back up with ease. *One.* She bent her arms again until her face nearly met the floor before straightening them. *Two.* Her preferred outlet had always been running. She lived for that release, had come to depend on it when she was stressed or trapped or needed to think. Being confined in the narrow cell had nearly driven her mad. Thank God she had learned so much about working out with Kade in The Pit. She had options now. She would not be broken.

When she finished the set of push-ups, she started with planks and crunches. It wasn't a run, but it would do. She pushed herself, straining and drenched in sweat, until she could breathe again. Then she pushed some more.

As Nori brought a knee to her forehead in an alternating side crunch, she heard something in the hall. She stopped, her abdominal muscles still engaged, and listened.

Feet shuffling. A door latch. Groaning. Another latch. Footsteps fading to nothing. She put her ear to her door, but heard no more clues.

"Hello?" Nori called, her voice tight and tentative. "Is that you?"

"Ungh." Not a word. A grunt.

"Oh, God, it is you," Nori gushed. "I thought you'd been killed. Or that you'd escaped. Where've you been?"

The woman's answer came slowly, her voice strained. "Your *friend*," she spat the word "visited me when you were... unavailable."

The woman groaned again, and Nori's heart stopped. Though she tried, she couldn't form a single word. And even if she could, what would she say? She was disgusted with herself for feeling relieved, and guilty the other woman had been harmed instead. Nori's world spun in a silent vacuum of nauseous guilt.

"God, I'm so sorry," she finally said. "Are you — will you be okay?" Nori still didn't know her name.

"Not my first time." The woman's words were saturated

with hate. "Don't worry. I don't think he'll be back anytime soon. Not if he wants to keep both eyes."

"It was you," Nori gasped. "You gave Iberville that black eye."

"I did. And I tried to break his knee."

"Oh, he's limping bad," Nori said. She couldn't help but smile.

"Good."

A minute— or maybe a hundred minutes— passed. "I'm sorry he came to you." Nori swallowed. "I'm sorry he hurt you."

The woman's voice didn't quaver. "I can handle it. I always have."

"Still," Nori said, then, "Why were you gone so long?"

"Infirmary."

Nori closed her eyes and breathed through the guilt, through the dread and fear that this torture and abuse might be her own future.

"Nori?" the woman asked.

"Yes," she answered, then, "I'm sorry… I don't know your name."

"I'm Indigo. Listen, I know you've had a visitor, too." Before Nori could argue, the woman spoke again, her strong voice hushed. "Someone on the inside."

Nori didn't answer.

"Sound bounces around these hard surfaces," Indigo said. "I heard everything before I left."

"Yeah," Nori bluffed, "Iberville came again. His persistence is impressive, I'll give him that."

"No. Not Iberville. Someone named Cooper who swore to get you out of here."

Nori squeezed her eyes shut, her brain on repeat. Oh God, oh God, oh God.

"Listen," Indigo said. "I take no pleasure in blackmailing somebody in the same bad situation, but I need out of here."

"What…" Nori cleared her throat. "What are you saying?"

"I'm saying if you don't find a way to take me with you, I'll tell them what I know before you ever get the chance to escape."

28

BUSTIN' OUT

The absence of nutritional food was having visible effects on Nori's body. She clicked her tongue as she looked down at herself. Was she imagining it, or were her breasts smaller, her middle thinner? Running a hand over her ribcage, she found bones too close to her skin. She was weaker, too, though she continued to push her body to protect her mind.

At a faint shuffle outside her door, Nori looked up from the remains of what were once powerful legs. A scrap of paper slid beneath the door, and she scrambled toward it. Snatching up the note, she devoured a single scribbled word. *'Tonight.'*

With no way to tell time, she paced the cell like a caged tiger for hours. She listened for voices, noises — anything. But the only sounds were the ones she had grown used to: the drip of a leaky pipe somewhere nearby, the faint hum of generated electricity that was the background noise of her new hell. She had long since bitten off her nails and moved to the skin at the tips of her fingers.

"You remember our deal?"

Nori had been listening so intently for a distant sound that the one from the neighboring cell jarred her. She bit down hard on her finger at Indigo's reminder.

"I know something's going on," Indigo said. "I can feel the tension. You can't leave here without me. We have a deal."

Nori squeezed her eyes shut. Cooper was gonna kill her for this. "I remember," she said around the skin of her thumb. "I'll get you out if I can."

"No." The woman's voice was closer, as if was pushing against the wall. "No 'if's.' You'll get me out or I'll get you caught."

"You wouldn't," Nori said.

"I would. I want out of here as bad as you do, girl. Maybe worse. And right now, you're my only chance. You take me with you or we'll rot here together."

Nori leaned her forehead against the cold wall. "All right," she said. "I'll get you out."

The promise sounded hollow even to Nori, who had no idea how she was getting out herself.

***

It wasn't Cooper who opened the door to her cell hours later, but a hazel-eyed guard in a CCC uniform.

Nori scrambled against the wall. "What— what do you want?"

He took a step toward her, and she crouched, clenching her fists for a fight. "Stay back," she warned.

The man held his hands up in a non-threatening way, and a ring of keys dangled from one thumb. "I'm a friend, Nori," he said. "Cooper sent me."

She didn't drop her fisted hands. Not yet. How could

Cooper possibly have a friend at the enemy's home base? The only name he had ever mentioned was Lindgren.

"I'm Cal," the stranger said.

Nori heard the click of a flashlight, then a thin beam cut through her cell. He shined the light at her face, blinding her, and she threw a hand in front of her eyes. It was too late. No way he would have missed the blue-green shine of her eyes. If she could have crawled into the wall, she would have. There was nowhere to go, though. She was cornered. Panicked and jerky, she pulled her hand from her eyes and made it back into a fist.

"Sorry," Cal mumbled and pointed the light at his feet. "I… Ah… Cooper failed to mention…" He took a deep breath and moved slowly toward her again. "I'm here to help you."

Nori shook her head. "No," she said, just over a whisper, then with more force, "No. I want to talk to Cooper." An edgy panic was taking over, and she couldn't think. "Where is Cooper?"

"I'm taking you to him." Cal took another step.

"Stop." Nori's voice was louder than she intended, and she reined it back before someone heard her. "Just stay where you are. Why didn't Cooper come himself? Where is he?"

Cal nodded, resigned to answer her questions, though he looked around as if in a hurry. "Cooper's fine. It's just that he's being watched and I'm not. He couldn't come without being discovered, which would ruin the whole plan."

Nori found some of her nerve and stood a little straighter. "What is the plan? And how do I know this isn't a trap?"

The nostrils of the man's slim nose flared. "I guess you don't. But why in the world would I sneak you *out* of a cell? Listen, we don't have time for this. Those guards will be back on rotation any minute."

When he reached for Nori's arm, she yelped and pulled it back so hard she hit the concrete wall behind her. Her elbow screamed in pain, but she didn't let it show. "I've been grabbed enough," she growled.

After a beat, Cal nodded, a trace of sympathy in his hazel eyes.

Their footsteps were muffled, and the click of the door faint as they left her cell behind. Cal walked past the cell next to hers, and Nori inhaled slowly before tiptoeing by, too. Then, just as she lifted her foot, two hands shot from the thin food slot in the door. Nori gasped and glanced down to see Indigo's brown knuckles, marred both with old scars and fresh scabs. Though it would make things easier, Nori wouldn't— couldn't— leave the woman behind to suffer more.

She closed her eyes and hoped for the best. "Open this cell, too."

Cal's face twisted. "What? No. Let's go." He jogged down the hall, but Nori didn't follow.

When he finally noticed, he threw his head back and stomped toward her as he ground out, "We don't have time for this."

"If I go, she goes." Nori squeezed the too-prominent bones at her hips. "I made a deal."

"I don't care about *your* deals, sweetheart," he snapped. "I care about mine and Cooper's."

"My deals *are* Cooper's," Nori retorted reflexively. "You'll honor it, or we won't honor yours." Okay, that may be over-stating their relationship, she thought, but it was too late to back down now. She stood taller, daring him to deny her again.

Cal stared at her for several long moments, his eyes

twitching with fury. But Nori held her ground. Finally, he shook his head as he fumbled through the keys, mumbling about a bullet to the head. Whether he meant his or hers, she couldn't be sure.

Indigo's cell door opened with a dry creak, and she stood in the door frame, a bronzed statue very much alive. Muscular and proud, she was nearly as tall as Cal, who'd backed away and leaned against the wall like a petulant child.

A smile pulled at Nori's mouth despite their circumstances. Though it had taken its toll on Nori, the time in a cell had hardly affected Indigo. She looked no less intimidating than when she had first met her on the road after escaping the Pit with Kade. Back then, the woman had gone out of her way to make sure Nori was not being held against her will. She had stood her ground against Kade, who towered above everyone, making sure Nori wasn't in any danger.

"It's you," Nori breathed. For an insane moment, she thought to hug the woman but stopped herself. Indigo seemed more likely to dislocate a shoulder than accept a hug. "I didn't know." Nori shook her head. "But, how... " She stuttered, then remembered suddenly. "Where's your husband?"

Indigo stretched toned arms above her head and twisted her back, readying herself for battle. "He's here somewhere." She looked to Cal as if daring him to stop her. "And I'm going to find him."

"We could actually use the distraction," Cal said, shrugging and pushing away from the wall.

Indigo raised her chin and eyed the ring in his hand. "I'll need those keys."

Cal's nostrils flared again as he shot Nori a murderous glare, but he twisted a single key from the thick ring. "This one opens cell doors," he said through his teeth. "It's the only one you're getting."

It was irrational, but Nori felt a twinge of sadness at the thought of parting ways with the woman. "Good luck finding your husband," she said, "And good luck getting out of here."

Indigo's dark eyes were at the same time weary and fierce, and when Nori met them, they somehow gave her strength. "You wanna stay alive, girl, you keep your head down and your fists up. You hear me?"

Nori swallowed hard and blinked her understanding.

Indigo's tight nod was the only goodbye before she charged down the hall.

Nori followed Cal in the same direction, but she struggled to keep up as they plowed through stark hallways and into dim stairwells. She was weak, her legs and lungs screaming for a rest that never came. Cal didn't dote on her. He didn't ask if she was all right, and he never bothered to make sure she followed. He assumed she would, and Nori clung to the implied respect when she had little else to go on.

At the end of yet another long hall, Cal stopped outside a set of double doors. Nori bent, bracing her hands on her knees and fighting for breath. When she was finally able to think past her raging lungs, she raised her head. Cal's posture all wrong. His legs were bent and ready as he reached for the gun at his belt.

"What—?" she began.

Cal didn't look at her, but threw his free arm to the side in a silencing motion. She heard them, then. Footsteps. Multiple sets, and voices. Nori backed against the wall, making herself as small as possible.

With another nervous glance in the direction of the voices,

Cal twisted the silver handle of one of the doors and motioned for Nori to follow him inside.

Her knowledge of the underground facility was limited, but the rooms she had seen were all the same. Artificially-lit with hard, institutional furniture, they were cold and stale, permeated with decades of dampness. And men.

The room she and Cal entered, though, was different. There was a faint chemical or electrical smell and the air was fresher, like it was filtered. A low but constant hum drew her eyes to a large dehumidifier in one corner. It was then she processed an entire wall of computer monitors and a dozen keyboards below them.

Moving toward the panel, Nori held her fingers reverently over the keys. She hadn't seen much tech, though she had read about it. The monitors were dark, but she could imagine them lit in green and blue, with flashing numbers and maps of a world beyond their own.

"Careful now. One stray finger and you could blow us all up."

Nori's breath caught in her throat at the sound of Sam Cooper's voice, and she ran to him before it occurred to her to go. In that moment, she didn't care about what he said or did or their argument. She didn't care she hadn't seen him in days or that they had an audience. She wrapped her arms around his neck and held on for life.

How deeply she missed physical contact! It had not even occurred to her until Cooper's arms held her. She nuzzled in even closer, and the heat and the smell of him was reassuring. He could never let go for all she cared. Never.

But too quickly, he pushed her back and scanned her face and body. His eyes held a slight hysteria she had never seen even in their diciest predicaments.

"I'm all right," Nori said, finding his gaze and nodding. His breaths came fast, like he had been sprinting. "I'm fine, Cooper," she said. "Really."

"Okay. You're okay," he said, his eyes closing.

Then she was pulled into his chest again, and happy to be there.

"Care to tell me who your friend is, though?" she asked after a while, looking up from Cooper's chest and eyeing Cal, who watched with thinly-veiled astonishment. Cal looked back and forth between them, a goofy grin on his face.

"You failed to mention you were in love with the girl, Cooper," Cal said. "I would've taken a little more care— "

Nori inhaled too fast and choked. She coughed and cleared her throat, struggling to take in air that was uncomfortably thick all of the sudden. "What's the plan?" she blurted. "We going to use this control panel to blow the place up?"

"Something like that," Cooper smiled down at her, his hands still clasped at the back of her waist. He didn't look away, and she couldn't. Surely there were things they should be doing or worrying about, but for the life of her, she couldn't think of one.

The white overhead lights flickered milliseconds before the alarm sounded, ripping apart the silence. Both the relief and excitement Nori had just discovered fled, replaced by a cold dread as Cooper's face hardened.

The handheld radio at Cal's side exploded with chatter. *Code Orange. Code Orange. All stations be on alert for an escaped prisoner. Repeat. Code Orange. Escape in Unit D.*

"How do they know already?" Cooper asked. "Were you two seen?"

"Your *girl*," Cal angled his head at Nori, "made a friend on the inside and let her out."

"What?" Cooper's voice held both disbelief and scorn as he looked from her to Cal. "And you agreed to this?" he asked Cal.

Nori didn't give him a chance to explain. "We had to," she said. "She heard everything. Knew your name. She swore to alert the guards if we didn't let her out, too. I had no choice."

Cooper pulled away from Nori and locked his hands behind his dark head.

"They've probably discovered the empty cells," Cal said before releasing a string of curses. "I thought the woman might serve as a good distraction, but it might've backfired." He paced the wall of computer panels, then stopped, looking between Nori and Cooper as if an idea had struck. He lifted the radio to his mouth. "Control, can you provide a description of the escapee?"

Seconds stretched to days before the radio cracked back to life and someone on the other end answered. *Black female. Early forties. Dangerous, but not believed to be armed.*

Nori closed her eyes, her pent-up breath leaving in a relieved rush. Then she realized what Cal had already put together and her heart sank. "Someone has seen her, then? God, I hope she finds a way out."

Cal nodded. "This whole place is going to be on lockdown. It's going to either make our job a lot harder, or a lot easier. Certainly not what we'd planned."

"Then we do what we can while we can," Cooper said, and his expression was far more serious than his words had been. He looked to Cal, who nodded back, an entire conversation passing between the two without a word.

"Wait, what does that mean?" Nori asked as panic crept into her voice. "What do we do now?"

"Now," Cooper looked to Cal, who squared his jaw. "We proceed with our plan while they're busy looking for your friend."

"But…" Nori's hands fell to her sides. "How will we get out of here if the place is locked down?"

"We'll cross that bridge when we get there," Cooper replied, and she finally understood their silent conversation. They probably wouldn't make it out.

29

SECONDARY CONTROL

"Where the hell is Lindgren?" Cooper pounded his fist on the table with such force a keyboard clanked to the floor. "He was supposed to be here ten minutes ago to start up this instrument panel."

"I'm sure he's on his way," Cal said. "The escapee situation is probably slowing him down."

Though he sounded sure, Cal's confidence was slipping. If the pacing hadn't given it away, Cooper would've known by the twitch in his right eye, Cal's only tell.

When the door to the secondary control room opened, the tension in the room eased and they all took a breath.

"Lindgren, finally," Cal said and stalked toward the scientist. "Let's get this ball rollin'."

"It's a madhouse out zhere," Lindgren said and straightened his lab coat. "I don't know how ze prisoner escaped, but it's an excellent distraction. Zhis plan may actually vehrk."

"'Course it'll work." Cal's chest expanded. "Mine and Cooper's plans always work."

"What, exactly, is the plan?" Nori asked slowly, her blue

eyes somehow both dubious and hopeful. God, he couldn't wait to get out of this place and back on the road with her.

He nodded toward the scientist. "Dr. Lindgren is going to short-circuit the primary instrument panel from this secondary one, which will send the facility into high alert."

"It's not on high alert already?" she asked.

"Good point," Cal cut in. "But that's mostly internal. This instrument panel controls the exterior of the facility and its defenses. So, when the power shuts down, every soldier in the place will report to a pre-determined station. They'll be stationed throughout the facility, which'll hopefully lessen the likelihood we encounter anyone."

"Isn't the point of dispersing them to protect the exits?" Nori asked.

"No." Cal shook his head. "With Lindgren's short-circuit, they won't know what the actual threat is. They'll protect the arsenal, the food, the air filtration system— everything of value."

"Okay," Nori said and pushed a chunk of dark hair behind her ear. Her cheekbones protruded more than they had before. She had lost too much weight. "Then what?"

Cooper walked away from the conversation to find his pack, digging through it before returning to hear the end of Cal's reply.

"... The big guy, Commander Mills, will take the helm of the primary control station. Lindgren will get us inside that room, where Cooper and I will force Mills to unlock the box containing a self-destruct switch. We'll enter the numeric key and begin the process."

Cooper opened and unwrapped the Vitabar he found and handed it to Nori.

"'Begin the process,'" she repeated, her face pale. "For this place to self-destruct?"

Cooper's gut twisted at the danger he was putting her in—that they were all in. But he knew without a doubt she would have made the same choice.

"That's the plan?" she asked around a bite of the Vitabar. "To blow everyone here—and ourselves— up?"

Cooper shook his head before she ran too far with the idea. "No." He took her hand and found the skin on the back side soft, but her palms calloused. What had she been doing? "No," he said again. "Once self-destruct is initiated, the facility will evacuate. There'll be chaos, which we'll slip right into, and out of here. Hopefully there'll be minimal casualties, but the facility itself will explode. That's the goal. To destroy this place so they can never generate another sunscorch."

Lindgren, who had been working furiously at the instrument panel, stopped moving. "Standridge," he said without looking up from the monitor, "get on ze last computer and enter zis exactly as I say."

Cal sprinted for the rolling chair, slid into the seat, and held his hands above the keyboard. "Ready."

But before Lindgren could call out the numbers, the alarm that had been sounding since the orange alert was first issued grew suddenly louder. Cooper looked to the doors, and the blood froze in his veins.

Two men in uniform stood in the doorframe as flashing lights illuminated them from behind. Their matching looks of surprise at finding the group inside were followed by suspicion, and one of the soldier's hands moved to the pistol at his side.

"What's going on here," the soldier asked from the doorway. No one answered immediately, but when he caught sight of Cal and Lindgren in uniform at the electronic panels, he visibly relaxed. "Prisoner escaped," he said. "Killed one of our men in D1 and injured another. You haven't seen anything?"

Cal stood from the computer, slipping into the faux-friendly body language Cooper knew well.

"We heard the alarm," Cal said. "Thought it was a drill." His laugh was manufactured. "God knows we have enough of 'em around here. Wasn't it just last week we had that mock evac at 2 a.m.? I never did get back to sleep, and had PT the next day. I was so tired, man."

Cooper's heart had been in his throat since the door opened. He was ready for a fight, though he hoped Cal could talk their way out of trouble. He was babbling now, but they seemed to be buying it. Lindgren sat unmoving, his hands frozen above the keyboards. He couldn't have looked more conspicuous.

When the other soldier's posture changed, Cooper's nerves spiked. He bent his knees, ready to strike. Though she stood dead still in a dark corner, the second soldier had spotted Nori. She wasn't the prisoner they were searching for, but she didn't belong there.

The soldier went for the gun, and Cooper didn't think, didn't speak. He jumped. He landed on top of the soldier, a knee pressed into his stomach, forcing him to the floor. Cooper grabbed for the pistol with one hand and punched the soldier in the jaw with the other. The back of the man's head hit the concrete floor, but he didn't stay down. Cooper went for the gun with both hands and the breath flew from his lungs when the soldier punched him in the ribs. Struggling to breathe, he tried to stay focused on the gun but his chest was on fire and every impulse said to work to find oxygen, not a firearm.

Somehow, Cooper managed to raise an elbow in the air and came down hard on the soldier's nose. His grip on the pistol loosened, and Cooper wrestled it away.

Busy talking to Cal, the other guard had not noticed Nori — or his partner's discovery. But he caught on when the fighting began. Cal stood with his hands raised at the gun pointed directly between his eyes.

The second soldier attempted to raise up again, but Cooper smacked the hard metal of the gun into his forehead, knocking him unconscious.

"Drop the gun," the first soldier said, turning his pistol from Cal to Cooper.

That was a mistake Cal took quick advantage of and kicked the man's hand up. Cooper stood quickly, but the soldier had regained control and was pointing the pistol back and forth at he and Cal.

"Look," Cooper said, "there's no way you win against four of us. You can shoot one, but the others will jump on you the minute you do."

The man eyed Cooper with an ugly mixture of fear and hate, and reached for his radio.

"Nope," Cooper said. "I can't let you do that."

The soldier ignored him and pulled the radio toward his mouth, pressing the button at its side and preparing to report them all.

It was instinct. The man was endangering them, and Cooper could never reach the radio in time to stop it. He pulled the trigger.

There were a lot of moments in his life Cooper would rather not re-live. With practice, he had become adept at tucking unpleasant memories deep into the crevices of his brain. There were plenty of things he wasn't proud of. It came with the job. And despite his best efforts, sometimes they found their way into his dreams, forcing him to relive the nightmares in a world he couldn't escape.

When he saw the soldier's shoulder fling toward the wall, blood blossoming around the wound, he knew he would be seeing the image again soon.

Cal scrambled for the downed-soldier's gun and radio as Cooper worked to regain control. His hands were shaking, so he gripped the gun tighter. It didn't help.

"They'll have heard that shot," Cal said, dragging the injured soldier's body toward the nearby closet.

Cooper must have lost time because the trail of smeared blood disappeared behind the closed door and he had never seen Cal complete the task.

"We have to move," Cal said. "Now."

"But," Cooper shook himself and turned to the scientist, whose mouth hung open. Work the details, Cooper reminded himself. Focus on the task at hand. "We need the code," he said. "Lindgren has to enter the code. Our plan — "

Cal cut him off. "There's no way we'll be able to take over Mills at primary control. Not now. Not with this area crawling with soldiers."

'Not after that shot' is what Cal didn't say.

Cooper fisted his hands to stop their shaking. "We need a new plan, then," he said. "Quick, Lindgren, finish that sequence."

"Cooper, man, there's no time." Cal still held the gun as he spread his hands. "If we don't get out of here now we'll all be killed. We've failed. Do you understand? We failed. We have to get out of here and live to fight another day."

Cooper's stomach churned with nauseous regret and guilt, though he wasn't sure if it was guilt from shooting the soldier or from sabotaging their mission. Probably both. His impulsive shot had ruined their chance to shut down the CCC.

For the first time, he thought to look at Nori, and wished he hadn't. She stared at him, arms limp at her sides as she shook her head. She opened her mouth, but no words came.

"Lindgren." Cal took the man by the shoulders, shaking him from a stupor. "Leave. Now. You were never here." The scientist nodded and stood, face blank, eyes unseeing. "Do you understand?" Cal asked. "Never reveal you were a part of this. I'll get these two out and find you when this all dies down."

Lindgren nodded dumbly and stumbled out the door.

The tip of the pistol was still hot when Cooper tucked it into the back of his pants. He worried Nori would flinch when he reached for her, but she didn't. She was in too much shock for that.

What was the point, Cooper wondered angrily. What was the point of her misery, of her isolation here, if they couldn't stop the scorches.

"Let's go, Nor," he said. "We had a backup plan if the evac chaos didn't work. We'll have to use it now."

Nori nodded and blinked and came back online. Her eyes flared wildly, pain and disapproval clear in their depths. Cooper would do anything to wipe that look from her face. She wasn't afraid of the soldiers or disappointed the mission had failed. She was disappointed in him, afraid of him, and he was staggered by the realization he might never regain her trust. He felt the absence in his soul.

30

TUNNELED EXIT

The bloody scene played on a loop in Nori's head as she followed Cooper and Cal through a narrow door to an equipment room. The surprised look in Cooper's eyes a fraction of a second before he pulled the trigger. The way the soldier's body had jerked when the force of the bullet struck him. How he had slumped to the floor, his face white with shock. The bright red trail of fresh blood, and the smell of hot metal permeating the room.

Cooper had shot him. Pulled the trigger and shot the man like a practice target. As if his life was nothing.

Nori shook herself and concentrated on her surroundings, opting to take in details rather than face her feelings. Thick pipes hung low in the huge room, steam spewing where rusty iron elbows met bright red shut-off valves. Metal boxes the size of refrigerators shook as the machinery within them ground and whined, working to facilitate life for three-thousand residents.

Ducking beneath another set of pipes, Nori covered her ears with her palms and breathed in the too-thick, too-wet air.

"What is this place?" She asked the question of Cal, both unable and unwilling to look at Cooper.

"Maintenance room," Cal yelled over the heavy machinery. "We'll access the air filtration system from here." He shot a grin in Cooper's direction, but Nori didn't turn. "Cooper and I have experience with 'em."

"What are we gonna do when we find it?" she asked. "Shut the air to the facility off?"

Cal winked at her, his hazel eyes gleaming with mischief. "No, girl. We're gonna climb it."

"THIS PART'S GONNA SUCK," Cal warned.

He had led them past steaming boilers and through a maze of noisy generators and intricate wiring until they stood beside a pipe so enormous Nori could've fit a fist between its ridges.

"Up you go," Cooper said behind her.

She turned without thinking and met Cooper's gaze, nowhere near ready to answer the questions she found there. Images overwhelmed her of the soldier's face flashing white before the blood stained his uniform. She glanced away, blinking to clear her mind of the haunting visual. She concentrated on the pipe, on Cal, on anything but Cooper.

"You expect me to climb this thing?" she asked Cal.

"Yep. There's a ladder inside that runs all the way up," he said. "Here. Have a look."

He lifted the latch of a small door, and Nori ducked her head inside. The force of air being pulled in from the Surface whipped hair into her face and took her breath, but she saw the ladder. She backed out as claustrophobia threatened to steal what little air she breathed in.

"You sure we'll fit?" Nori's throat seized at the prospect of locking herself inside a wind tunnel, the end of which she could not see.

"It was built for men a lot bigger than you to climb in and repair it." Cal's face grew overly serious. "You're not scared, are you?"

"No." Nori's voice was shakier than she would have liked. "Just... cautious."

Cal lifted his head in understanding, but she wasn't fooling him, or anyone else, and she knew it.

It was better than going back into a cell. At least that's what she told herself as she worked up the nerve to crawl into a hurricane force metal trap. She took a deep breath, held it, and took the first steps of the impossible climb from the depths of the CCC to the Surface.

Nori's hands shook as she stepped through the tiny opening and onto the metal rungs of the ladder inside. The rush of air was overwhelming, and her shirt flew to her shoulders. With stiff, jerky movements, she tucked the shirt in at her waist and tried to force her body to move. It didn't work. She was confined and clunky and scared to death in the galvanized duct. And something was happening beneath her.

Risking a look down, she saw the top of Cooper's dark head. There was no way his wide shoulders would ever make it through, she thought. But as she watched, they did. Turning sideways, he squeezed through the little door, which closed behind him with a *snick*.

He nodded up at her encouragingly, so she took a deep breath and began the climb.

Several rungs up, though, she stopped. The little door hadn't opened again, and Cal hadn't followed. She risked another look down at Cooper.

"Isn't he coming?"

"I'm sure he — " Cooper stopped mid-sentence.

"What?" Nori asked, nervously eyeing the space around them. "What is it?"

Cooper held a finger to his lips, and she gripped the cold metal rung and leaned to the side to better see the bottom. Light stole into the tiny doorway below them, and Cal's head thrust in.

"You two go." His words were clipped, his voice authoritative. "Don't wait. Someone's coming. I'll catch up." He shot a meaningful glance at Cooper, whose back went rigid.

The door shut, and Nori heard voices outside. Though she strained, she couldn't make out the words.

A tap on her leg grabbed her attention, and Cooper motioned up with his head. He wanted her to climb. She mouthed "Cal," but he shook his head and pushed up at her legs. She climbed.

It had been long enough that Cal should've caught up. Nori stopped, leaning back against the pipe and wiping her hands on her pants.

"Let's wait here for Cal," she said.

Cooper nodded, but neither of them spoke for a while. Trying everything in her power *not* to think about what happened in the control room, Nori's thoughts turned to Indigo. She hoped she had found her husband. And she hoped they'd found a way to escape, though with the entire facility looking for them, the odds weren't great.

"He's not coming, is he?" she finally asked.

"He'll catch up." Cooper's dark head bent as he looked down the pipe in vain. "We can't wait on him any longer, though. He wouldn't want that."

"We can't just leave him." Her voice was too loud, too emphatic. "What if he's in trouble?" she said lower.

"This is the kind of thing we trained for, Nori. If Cal sacrificed himself so we could escape, it does none of us good to get caught. If he led them away from us and fell back with his unit, he'll find us again. Or he'll stay there and work from the inside. But none of those things move forward if you and I don't escape."

"But—" Nori's protest died in her throat. Everything he said was true. It was hard to hear, but it made sense.

"I've known Cal my whole life," Cooper said. "He did what I would've done. And if the tables were turned, I'd have wanted you to go without me. He's probably formed a new plan by now, but we still have to follow through with ours."

Nori nodded and resumed the awful climb. She was weak, tired, and when she slowed to rest again she braced her back against the cold metal.

"Why didn't you tell Cal about me?" she asked. At Cooper's questioning look, she clarified. "About the Lumin and my vision, I mean."

He was just below her, his head nearly to her knees. "It's not my story to tell."

They had a lot more to discuss than her night vision, but she dare not open that pandora's box. Not yet.

Would talking to Cooper now, and pretending nothing happened, say she was okay with what he had done? Because she wasn't. Sure, they'd been in danger, but he *shot* someone.

Nori looked up at the seemingly endless expanse of ladder above her, searching for a way out of the intimate space she shared with Cooper. But the only way out was up. She was too close to him in the too-tight space and too-still silence. When he touched the calf of her leg, she jumped.

"I'm sorry about what happened back there," he said. Though it was low, Cooper's voice echoed in a deep, sorrowful rumble. "I know it was hard for you to see, that it might change the way you see me. But I had to think fast to save us, Nori. I operated on instinct, on years of training." His thumb was warm on her calf as he ran it back and forth across the leg of her pants. "I don't know what else to say."

Nori held at bay the well of confused emotions growing deeper with his every word. Angry, frightened, sorrowful, relieved; she couldn't land on one. But if she had learned anything in the Subterranean world, it was that life was rarely black and white. Actions and reactions and their repercussions all formed shades of gray.

"There's nothing to say." Nori's words were barely above a whisper. "I've seen enough to know the world isn't the utopia my parents tried to build for me. I've seen death. And I know it wasn't cruelty that caused you to pull the trigger."

"Then why won't you look at me?" Cooper's voice was urgent and pained. "I can see the disapproval in your eyes and it's killing me." He squeezed her calf. "Don't you know I hate myself for what I had to do? That I feel guilt enough for both of us?"

Nori's heart shattered at the admission, at his vulnerability. She wanted nothing more than to hold him, but in the tight space she could do little more than bend to catch his hand. His fingers tightened around hers almost painfully, but she held him just as hard. "We'll be okay, Cooper," she said. "We'll get past this, too."

"I DIDN'T REALIZE we were so far down," Nori said as she hauled herself, heavy and exhausted, up another rung.

Cooper grunted. "Control room was 15 levels down."

His breathing was heavy, but nothing compared to Nori's. The muscles of her arms and legs were rubber, and her energy had long since faded. Cooper was always right below her, though. Moving when she moved but never rushing.

At last she stopped, leaning against the wall to rest her arms and stretch her neck. When Cooper pushed a canteen of water up, she took a long swallow. "Does this vent open up directly to the Surface?" she asked.

"Yes." Cooper took a drink. "But we're looking for an offshoot before we reach the top."

She flexed and bent her fingers and rubbed the sore spots that had developed on her palms. "An offshoot? To get us back to the tunnels?"

"Exactly," Cooper said and offered her another Vitabar. "We'll be on foot back in the tunnels, but it beats the alternative."

She shook her head at the food he offered and held in a groan as she gripped the cold metal to resume their ascent.

Six rungs up, she noticed a subtle change in shadows and laid her forehead on the metal bar in front of her to peer down at Cooper. Relief and excitement sent a much-needed jolt of energy downh her spine. "Would this offshoot you mentioned be a metal door cut into the side of the pipe?"

"Probably, yes." Cooper looked up at her, his eyes hopeful and his face filthy. "You see one?" She nodded down and smiled at his mumbled, "Oh, thank God."

31

—

LIZ

Nori gripped the rusted handle and groaned when a blister on her palm burst. It had been years since the door was opened, if ever. Like the rest of the old air duct, it was covered in a thick layer of slippery brown grime. She wanted nothing more than to get out of the ventilated hell, but the heavy door wouldn't budge and Cooper's encouragements only irritated her more.

"Come on, Nori," he said. "Push."

"I. Am. Pushing." She forced the words around grinding teeth. Hands raw and stinging, she wedged her shoulder into the door and pushed again using the muscles of her legs and back.

When it finally gave, she fell into the opening, barely avoiding a face-plant by throwing down her elbow. She whined and rolled onto her back, pulling her legs into the new space.

"You did it," Cooper cheered from beneath her. She was still on the ground holding her throbbing elbow when his face emerged from the vent. "I knew you could do it."

"Oh, God, Nori," Cooper scampered up the last rung of the ladder and out of the vent. He bent over her as she lay on her side.

She never dreamed she would miss the cold, filthy floor of the tunnels. But she was so happy to be on the solid ground again she inhaled the sharp, rich scent of earth and stone, cherishing it like a childhood home.

"What's wrong?" Cooper's hair fell forward as he bent over her, his green-gold eyes scanning her for injuries. "Where are you hurt?"

"Everywhere," she grumbled. "Nowhere serious."

The crease between his eyes deepened. "Then why are you crying?"

"Am I?" She raised a shaking hand to her cheeks and felt the wet tracks. She shook her head but didn't answer, clearing her throat and attempting to get up.

Cooper wrapped his arms around her. "Don't move. Not yet."

"I'm okay." She tried to wiggle from his embrace. "Really."

"I know," he said and inhaled the air around her hair. "I just need a minute like this."

"My best guess is we're north of the CCC headquarters." Cooper's arms swung as he walked, and Nori hustled to keep up. "If we keep on this road, we can reach the old U.S.-Mexico border in a few days."

"We'd travel a lot faster with a motorcycle," Nori said around a bite. She was starving, but Cooper had hardly eaten. "Don't you think ours might be where we left it?"

"That's at least another day's walk," he answered. "In the

wrong direction. And the place is probably still on high alert and swarming with soldiers." He shook his head slowly. "No, we can't go back there."

"What's our next move, then?" Nori threw up her hands. Exhaustion had teamed up with hopelessness to form a truly foul mood. "Your precious Settlement refuses to take action. We can't go back to the CCC. We don't know what happened to Cal. We're no closer to stopping them than when we left my parents." Her emotions boiled just below the surface, and she inhaled to slow them, to keep them from rising to the top.

"I don't know what you want me to say here, Nori." Cooper dropped his pack and stalked toward her. "Is our situation ideal? No. It's not. I don't like not having a plan any more than you do, and I'm not used to operating without resources or transportation." He scrubbed his face, and when he pulled his hands away, his gaze was fixed on hers, his voice steady. "But we'll get them. I've got a friend near the border."

"'Course you do," Nori knew her tone was snide, but he didn't respond to it.

"We'll rest and clean up there," he said, "and try to find some wheels. I'll need to give a report to the Settlement anyway."

Nori snorted. "Why bother?"

"Just because they're useless doesn't mean I am."

"Does this friend of yours have a radio or something?" she asked.

Cooper nodded and threw his backpack over a shoulder.

The thought gave her some hope, at least. Maybe she could check in with her parents.

Cooper's friend's house was better suited for hobbits than humans. After turning off the main road, they walked several hours down a path so degraded at times they crept with their backs against the rock or risked falling into deep ravines. Eventually, they wandered up to a half dozen doors bolted into the rock face. Beyond the doors was a big space lined with little storefronts whose wares on display by torchlight. The street was clean, the buildings well-cared-for. It was the first place Nori had seen since going Subterranean that was... almost... charming.

Cooper wiped his face clean with his shirt before knocking on the very last door. The paint had been there a while, its red fading to orange at the corners and around the knob. But someone cared for the place, that much was obvious from the little trinkets and a rug woven of pliable plastic. Cooper smoothed his hair back, and if Nori hadn't known better she would almost think he was nervous.

When a woman's voice called "who's there" from inside, a suspicion took root. One Nori didn't like at all.

"It's me. It's Cooper."

"Who—" Nori began just before the door opened to reveal the woman inside. She was older than Cooper, but not old. She was lovely, actually. Curly brown hair trailed down her back to meet the flowing purple skirt of her dress. Her eyes were large and round, like her lips, which spread into a wide grin when she caught sight of Cooper.

A sick feeling settled in the pit of Nori's stomach, and when the woman reached to hug him, the sick feeling became very *un*settled.

The woman gave a shocked little jerk when she finally noticed Nori. "And who's this?" she asked, her smile curious but polite.

"Liz Balfour," Cooper said as he put a hand on Nori's shoulder and drew her closer. "This is Nori Chisholm." He gave an encouraging nod. "Nori, this is Liz."

The woman looked too long at Nori's face, but then, she was used to that. She could even anticipate the woman's next move— it was what everyone did after noticing the light scarring across her cheeks and forehead. Pink, barely there. Not deforming, but imperfect all the same. The woman quickly averted her eyes, as if Nori wouldn't notice she noticed. Without a word, the woman rushed her with a swift, too familiar embrace that left Nori feeling both thoroughly dominated and pitied. She didn't like either feeling.

"Nori, welcome," Liz said, the low timbre of her voice nearly patronizing. "Come in, come in."

She followed Cooper into the small home, which smelled earthy and almost green, like dried herbs. She noticed pretty quickly there were no signs of a man. No shoes at the door, no coat across a chair. It was a small space, but tidy. A woven tapestry hung on the wall and other handmade things decorated the little dwelling, making it homey and comfortable— a reaction Nori despised.

Because it was so small, it was also too-intimate. "We're sorry to show up unannounced like this," Nori said, feeling thoroughly intrusive.

Liz smiled, but her gaze bypassed Nori and landed firmly on Cooper. "Oh, please," she said. "I'm happy to have you." Though her words were kind, Nori did not like the way her eyes glazed when she said, "Sam Cooper is welcome in my home any time he passes through." No. Nori chewed her tongue to keep from swallowing it. She did not like that at all.

"What are we doing here?" Nori whispered the words, but

the tiny kitchen, where Liz was busy making a strong-smelling tea, was only five feet away from the sitting room.

"Liz is an old friend," he said, and when Nori shot him a sharp look he did not acknowledge it. "She has access to a radiophone in town, and we needed a place to clean up. To rest."

"I don't like the way she looks at you." Nori watched her own hands clench and unclench in her lap. "I don't want to stay here."

"We don't have a lot of options," he said. "Don't be— "

"Here we are." The *swish* of Liz's broom skirt preceded her arrival with the tea. "What are you two whispering about over here? Top secret stuff, if I know Sam Cooper." She served his tea first. "Which I do."

Whether the woman was intentionally baiting or blatantly ignoring Nori to flirt with Cooper, she couldn't be sure. But she had a strong sense earlier of being weighed, measured, and found wanting, as if Liz had sized her up and determined Cooper couldn't possibly see her in a romantic way.

"I was saying it was such a shame we can't stay longer," Nori said, eyeing Cooper over her teacup and daring him to contradict her. "Your hospitality is really... something." She put the force of her feelings into a razor-sharp smile. "But Cooper says we really must go after freshening up and going into town for a bit."

"Oh, don't be silly." Liz placed her cup on the table. "I insist you stay. You look tired, honey, and it's so cold out there on the road."

Looking back, it was the 'you look tired' comment that sent Nori over the edge. She was a big enough person to admit that. But in the heat of the moment, when Liz had made it so very obvious she wanted Cooper to stay, coupled with

the fact Nori probably did, actually, look like a ragged mess…
well, her temper got the best of her.

"Oh, don't worry about us," Nori said, her smile saccha-
rine sweet. "Cooper and I have found very inventive ways to
keep warm."

The sound of Cooper's cup shattering on the flagstone
floor drew Nori's attention from Liz's face, but not before she
had the satisfaction of seeing the shocked and belligerent way
the woman blinked through her disappointment.

"THE SUB-TO-SURFACE RADIO is strictly for emergencies."
Liz's demeanor had grown far less friendly since Nori's
announcement. She was tapping her foot impatiently when
Nori came out of the little bathroom, and wasted no time
ushering them into town and out of her house. "If anyone ever
discovered I'd helped you…" She shook her head. "Not worth
the risk."

"It's kind of you to help us with this very important
mission, Liz." Cooper shot Nori an accusing look. "And brave.
So many lives are at stake."

I probably ought to feel some sort of remorse or shame,
Nori thought. And she looked around for the feelings. She
really did. They simply weren't there. Her actions were
warranted, she was sure of it. If she hadn't staked her claim,
Liz would've continued to trespass on her… well, property
wasn't the right word, but the analogy worked.

And Cooper certainly had not disputed her. If anything,
he had gone out of his way to touch her fingers or the small
of her back when Liz was watching. He made sure to say
"us" and "we" and "our." All in all, Nori was glad she had

spoken up. If it was a test, then she and Cooper had both passed.

"We little guys do have to stick together," Liz said and scanned the town square while flipping through a keyring. "Inside, now. Quickly."

She ushered Nori and Cooper into a small square building that had little more than a desk and a single, metal-barred jail cell. Nori shivered and stayed near the door. Liz opened the top drawer of the old desk and pulled out a black bag, which she unzipped to reveal a complicated-looking radiophone.

Cooper's face was tight with tension as he tuned and dialed the phone. When he finally made a connection, his gaze shot to Nori's, and she let out the breath she had been holding.

"Brown Fox to Hen House," he said. "Requesting a secure channel." Cooper listened for a moment, then, "Copy that." He ended the call and began another.

"What was that?" Nori asked. "What now?"

"Finding a channel we can't be overheard," he said. "I— " he stopped and raised his eyebrows meaningfully while pointing to the phone. He had found them again.

Cooper relayed much of his time inside the CCC to whomever was on the other end of the line. He even told them he found Sand Fox, who could only be Cal. After that, he did a lot of listening and quite a bit of fist-balling.

"Yes, ma'am," he gritted over the line. "But— No. No ma'am." More listening. "The old silver mine? Copy that…. I will… Over."

Cooper laid the phone on the desk and took several breaths before he turned to Nori. She couldn't read his face.

"Well," she prompted. "What did they say?"

"They're going to move," he said. "Tomorrow." He closed

his eyes and some of the tension around them faded. "It'll take several days, but they're coming."

Nori threw her head back and let out a long breath. She hugged Cooper, who held on longer than was necessary—until Liz cleared her throat and they remembered she was there.

"Thank you so much, Liz." Cooper gave the woman a stiff side hug. "This has made all the difference."

She looked uncomfortable, but Nori couldn't find it in herself to spare much time for the woman's feelings. "May I use the radiophone, too?" she asked. "I'd like to check on my family."

"Of course," Liz nodded. "Quickly, though."

Cooper helped Nori find the right frequency, but they couldn't get an answer from her family. She tried again and again with no luck. When fear crept in, she bit at the skin of her thumb before catching herself and throwing her hand down.

"I'm sure they're fine." Cooper's touch had always calmed her, but when he rubbed her arm it felt too close to pity. "Probably just out somewhere with Grant and Kade. Let's try one more time."

They did, but it was no use. There was no answer at the other end of the line.

"I'm sorry, but we really have to go." Liz packed the phone into its case and locked it in the drawer. "Calvin will be back any minute." At Nori's questioning look Liz added, "The sheriff."

Her mind on the cliffside home where she had last seen her parents, Nori shot one last longing look at the drawer before leaving the place— and the phone— behind.

"Are you sorry I forced us to leave?" Nori asked.

Camped beneath an outcropping of rock, her butt and back regretted not accepting Liz's offer of a bed, but her pride didn't.

"No." Cooper scooted closer to her, pulling the one blanket in their possession around them both. "I mean, do I wish I was in a bed right now?" He arched an eyebrow. "Yes, I do." He squeezed her hand. "But I understand why you did it."

"Do you wish you were in *her* bed?" Nori regretted the words before the last one left her mouth. But what was done was done, and she waited for his response.

"Nori."

She raised her eyebrows but wouldn't meet his gaze.

"Nori," he said. "Look at me."

She closed her eyes, then forced them wide and turned to find Cooper's gaze.

"I have no interest in Liz." He pulled her closer. "Not anymore."

She had suspected as much, but it was nice to hear him say it. Smiling, she snuggled into his shoulder.

"Now," he said. "What were you saying about those creative ways of staying warm?"

32

A CHANGE OF PLAN

The militant clip of Cooper's pacing was Nori's first clue. He had been thinking again; forming a plan. That was always dangerous.

"We can't stay here," he said.

"We can't?" She groaned and rose from the rock floor.

"No. We need to be on the north side of the headquarters, near the *cenoté* we entered. It's the entrance Settlement troops will use."

"But you said that was too risky, that CCC troops would be scouring the area, that it was on high alert."

"Well, I've been thinking." He crossed his arms. "It's risky, but there is a way around."

"And you want to meet up with your buddies from the Settlement and storm the castle together?"

"Well." He shrugged. "Yeah. But I do worry you're not up for it."

"I'm feeling much stronger, actually. Couple of Vitabars and a few hours rest and I'm good as new."

Cooper's intense gaze raked across her body before resting

on her face. He frowned and shook his head, his expression bleak. "I don't know where this is going, Nor." He moved toward her and stopped just short of touching her, his hand falling limply to his side. "I don't know if there's a future here. For us, I mean. It's just…" He shook his head. "Well, skinny girls have never been my thing."

Nori's head snapped back in shock and she looked up at Cooper. That's when she saw the evil grin spoiling his handsome face. A breath she didn't know she was holding escaped in a rush.

"You, Sam Cooper, are an epic jerk." Her panic had made the easy transformation to anger, and she threw the thing closest to her at his head. Unfortunately, it was a rock. Fortunately, she missed his head.

Cooper rubbed his shoulder where the rock had hit. "Oh, don't be mad," he said, a grin splitting his face as he closed in on her.

Too close. Too much. Too soon. That was Cooper, though. One extreme to another in the space of a breath.

"You had to know I was kidding," he said and ran his hands around her waist. "I love skinny girls."

Nori mock pouted and flicked him in the same spot the rock had hit. His laugh was light as lifted her to his eye level with ease.

"It's you, Nori. I love you. However you come."

They'd been on the road a full day, resting when she got tired and avoiding contact with anyone, which was tricky in the tight pass. But Nori's sight had proved invaluable. She could see the nooks and crevices Cooper couldn't. At the first signs of people or vehicles, the two took shelter in the tight spaces she had located until the threats passed.

This forced togetherness had quickly become Nori's favorite part. Her heart pounded with anticipation each time she heard something. It was thrilling to race to a tiny alcove and squeeze inside with Cooper. They shared the same air, the same space, their bodies forming an alliance.

At the sound of another engine, she and Cooper raced to the last shadowy crevice they'd passed, squeezing inside. The alcove faced away from the approaching vehicle, hiding them even from headlights. With practice, Nori had learned to distinguish a few types of motors. She could tell this one was a motorcycle even over their labored breathing.

As it neared, Cooper traced the shell of her ear, sending shivers to her toes. When she closed her eyes, he kissed her—something he had grown quite good at with so much practice. Wrapping her arms around his neck, she touched the soft curls at the back of his head. But her fingers went still when she realized the engine had stopped. Her eyes popped open and found Cooper's. He shook his head ever so lightly. Don't move.

She didn't. She stood as still as possible, pressed up against the man she had come to... love? Did she love Cooper? She was crazy about him. She trusted him. She was definitely attracted to him. But love? Were they there yet? Could he have possibly meant it when he proclaimed his?

Gravel ground beneath approaching feet. The footsteps crunched past their crevice and back again, but the engine didn't restart. Nori's gaze shot up to Cooper, who shrugged as well as he could. She dared not risk sticking her head out to investigate. Cooper must've read her thoughts, because he shook his head and mouthed, "no."

They stayed that way— still and silent— until Nori's neck ached. She laid her head against the rock wall behind her, and after a few moments, felt the vibration of the engine roaring to life. Cooper closed his eyes, relief clear on his face, and Nori stuck her head out just inches beyond the edge of the crevice to catch a glimpse of their guest as he passed.

He was leaving, but not quickly enough. Not nearly quick enough to mask the imposing silhouette that belonged to no one but Keegan Kade.

Nori tried to jump from the crevice, too shocked to find words. "Hey," she finally yelled as she worked to get free. "Come back."

"Nori, what the he—" Cooper sputtered and grabbed her hand, pulling her back.

"Kaaaaade." Nori's desperate cry cut him off.

"Kade?" Cooper looked from her to the fleeting bike and back again, his face struck pale. "Are you sure?"

She nodded.

"Can you run?"

She nodded again, and bolted after the motorcycle.

"We'll... never... catch him." Nori struggled to breathe, and even more so to speak.

"Maybe get... lucky." Cooper was stalling to stay with her, but she could hardly object, and not just because she was too short of breath. Cooper bent to pick up a rock, and threw it just as the bike disappeared around a corner. When the motor faded in the distance, Nori lost hope. Cooper trotted back to her, but then turned his head, listening.

"He stopped."

Nori bent at the waist, hands on her knees. "You think... you hit him?" she asked.

"We're about to find out."

Nori heard the grinding crunch of footsteps around the corner, but no motor. No voice.

"Kade?" Her voice was shaky, tentative. "Kade, is that you?"

Her friend's dark brown head crested the incline. She waited two heartbeats, until she saw his eyes, and ran for it. For him.

"Can't breathe," Nori said after a while. Something in her chest cracked.

Kade loosened his hold on her, but didn't let go. "God, I've been looking everywhere for you," he said. When he finally released her, he stepped toward Cooper and shook his hand, but Cooper pulled him into a tight hug. Kade's eyes widened in Nori's direction, and she shrugged.

"I'm so happy to see you, friend." Nori couldn't stop smiling. And why should she? Her best friend just turned up unexpectedly with a mode of transportation. They'd have to make two trips, but still, a set of wheels would save a lot of time. Wait, what was he doing there? She turned to ask him, and saw the reluctance in his eyes.

"What's happened?" Nori clasped her hands together to keep them from shaking. "Is it my mother?"

Kade closed his eyes, his wide chest rising and falling before he answered. "I'm so sorry."

"No." Nori shook her head wildly, backing away. Cooper tried to hold her, but she twisted from him, too. "No."

"She's gone, Nori," Kade said. "It was peaceful. I'm... I'm so sorry."

"No," Nori repeated. "She was fine. She was fine when I left."

"She was so weak," he said. "More so every day. You could see that."

"But the day I left… She was so strong. She… she was getting better."

"I think she did that for you. So you wouldn't stay behind. So you'd go."

"But that's not fair." Nori swiped back the hair that had fallen into her face. "Why would she do that? I should've been with her when she… when she…" She couldn't force the words past her lips. This wasn't real. This wasn't happening. He must be wrong. Her knees hit the hard ground, but she didn't feel it.

Kade knelt next to her and took her hands. "Your dad was there until the end," he said. "Holding her hand. Grant and I were there. She was surrounded by love, Nori. She left quietly, peacefully, surrounded by love."

"Without me." Nori's words were garbled as they made their way through her sobs. "I wasn't there for her. I left her. And now she's gone."

"That's what she wanted, Nori." One of Kade's big hands pushed her head back and he insisted her gaze meet his. "She wanted you to remember her strength. She wanted you to be happy, to pursue your truth. You know better than anyone how selfless she was, how strong."

Nori closed her eyes as tears trailed down her cheeks. She lay her head on Kade's big shoulder and let him support her as she fell to pieces.

WHEN NORI WOKE, she saw Cooper loading his pack onto the motorcycle. She stood and wiped her eyes, which were tender from overuse. "Where are you going?" she asked.

He opened his arms as he approached her, and Nori

tucked herself inside, breathing in his warmth. "I'm going to take the bike to the other side, to meet Gisa and the others from the Settlement."

Nori's head snapped back. "But what about me? We're doing this together, Cooper. You can't just leave me here."

"You're in no shape to be riding into battle." His cheek against her head felt more like condescension than concern. "You're grieving. You're weak. You need some time to recover."

Nori jerked from his embrace. "When did you develop the ability to decide what I need better than I can?"

Cooper's mouth opened and closed several times. "I... I—"

"Yeah, you." Nori threw her hands up. "You, you, you. It's always about you. *You* want to meet up with your people and ride in like a hero. *You* think I can't handle it. *You* think I'm too weak. I'll tell you what, Sam Cooper. Screw *you* and the bike you rode in on."

Cooper's face both fell and hardened, but she didn't care. If she hadn't woken, would he have even said goodbye?

Cooper's jaws flexed as he approached her, but she backed away. "Nori, please," he said. "I don't want to leave like this."

"Nobody's forcing you to go."

"This makes sense, Nori," Kade said, stepping into her line of sight as he spoke up for the first time. "Cooper will go ahead of us. He'll tell them what he knows so they can plan the invasion."

"I'll come back for you as soon as I can," Cooper said. "Or I'll send someone for both of you."

"So we're not a team." She shrugged. "Not really. Not when it counts."

"What do you want me to do, Nori? They're probably

waiting for me. They need my help. Do you want to leave Kade here alone and go with me?"

God help her, but she did. The most humiliating thing was she knew Cooper and Kade were right. Cooper going ahead was the sensible route. She and Kade should travel together, and wait for him to send someone. The rational part of her brain had already analyzed the situation and come down on their side. The rational part of her brain knew she should get hold of herself and kiss her man goodbye.

But the irrational side, well, it was in control. The irrational side felt angry and abandoned. Hadn't she endured enough? Her mother was dead, for God's sake. Her mother was dead and the man who professed to love her was leaving her. Again.

Nori closed her eyes against the grief that threatened to pull her under. She shook her head. "No." It was all she could say.

"I'm sorry." Cooper's words were emphatic, but she didn't look at him. "I have to go. It's too important. I'm sorry, Nori."

She nodded, and when she finally looked up he was gone.

33

STEALTH

The guilt was the worst part of it. Cooper could get past the pain in his chest at having to leave Nori. He'd done it before. He was practiced and efficient at ignoring his own needs. It was being the cause of her pain, her sadness, that withered his insides. As he'd mounted the bike to leave, he'd wanted one last look at her face, and found a storm in her sky-blue eyes.

What choice did he have? Settlement forces were on the move. Gisa and Franks would probably beat him there. For the attack to be successful, they needed his intel on the *cenoté* entrance, on the new surveillance, and on the emergency procedures he'd seen in action.

Oh, Nori had wanted to come, all right. But that made no sense. She tried to hide it, but she was still so weak. And there were huge risks involved. He could hardly drag her into battle as she was. Hell, if he was being honest, he was glad she wouldn't be there for it. She was too important to risk. Too precious. And, God, wouldn't she kill him if she knew he thought that.

No. He gripped the handlebars, their familiarity lending some confidence. Leaving her with Kade was the right thing. He would go back for her later. She would be safer this way.

Cooper's head snapped up at the sound of another motor. It was too close. He'd been lost in his thoughts and hadn't heard the other bike approaching. No time for another plan, he pulled his collar up and ducked his head as the bike passed.

Breath held. Heart in his throat. Fingers clenched around the handlebars. At the last second, he turned and stole a glimpse of the rider from the corner of his eye. And froze. He'd know those pock-marked cheeks anywhere.

The biker didn't slow. He hadn't recognized Cooper. Lucky. Impossibly lucky. His shoulders, which had crawled toward his ears, relaxed, and he laid on the throttle to get as far away as possible before the killer realized his mistake.

The memories of the night he'd last encountered Stealth triggered the same panic. Cooper had been shot, cornered in an alley, and as he'd stared into the bounty hunter's feral black eyes, seen his own death. No one escaped Stealth. He was the most prolific and feared hunter alive. His cold cruelty was renowned, as was his preference to take bounties in dead.

That night had ended not only with Cooper alive, but with a newfound curiosity. It was the night he met Nori. She had saved him by throwing Stealth off his tracks, and again later when he had passed out from blood loss. He had woken hurt and confused, and tucked inside a tiny room with the most delicate and beautiful thing he had ever seen.

He smiled at the memory of Nori's blush, at the nervous twist of her hands when he quizzed her about the tourniquet on his upper thigh.

His smile evaporated, though, when he realized who Stealth would next encounter on the road.

His blood ran cold when he thought of the bounty hunter's snake-like grin and wicked pistol. Kade was a great fighter, but Cooper had taken the only gun. Lead beat flesh in any matchup. Nori was in trouble. He had abandoned her, left her to the wolves— or worse. Stealth never avoided an opportunity for violence, and his dark focus would land directly on her.

Clearing his mind to weigh his options, Cooper repeated his mantra. Rational. Judicious. Concise. It was how he had survived this long. He hoped he could save Nori and Kade, too.

Gravel flung across the tunnel wall as he whipped his bike around and sped in the opposite direction. Toward Nori and Kade. And Stealth.

Cooper saw Stealth's back stiffen. The hunter knew he was being pursued. The right side of his riding jacket rose as, without turning to look behind him, he pulled a gun from its holster. Cooper was safe from the gun in this position, at least. Stealth could hardly aim backward. Scare him, yes, but actually hit him? Probably not.

The man still hadn't turned to see who followed him as he rounded a curve in the road. Cooper followed, debating whether to pull alongside and knock Stealth off the bike, or to run his front wheel into the back of the other bike and cause a collision. The problem with the latter plan, of course, was that the crash might kill them both.

The dilemma was solved when Stealth jumped to the ground from his moving motorcycle. Cooper rounded the corner and nearly plowed over the man who stood, legs spread and gun aimed, in the middle of the tunnel.

Thank God the white beam of Cooper's headlight was blinding, or he would be dead already. In the milliseconds before he jumped out of the way, Stealth had gotten off one shot that whizzed so close to Cooper's ear he had felt the heat of it.

Stealth struggled to get up. Seizing his only chance, Cooper was off the bike and on the man before he could aim again, knocking the gun from his hands in the grapple. Stealth was strong, and fought like a wild man to break Cooper's hold and snatch the gun back.

Before he could reach it, though, Cooper delivered a gut punch with the full force of his body. Stealth doubled over and fell to his knees, one hand pressed to his stomach and the other on the ground.

He wouldn't stay down for long. Cooper drew back to deliver another blow— this time to his jaw. But before he could land the punch, Stealth surged and hammered the side of Cooper's head with a rock he must've found on the road.

Cooper stumbled back, blinking, trying to think, working to stay conscious, but blackness faded in and out like a persistent sleep. He threw a hand wide to brace himself on the tunnel wall.

"Knew it was just a matter of time before I'd find you again," Stealth said. Cooper couldn't focus on the hunter's face, but his voice was snide, boastful. "I worked hard for the money this time, but I always get my man."

"It's not over yet, gorgeous," Cooper said and groaned as he stood upright. He couldn't see Stealth's gun, but knew about where it had fallen. He inched in that direction.

"You didn't catch me in Ralston," Cooper said in an attempt to distract the man. He sought out the gun with the toe of his boot, but only connected with rocks.

"A mistake I'll soon rectify," Stealth said, and the confidence in his voice caused Cooper to look up. "You looking for this?"

Cooper's head, which had a gun pointed directly at it, fell forward in defeat. He didn't have many options left. He could run. The darkness would offer some cover. But he would be on foot. His bike was behind Stealth. To get it, he would have to go through the bounty hunter, and considering he held the gun, well, the odds were not in Cooper's favor.

"What are you doing here?" Stealth asked, his gravelly voice unusually high-pitched.

Cooper looked up just in time to see Kade's ferocious right hook knock Stealth to the ground.

"Nice to see you, too, *Papa*," Kade said.

His disgust rolled not just from his tongue, but all the way through his body. He shook with emotion, vibrating with anger... and something worse. Hatred, Cooper realized. Kade hated the man he had just named father.

"QUICK, NORI." Cooper motioned to the saddle bags of his bike. "Grab some rope before he wakes up."

"I hope he does wake up," Kade said. He hadn't moved from his fisted position at Stealth's side. "I'd love to knock him out again."

At Nori's questioning look, Cooper shrugged and shook his head. He crept toward Kade, who turned, his expression deadly. Cooper stopped.

"Ah, Kade?" Cooper asked.

The big man's murderous gaze had drifted back to Stealth, who lay face-down and unconscious on the silted ground.

"Is this guy your… father," Cooper asked. "Is Stealth… Is Stealth your *father*?"

Kade jerked his chin to his chest.

Cooper looked at Nori again and shook his head in wonder. How Keegan Kade was the flesh and blood of the most feared killer in the Subterranean, Cooper had no idea. Kade, who'd chosen to love instead of to fight time and again. Kade, who was built for destruction but created some of the most beautiful paintings Cooper had ever seen.

"A little help?" Nori's request brought Cooper back to the present, and he snapped his gaping mouth.

"Here, I'll finish that," Cooper said and tied the synthetic rope, pinning Stealth's hands behind his back.

He moved to tie his feet, and had just circled the man's ankles with the rope when one leg jerked free. Stealth thrust the heel of his boot into Cooper's face. Blinding pain shot through his nose and between his eyes. He was dizzy, nauseous, and mad.

Fighting to stay conscious, Cooper growled and tried to grab the kicking leg, but Stealth twisted onto his back and pushed himself away.

Worried about Nori, Cooper searched and found her—smartly backed away from flying boots. Stealth's legs abruptly stopped scraping in the gravel. Kade stood over the man, his lips pulled back and his eyes throwing flames. One foot was pressed into Stealth's neck.

"Move again and I'll crush your throat," Kade said.

Stealth's eyes narrowed as if he doubted the threat.

"You think I won't do it?" Kade's eyebrows raised as his foot lowered, and Stealth made a coughing, gagging sound. "I told you if I ever saw you again I'd snap your neck."

Cooper watched the scene, unsure if he should interfere. The two obviously had a volatile history.

Stealth kicked his legs again. Probably because he couldn't breathe.

Nori, though, had a different idea. Her eyes were wide as she approached her friend.

"Kade," she said. "Kade, I don't think this is something you want to do." At his scoff, she said, "Not really. You don't *really* want to kill your father."

"He sure as hell tried to kill me," Kade spat. "More than once."

Nori wrapped her small hands just above Kade's elbow. "This won't help you heal," she said, but Kade's gaze never left his father's increasingly-purple face. "It'll only give you more wounds."

Kade blinked, and she stepped closer. "I think you have to ask yourself if you can stand any more injuries from this man, or if you've endured enough." Her throat bobbed on a swallow. "Haven't you endured enough pain at his hands?" she asked. "Don't give him this, too."

Kade finally looked up. He held Nori's gaze for the longest time, and Cooper held his breath. It was clear when Kade released the tension at Stealth's neck. The man coughed and wheezed and closed his eyes to breathe.

Cooper quickly tied his feet together and tethered them to his bound arms so he couldn't stand.

"What now?" Kade asked, his face blank. Shocked.

"'What now'?" Stealth mocked his son from the ground and then spit out blood. "Don't have the balls to make decisions. Don't have the balls to kill me. Must have no balls at all, considering what you choose for *girlfriends*."

Fury and disgust rose quickly within Cooper and it was all

he could do to keep from kicking the bigoted idiot in his vulgar mouth.

Nori, apparently, felt no such restraint, and delivered a kick to the downed man's gut that sent him into another coughing and gagging fit. Cooper nodded approval in Nori's direction, but she didn't need it. At least, she didn't seek it from him.

"The good news is we have two bikes now." Kade shot an evil smile in Stealth's direction as he stood the man's sleek bike.

"Get your filthy hands off her." Stealth's savage command roared through the tunnel, but it had no bite, bound as he was on the floor.

When Kade kicked the motorcycle to a start, Stealth surpassed savage and grew apoplectic. Hate spewed from his mouth like acidic spittle.

"That's enough," Cooper growled as he tore the bottom of Stealth's shirt off and tied it around his mouth. He jerked one last time on the knot, maybe a little too hard, and lifted his own motorcycle.

"Nori?" Cooper's emotions ran high, and there was no possibility of hiding how much he wanted her with him. "Ride with me?" he asked.

BREAK DOWN; RISE UP

It was a good thing all Nori had to do was hold on to Cooper as he navigated them through the dark tunnel. It's all she could do. Her heart had been scooped out, leaving only a thin, faintly pulsing husk. It had been so full yesterday, brimming with hope and bursting with the prospect of love and a future with Cooper. But that was before. Before Kade arrived with news she wished she had never heard. Before she learned her sweet, nurturing mother was gone.

With her cheek against the cool leather of Cooper's jacket, Nori grieved until her throat ached with the need to scream. If Cooper heard her anguished moans or felt the tremors rocking her as she sobbed, he didn't show it. He rode on and gave her as much privacy as he could. Occasionally, he would reach to his waist and squeeze her hands, but he didn't try to quiet her, and he didn't stop to coddle her.

Her sinuses were a mess, her head achy and full after hours of grief. She sniffed back tears and wiped her nose one last time. It was enough crying, enough grieving. For now. When this was all over, when she saw her father again, she would let herself feel the pain of her mother's loss. But for now, they had work to do. She didn't have to be one-hundred percent, but she did have to function. She could hold her mother in her heart and still focus on their mission. At least, she thought she could. She was going to try.

A look back at Kade found the big man's shoulder's tense. The grips of his handlebars probably regretted the day they were made. His jaws were flexed and his eyes were on the road, but his thoughts were obviously miles away. Or more accurately, miles back.

They'd left Stealth bound and gagged in the tunnel where they'd fought him. Leaving him alive was something she hoped they wouldn't regret. But what more could they have done? It's not like Kade could kill his own father. Though, at one point, she was afraid he would do just that.

God, to have a father like that, who could *say* things like that to his own son. A chill ran down Nori's spine at the thought of the abuse Kade had probably endured in his own home. She had known he was special, but to be such a beautiful human being after a life with such a monster... her friend had an exceptional soul.

Nori tapped Cooper's thigh to get his attention. His legs were strong beneath her fingers, and she concentrated on his strength, borrowing against it until she found her own. When he turned, she caught his gaze and mouthed "stop" over the roaring motor. He nodded, and she motioned the plan back at Kade.

"You hungry?" Cooper asked, already unwrapping a Vitabar.

"Thanks," she said, and couldn't help smiling at his adorable doting.

Kade hadn't joined them right away, and as she chewed,

she caught sight of him several feet away, sinking to the ground with his head leaned against the rock wall.

"How are you feeling?" Cooper asked, but didn't wait for her answer before folding her into a hug and rubbing his hands across her shoulders.

How was she feeling? That was a tricky question. For the first several hours back on the road, she had felt the most acute grief of her life. She wanted nothing more than to curl up in a cold corner and join her mother.

But then her pain had changed, morphing into something like determination, or maybe vengeance. Her grief had been consumed by a raging blackness, a drive to see her mother avenged. Her mother, who had been crippled during the last sunscorch, the paralyzation from her accident responsible for her pain and, ultimately, her early death. Her mother, who had been deceived while pregnant with Nori and injected with a substance that changed her unborn child's chemical makeup. Her mother, who had lost two young children to a sunscorch.

And who was responsible for her mother's pain, deception, and death? Who was responsible for all the misery Nori had endured in her own life?

The freaking CCC.

How was she feeling? At that moment, she was filled with fire and vengeance and it felt goooood.

"Better," she finally answered. "Stronger." She pulled from his arms. "How long until we're there?"

"Another few hours, probably."

Cooper turned to Kade and yelled, "You on board for this?"

Kade stood to his full height, his massive chest expanding on a deep inhale.

"I'm ready," he said. "I want these idiots to burn. I'm tired of their manipulation and abuse. This 'might makes right' nonsense has got to stop, and I'll do everything I can to help."

"Me too," Nori said, a deep sense of belonging, of purpose, filling the cavity in her chest. "I'm done being a victim," she said. "I'm done crying, and I'm done biting my nails as other people determine my fate."

Her back straightened and strengthened with an infusion of pride. "I have a gift," she said. "Despite the way I acquired it, it's mine." She met Cooper's gaze and found his eyes blazing with pride. "And I'm going to use it."

35

CATHEDRAL CAVERN

As they neared the abandoned silver mine, Cooper caught the scent of campfires and cursed. They'd been beaten to the rendezvous point. His wrist twitched to flood the throttle, but conditions forced him to keep slow. The old mining tunnel was so low in places he had nearly taken Nori's head off before remembering to yell "duck." And Kade sat his motorcycle so tall he had dismounted and walked twice.

The composition of this part of the Subterranean was different. Slate gray rock had given way to orange and deep copper-colored stone, chipped away over decades until it resembled a scaly bowel. Occasionally, the bike's headlights reflected bits of metal in the rough-hewn walls, veins of silver once prized but long-abandoned.

Cooper's breath caught in his throat when he rounded a corner and his headlight tumbled into darkness. They'd finally made it. One moment he was crowded on all sides by chiseled stone, and the next he steered into the mouth of a cathedral-sized cavern.

The vaulted dome should have eased some of the pressure

he felt after navigating tight spaces for so long, but instead he felt more claustrophobic. The cathedral cavern's nave crawled with Settlement troops.

Behind him, Nori pressed close for a better look. He would be glad to rejoin his people— if he could still call them that— but he would miss the warm presence of her at his back. As he navigated the new space, his gaze snagged on familiar faces and he nodded at people he had known his whole life. Curious eyes followed as they passed, but the focus wasn't on him.

Nori's grip tightened at his waist. She had noticed the looks too, then. Probably best to avoid a mass introduction for now, he thought. Nori could handle herself, but she had been through a lot lately. She had been through a lot her entire life. If he could save her this small thing, he would.

As he steered the bike through the twisting mass of people, memories resurfaced of the time he delivered Nori to Hank. It seemed like a lifetime ago he had found her in that tunnel, alone and utterly clueless, and saved her from Sarge's slimy grasp. She was a walking contradiction, the most delicate spitfire he had ever seen. Finding a place for her with Hank had been the right thing to do. He knew that. And yet he hadn't been able to resist going back. It had become the story of his life— finding safe places to stow Nori Chisholm, and then abandoning his resolve to leave her.

That part of their story was over, though. He squeezed Nori's hand at his waist, whether to reassure her, or himself, he didn't know. From now on, they'd be together. Wherever he went, so would she. At least, he hoped that's what she wanted. No, she did. She felt the same way. Didn't she?

Shaking himself, Cooper refocused on the tasks at hand. Despite friendly waves and invitations to stop and catch up, he steered the bike directly into the middle of the encampment. It's where Gisa would be. Franks, too, whose throat Cooper wanted to squeeze until the veins of his wrinkled forehead popped out.

"Cooper." The words were mouthed, but unmistakable. Gisa Meir's eyes lit, but her mouth did not form a smile. She was known for her skill as a fighter, her strength as a leader, and her stoicism. Not her emotions. Cooper had always followed Gisa's lead where those were concerned.

He turned off the engine and dismounted. "Gisa," he said and nodded professionally, though his relief at seeing the woman was so intense he ached to hug her.

Instead, he extended a hand to Nori as she hopped from the back of the bike. "This is Nori Chisholm."

They'd been riding a long time and Nori grimaced only slightly before straightening and cutting curious eyes at Gisa. "Hello," she said.

Gisa bobbed her head once, cooly assessing Nori, but then her attention snagged on their escort. "And your other friend?" she asked.

Kade approached with unhurried confidence. "Keegan Kade, ma'am." He shook her hand as he said with trademark meekness, "Everyone calls me Kade."

Gisa's attention swung back to Cooper for an explanation, but he didn't have time for that. "We came as quickly as we could," he said. "I'm sure you'll want to form a plan."

"We've already got a plan." Zenon Franks' strident voice cut into the conversation before he came into view. "We're all set to go in," Franks said and stepped around Kade, giving him the same notice he would a boulder.

Cooper's vision blurred as his blood pressure smacked the cavern ceiling. Franks might outrank him, but this was *his* intel. *He* had been inside the CCC. Franks had no idea the scope of what they were up against, of the systems and alarms in place, of the sheer number of armed troops ready to defend the facility and take them out in the process.

"That's enough, Zenon." Gisa's tone could've cut the stone wall. "Cooper, we've been waiting on you to sketch the interior." She nailed Franks with a mortal stare and her top lip rose as if something stank. "Sometimes I think you live to enrage him," she said.

"Guess you've been put in your place." Cooper had only meant to think the words, but when Franks eyes flew wide he knew he had said them aloud. He fought a grin, but Franks, who needed no excuse to fly off the handle, lunged for him.

He was in Cooper's face in a split second, hot breath and spittle flying. Cooper turned his head, but the stout old man grabbed the shirt at his throat in one fist. He yanked, trying to shake Cooper, to immobilize him with fear like he had so many times before. But Cooper had been a kid then and believed all of the Subterranean revolved around Zenon Franks. He and Cal had pretended to *be* Franks, tucking too-long uniform pants into their boots, their posture stick-straight and their lips tight.

As a Sixth Tier trainee, Franks had targeted Cooper almost immediately for the brunt of his abuse. He never knew why; only that his friendship with Cal had caused Cal to suffer, too. Cooper had been too small to stand his ground then. Too small to defend himself.

It was thoughts of Cal that sent Cooper's blood boiling again. He pushed Franks with such force the man stumbled back, shock yielding his eyes the same color as his age-bleached hair.

"You lied," Cooper seethed. "You lied to all of us. You let

us believe he was dead. Or worse, that he abandoned us." Cooper stalked toward Franks, who'd recovered and stood on bent knees, ready for another attack. The spark in his eyes said he was hoping for it. "All this time," Cooper said. "He was alive."

"Cooper, get control of yourself." Gisa's reprimand was all bark and no bite. "What are you talking about?"

"He thought we knew where he was. He thought his work was sanctioned by the Settlement." Cooper shook his head and looked to Gisa, who'd gone still as death. "Franks sent Cal to the CCC. They've been in communication all this time."

Gisa didn't say anything, and for a glorious moment Cooper played out the scene in his head. She would be furious Franks had conducted operations without her knowledge. She would charge him with insubordination on the spot. Or shoot him. Maybe both.

Grim satisfaction settled in Cooper's spine at the thought of Franks finally getting what he deserved. He smiled in the man's direction, and noticed for the first time Franks' expression. He wasn't worried. He wasn't searching for escape or to explain himself. His mouth formed a familiar impertinent sneer. His frosty eyes held hatred, not fear. And certainly not remorse.

Cooper's gaze snapped to Gisa. He looked between her and Franks and felt once again like a defenseless child.

"What?" he asked her weakly. Then it hit him. "You knew."

The last words were choked, barely scraping through his deflated lungs. He looked down, certain his chest had been impaled. His mouth opened again, but no words came. Blinking foolishly seemed to be the only thing he was capable of doing.

Nori was suddenly at his back, once more the strong presence he had come to count on. He siphoned from the certainty of her.

"You freaking knew," Cooper spat at Gisa. "I can't believe this." He shook his head, and the jaded laugh that escaped his mouth sounded like someone else. "No, I take that back," he said. "I believe it of him. But you. I can't believe *you* would do it. To *me*."

"You always were a whiner."

Franks' snide voice was the pin pulled from the grenade of Cooper's fury. He exploded into fists and snarls and blew up at the man, who'd been spoiling for a fight as long as Cooper had known him.

Franks ducked the first punch, then twisted to catch Cooper in the kidney. He fought through the pain, limping in a narrow circle. For an old man, Franks still packed a punch.

There was only one place Cooper wanted to hit Franks, and that was his arrogant mouth. He did just that, though he suffered for it when the flesh of his knuckles gave way to Franks' front teeth.

When Franks spat blood, Cooper's anger was nourished.

When he charged, Cooper was ready.

He wasn't a kid anymore.

36

RALLYING CRY

"You shouldn't have done that," Nori told Cooper as she cleaned a cut on his knuckle.

She had been so scared when he had attacked Franks. Not just that he would be hurt; but at the way blind fury had transformed him so completely. It was another side of Cooper she had not seen.

"Actually, I still can't believe you laid into him like that," she said. "You *always* think first. You're *always* in control of yourself. What *was* that?"

Cooper shrugged and looked away. She followed his line of sight, which was directed at Franks as his fists flexed angrily.

"Listen," Nori said, "whoever that is, and whoever he is to you, he is not our priority."

When Cooper didn't answer, she squeezed his still-swelling hand.

"Ow!" He frowned, but finally looked at her.

"Forget about him," she said.

"It's not just him," Cooper said and forced air through his

nose. "It's her, too. They lied to me. They let me believe my best friend was gone." He swallowed. "When they *knew*."

"Did… " Nori stopped and shrugged. "What am I supposed to call her, anyway? 'Gisa' seems awfully informal for the leader of your group. Shouldn't I call her General Meier or something?"

"The Settlement doesn't use titles," Cooper answered. "Too defining for a commune of equals." His mouth twisted. "Though I can think of a few choice names for both of them right now."

Nori sighed, the closest she could come to a reprimand for his actions. Those two deserved Cooper's anger, and more. She had wanted to kick Franks in the gut herself after the insolent way he had talked to Cooper.

Growing up, she would have given anything to have a friendship like his and Cal's. That these horrible people had not just stolen something so precious from Cooper, but tried to kill it? No, she would not have been able to forgive that, either.

"Well, did… Gisa… say why they kept Cal's mission from you?" Nori asked. "When you talked to her a minute ago did she give an explanation?"

"She said we were too close." Cooper's derisive laugh made Nori cringe. "She said we were inseparable, and if I'd known he was embedded somewhere I'd have found a way to sneak in, putting the mission at risk."

Nori had to admit that, cruel as it was, the reasoning was not unsound. "Do you think they were right to do it?"

Cooper bolted upright, pulling his hand from her in an angry jerk. "No, I don't think they were right," he said. "God, Nori, you've lost someone you cared about. It's devastating. Why torture me like that when they could've told me about the mission? I'd have been satisfied with the updates he sent, no matter how infrequent."

Nori nodded up at him as her heart broke. She suspected their lack of faith in Cooper played as big a role in his pain as the deception.

"Thankfully you never ran into Cal during your own undercover work," she mused. "That could've been bad."

"But I did! Don't you see? They very nearly got us both killed." Cooper shook his head. "Stupid decision. Stupid and short-sighted. I'm sure it was Franks' idea and she went along with it."

Nori nodded, then stood to dust the dirt from her pants. "How long until we leave?"

He closed his eyes and took a deep breath, and she could tell the moment he decided to put his anger aside. Then movement at the center of the cavern caught both their attention.

"She's going to address the group now," Cooper said. "We'd better go."

<hr>

"SETTLEMENT TROOPS," Gisa Meier's smooth, powerful voice echoed through the cavern on a wave of authority. "Settlement *family*." She held her arms out and turned to address the hundreds of soldiers surrounding her. "This is the day we've trained for. The day for which we have prepared and worked and sacrificed."

No one spoke. They hardly moved. The hungry audience was starving for its leader's next morsels.

"Today," Gisa said, "we face not just *our* enemy, but the enemy of civilization itself. We charge to battle against those who have destroyed the world to save themselves. We fight those who have taken not just our land, our way of life, but the people we love."

Gisa paused, and the tip of her words pierced Nori's soul. "We fight those who destroyed our past so that we might all have a future."

Like the soldiers crowded around her, the hair on Nori's arms stood at attention. The air in the cavern had changed, charged. Her heart was heavy in her chest, and an overpowering sense of purpose raced through her veins, its scarlet hair trailing behind.

For the first time in her life, Nori grasped what it might feel like to be a part of something bigger than herself, to be a spoke in the wheel of a vehicle for change. Gisa Meier had called her people to action. She had called them to fight. Despite having never set foot in the Settlement, Nori felt driven to fight beside them, to protect it.

"The fist of our attack has several fingers," Gisa said, hammering the point home with her hands. "Sub-to-Surface troops, you'll leave at once to support the mission above ground.

"Lumineers, as usual, you're the front line. You'll break into four groups, leading our forces into four entrances."

She extended a third finger from the fist. "Ground troops, you'll follow the Lumineers, and once inside will be the primary offense."

With a final nod, she somehow met the gaze of each soldier gathered. "Report to your battalion leaders for further instructions. We march in thirty."

"God, she's amazing," Nori said as she followed Cooper to the motorcycle. The crowd had quieted its cheering after two or three minutes and disbanded to form smaller groups. "No wonder she's your leader," Nori said. "I'd follow her anywhere, even back into that fiery pit to fight the creeps at Yahweh, and I just met her."

Cooper raised his eyebrows, his smile tight. He was less affected by Gisa's speech, but of course he had heard her before. For Nori, it was all so new. Being a part of the action and, more importantly, part something meaningful... Like love, it was one more thing she never thought she would have a shot at.

Her gaze gravitated to Cooper, who jerked a little too hard at the saddlebags of his bike. This thing with Cal had really upset him. He had talked to Gisa for an eternity after she had broken up his fight with Franks. He had come back sullen and mute — inconvenient since she had a thousand questions.

Nori moved behind Cooper and ran her arms around his waist. She pressed her cheek into the valley between his shoulder blades, a move that had become as natural as blinking. Being close to Cooper, breathing the scent of him, grounded her. She had been as inspired as the rest of the troops by Gisa's speech, focused on defeating their shared enemy. But it was Cooper and the life they might have together that she was really fighting for.

He exhaled, long and low, then turned in her arms. He closed his eyes and pressed his forehead to hers, their breaths coming slower and slower until they synchronized. Nori didn't move, didn't dare break the spell of the moment he so obviously needed in the midst of betrayal and battle. He leaned back and searched her face as she stared, transfixed on the swirling gold of his irises and the thick black lashes framing them.

Cooper smoothed the hair from her face before confining it into to a handful of ponytail. When he pulled so her face angled up and lay a reverent kiss on her lips, the cathedral-sized cavern could've been empty for all she cared. It was the two of them alone again in the crevice of a tunnel, building something precious just feet away from danger. It was the two of them cuddled around a fire, sharing childhood memories and secret dreams of the future.

Nori was so lost in Sam Cooper she didn't hear them approach. Only when his lips ripped from hers, his fingers tightening in her hair, did she open her eyes.

"Looks like Coop's too busy to notice his friends."

The unfamiliar faces registered before the words could embarrass her, though they quickly caught up. Two men, maybe twenty years old, stood behind Cooper. They were obviously twins, but one's face looked older than the other somehow. More severe.

"Newt." Cooper nodded to the Twin-In-Charge, then at the other. "Jake."

He hadn't moved from her side, though he dropped his hands.

"You not happy to see us, Coop?" It was the younger-looking twin, Jake. Like most of the Settlement soldiers she had seen, his dark hair had been cut close to his head. "We sure are happy to see you."

Gray-blue eyes cut to Nori and his smile was shy. "Who's this," he asked, and then more quickly "and were there any more where she came from?"

Nori snorted a laugh. At least he was transparent.

His brother elbowed him in the ribs, though, and shoved him aside. "What'd I tell you about talking before you think?" Newt said severely.

His eyes were the same color as Jake's, but the similarity ended there. Where Jake's were open and friendly, Newt's were suspicious, calculating.

"Sam?" A woman's voice was soft and full of emotion. Nori looked up to find its owner who stood several feet away with a flashlight. The beam found Cooper first, then swung past the two brothers. Whether the woman was young or old, plain or lovely, Nori didn't spare a moment's thought. It wasn't the woman who had her attention; it was the twins.

She had seen the same reflection a thousand times before. Like her scars, it was a part of her people had always found unnerving. "Uniquely gifted," was her mother's term, and though Nori's heart stuttered at the thought of her mother, it didn't stop this time. Not when two people stood beside her with eyes she had only ever seen in the mirror.

"Your eyes," Nori breathed, stepping toward them.

"Yours, too." Newt's retort was instant, and mildly offended.

"Yes, but…" There was an end to that sentence somewhere, Nori knew, but all she could think was no wonder she had freaked people out her whole life.

When the beam of the flashlight had caught the brothers' eyes, they'd shone a shocking blue-green. *Tapetum lucidum*, the mirror-like membrane that reflected light back through a retina. It was a nocturnal device she had only ever seen since she had been Subterranean. In spiders and mice. And herself.

The woman switched off the flashlight. "I'm sorry," she said. "I didn't mean to blind you."

Despite the storm in her mind batting questions and theories around like dust particles, Nori now noticed the woman was young. Bold, light brown eyes inspected Nori, who stood straighter after a deep breath, resigned to meet yet another woman from Cooper's past.

"Meggie," Cooper said, and there was something in his tone that caught Nori's attention. She whipped her head in time to catch the droop of his shoulders and a long, slow blink. He cared about this girl. When he wrapped his arms around her, Nori fought the urge to puke.

"Meggie," Cooper said again as he released her. "I want you to meet Nori, my… " he shrugged and an embarrassed grin rippled across his mouth, "… love," he finished weakly.

Everything had happened so fast Nori wasn't sure how to react first. The choice was made for her when the girl beamed and rushed her in a hug completely inappropriate for strangers. Nori made sure her tongue was inside her teeth as the girl jumped three or four times.

"I'm so happy to meet you," Meggie said, still holding on tight.

Nori bugged eyes at Cooper, whose smile took up his entire face. Jake seemed entertained by the whole thing, too. But not his brother. Newt's face was etched in stone.

Pulling from the girl, Nori straightened her shirt. "I'm glad to meet you, too,… "

"Meg!" she cut in before Nori could finish. "Sam's sister!"

"'Sam's sister,'" she repeated dumbly. "You're Cooper's sister. Meg."

The girl's enthusiastic grin could've lit the entire cavern, which reminded Nori of the other big thing hanging over their heads.

"Wait," she said, stomping toward Cooper. "Just." She shook her head. "Hold up."

Glancing at Newt and Jake, Nori took in their uniforms. She recalled Gisa's emboldened speech and the units being deployed.

"What the heck are Lumineers?"

37

LUMINEERS

Cooper didn't need to explain. She *knew*. Newt and Jake — Lumineers— they were like her. Nori's hands trembled as the twins walked away to join the throng of soldiers who were busy checking weapons and readying supplies.

An excited current thrummed through the room, but there was something else, too. An underlying thread of fear. Barely noticeable, but it was there. The Settlement army was strong; fearless, even, but it was preparing to take on an enemy with far greater resources.

Did these soldiers know that? Did it matter? How many of them could see in the dark as she could? A dozen? A hundred?

When Cooper had told her there were others like her at the Settlement, she had never imagined they were special. Not that she had imagined them shrinking from the sun like vampires. It simply hadn't occurred to her she could be valuable. She never dreamed the thing that had always handicapped her was considered here a gift. No, not a gift. A *weapon*.

If Lumineers were like Newt and Jake, fighting on the front lines and using their abilities to conquer the bad guys… Nori squared her jaw and turned to Cooper, her mind made.

"I'm joining the Lumineers," she said. "I'll fight with them."

Cooper coughed up the tongue he nearly swallowed at her pronouncement. "The hell you will," he said with a derisive snort.

Nori's temper flashed white hot as a lifetime of simmering revolt bubbled up to spew at him. The look on her face must have matched the combustible tension in the air because Cooper's eyes shot wide when he finally looked at her.

"You do not tell me what to do, Sam Cooper."

It was a staring contest, a battle of wills. Nori breathed through the rage, and through little stings of pain as finger-nails dug into her palms.

Eventually, Cooper backed off, waving away the tension. "I didn't mean you *couldn't* join them. *Someday*. Just that you couldn't fight with them *now*."

"And why not?" The cliche of an affronted woman, Nori's hands flew to her hips. "I'm like these people and you know it. I want to fight. I can be useful."

Cooper stepped close, his voice low and urgent. "Because you haven't trained for it," he said. "Because their jobs are too important to risk even a single mistake. And because you might get more people killed than you'd help rushing in unpracticed and unprepared."

Nori swallowed her retort. Her face heated again, but it wasn't with anger this time. She hated it when he made sense.

"I have to do *something*, Cooper," she said. "They killed my people, too."

"I know that." He slid his hand into hers. "I'd hoped you'd

go in with me— behind the Lumineers. We're a good team, you and I."

Nori sniffed and backed out of his arms, satisfied but too edgy to be comforted. "When do we leave?"

"KADE, you don't have to do this," Nori said.

He had disappeared sometime during Gisa's speech, and when he finally reappeared he began readying for battle, too.

"You can go back home," she said, "to the 25th. See Grant and Mo—" Nori shook her head. She couldn't think of her mother, couldn't lose control. Not now. "— see Grant and Dad. They'll be wondering where you are."

"Yeah?" Kade arched an eyebrow. "They'll be wondering where you are, too. You want to go home?"

He had her there.

"But I've been inside this place before," she said. "I know the layout and can help find the control panels."

"Well, I've got a knack for electrical and their guy's puking his guts out from a run-in with gray water," he said. "So. Looks like I'm going."

"Kade," Cooper said and thumped the fighter on the back. "Just heard you're a whiz with circuitry. Welcome aboard, man."

Nori's mouth fell open, but she kept it shut. "What's the plan again?"

"We'll evacuate the cavern together, but separate into four groups. Each group will conduct a coordinated attack on the CCC headquarters at 2100." Nori shot him a look, and he quickly added, "which is about three hours from now."

"I'm going in with you two?" Kade's voice was absent of fear, as if he was asking for directions.

"Exactly," Cooper said, then turned to Nori. "You'll get to see first-hand what Lumineers can do since a quarter of the force will lead us in from the *cenote*." His voice skewed sarcastic. "Then you can decide if you still want to join them."

***

THOUGH THEY'D MARCHED for nearly two hours, Nori wasn't tired. She was wired, jittery with nerves. Her spastic heart beat so loudly she worried Mathers and Iberville would hear it through the reinforced concrete.

Lumineers had led the way, their expert reconnaissance skills leaving Nori both impressed and jealous. She trailed them as closely as she could, often forced to sprint. Their quick movements and sharp reflexes had been honed to a fine point. With no need for spotlights or lanterns, they crept quickly through the darkness. The regular soldiers either took their cues from this elite force... or were left behind.

Nori did a double take, surprising herself when she recognized a deep groove in the stone wall. There was nothing special about it besides the shape, which she had imagined the first time she saw it to be an exact molding of a front fender, as if someone had taken the corner too quickly and lost control. She looked where she remembered it being and found the crumbled opening into the *cenote* gaping just ahead.

"You're sure the Sub-to-Surface troops have taken out the alarms?" Nori had already asked the question twice. But it was pretty freaking ominous to sneak into a place she knew for certain was being guarded.

"That was their objective." Cooper's whispered answer

was the same as last time. "We have to trust they did their job, that they took out both the alarms and anyone watching. Just as they trust us to take out the controls and personnel inside."

Nori exhaled at least three-breaths' worth of air. There was an awful lot of trust involved in a military operation. It suited her better to only rely on Cooper.

But the fact was she and Cooper had failed to take out the control panel and the people inside who were creating scorches. So here they were, part of a team.

The Lumineers stopped abruptly and Nori mimicked their action. Cooper didn't catch the halt as quickly, and bumped into her. He backed away, but not far.

Nori leaned into him as he supported her weight. She could feel his breaths at her neck, a private, tender moment before the violence began. It was full of emotion, of things left unsaid. And painfully brief.

A rippled nod began with the Lumineers and made its way back to the rear forces.

"Cover your ears," Cooper whispered and squeezed her waist.

No sooner had she put palms to the side of her head than an earth-wrenching *boom* shook the ground. Chunks of rock from the hole they'd just come through splashed into the water and particles fell from the stone ceiling. Dust and gun powder permeated the small space, and Nori pulled her shirt over her nose. She could smell her body's chemical makeup changing, her skin made sharp with nervous energy and fear. But it was better than the stifling air around them.

When the bomb detonated, silence and stealth were abandoned. Whether she was moving because someone yelled "Go, go, go!" or because everyone around her was go, go, going, Nori didn't know. But she went.

Someone had blown the locking mechanism off the thick metal door she and Cooper had gone through days— or was it weeks— before. Their mission accomplished, the Lumineers stood aside, backs against the water-worn wall as armed soldiers replaced them at the front line.

The *cenote* was a war zone now, hazy with smoke, filled with soldiers, and deafening with the alarm the bomb had triggered.

Cooper stood between Nori and the door, and Kade was... her search quickly became frantic when she couldn't find him.

"Where's Kade?" Nori screamed to be heard over the alarm, her voice pitched high with panic.

"Don't know," Cooper said and she barely heard the words. "... probably behind us somewhere."

"We have to wait for him."

Cooper didn't seem to understand her. Or didn't seem to agree. She planted her feet. "We can't leave Kade."

"... be fine," Nori heard him say between pauses in the the shrill alarm. "... no time."

"Yeah, but—" She shook her head, horrified. They couldn't leave Kade. She wouldn't.

"... can't wait, Nori. ... depending on us... on you.... big boy... his own job to do." Cooper's eyes never left hers, as if he willed her to understand, to do her part.

She was nauseous at the thought, but he was right. Kade was amazing, a survivor. He was probably ahead of them.

"Ready?" Cooper yelled.

She nodded and watched his face for the signal to enter as blinding white lights flashed in time to the blaring alarm.

Even through the haze she could read every thought that passed behind Cooper's eyes. She let his thoughts roll over her, like smoke over a stone. The one she looked for, and the one she acted on, was the final one that said, "Let's do this."

The farther into the ruined entrance they ran, the louder the alarm screamed. If her hands had been free, she would have covered her ears again, but Cooper had thrust a gun into them a millisecond before he ran into the facility. She had no choice but hold it and follow him in. Where had he gotten it?

What she never expected was for the pistol to be a comforting weight in her hands. She squeezed the smooth hilt as she followed Cooper, the metal warming in her palms. For a split second, she worried she might shoot him, or one of their own, inexperienced as she was, but gunfire—not hers— shot holes into any such thoughts.

Cooper threw his back to the wall and held up his gun, ready. Nori did the same but her pistol wobbled like a toy in the hands of a toddler. She tightened her grip to stop the shaking, closed her eyes and breathed as she searched for focus, for clarity. She was no good to them this way. Either she was part of this team, or she was a drain on Cooper, on all of them. She had decided to leave helpless behind. From now on, she was a part of the team.

"Hear that?" Cooper asked over the sharp crack of gunfire.

Nori nodded. She didn't trust her voice yet.

"They're on the other side of this wall," he said and swallowed. "You remember the color of their uniforms?"

"Gray." Good, she thought. She hadn't whined.

"Right," Cooper asnwered. "And ours are green. On the count of three, we're going around this corner. You duck and I'll stay high. Shoot the gray."

"But I can't — " she began.

"One."

"Cooper?" Nori was lightheaded, not breathing so much anymore as panting.

"Two."

"No, just wait… " She wasn't ready. She wasn't ready. She was not ready.

"Three."

Cooper pushed off the wall without ever looking in her direction, trusting she would pull her weight.

"God," Nori growled before scrambling around the corner, giving what she was sure was a bad impression of someone from a SWAT team.

Her finger flexed on the trigger, but she wasn't even sure how hard to pull. And didn't these things have a safety feature or something? Should she aim for their heads or their hearts? What if she missed and caused Cooper to get shot? Those and a dozen more thoughts raced through her brain in the milliseconds before she comprehended the state of the hallway.

There were no gray uniforms, only green. Eight of them. All eight lay crumpled on the concrete, the scarlet of their blood ruining the pristine floors.

38

ON THE INSIDE

"Rodgers?"

Cooper would recognize that mess of hair anywhere, even fanned across the floor and tinted with the garnet stain of his blood. Cooper's heart stuttered as he skidded onto his knees.

"Rodgers?" he said again, his voice cracking as he laid a hand on his friend's chest and neck.

The skin was warm, but he was gone. Cooper closed his eyes and shook his head, fighting back panic and grief. He couldn't deal with this. Not here. Not now. It was cry or curse, and he made it a good one.

"You knew him?" Nori's whispered voice was close-by.

"I did." Cooper swallowed before he could speak again. "He— "

Gunshots cracked through the hall again, and Cooper bolted upright, swiping Nori's wrist and pulling her to the wall beside him. "We have to keep moving," he said.

Nori's face was pale, her blue eyes huge as she nodded up at him. Her bottom lip trembled until she pulled it tight.

What he needed was to find Cal— if he hadn't been discovered and put in jail. Or killed. *No.* Cooper kicked the thought away. He hadn't found his best friend after all these years just to lose him again so soon. Although, he never had reason to believe luck was on his side. Fate had so far been like a bipolar fairy godmother, bestowing favors and curses with equal generosity.

No way to know but to find out. *Follow me,* he mouthed to Nori before creeping toward the sound of gunfire. At the metal door leading to the stairwell, he found her gaze again. *Ready?*

He moved to throw the door open and storm inside but before he could Nori jumped into the open doorway with her gun drawn like a vice cop in chase. He watched with near-hysteria as she swung her head— and gun— from left to right, doing her best to clear the area.

Cooper forced air in and out of his nostrils, afraid if he opened his mouth he wouldn't stop yelling at Nori until his voice was completely gone. If they survived this, he was going to strangle her impulsive little neck.

No one shot her. The stairwell was empty. Thank God.

"What on earth were you thinking?" he seethed once they were both inside with the door closed again. "What if someone had been on the other side of that door?"

"I'd have shot them." Nori's narrow shoulders shrugged beneath the olive green shirt she had borrowed from Meg.

"You'd have shot… " Cooper closed his eyes and inhaled to three. "Five minutes ago you couldn't stand to touch the thing."

"Well, you can't have it both ways," she smirked, and, God help him but he wanted to kiss her right then and there. Whether it was to remember what they were fighting for, or to do it before it was all over for both of them, he wasn't sure.

"Look, you want me to use the gun or not?" she asked.

"Yes. I mean, no." He shook his head, at a loss how to get her to grasp the seriousness of their situation. "Nori, you can't take risks like that. I'll do the jumping into doorways. You stay behind until we know it's clear."

"So, we're not a team?" Bits of her dark hair had fallen from a ponytail and she brushed them from her face with the hand not holding the gun.

"You know we are," he said.

"But you're the only one allowed to actually fight, to take any risks?"

"That's not what I'm saying."

"Isn't it?" When Nori's eyes narrowed, he looked anywhere but at them.

"I'm not ashamed of wanting to keep you safe, Nor," he said. "We're good at different things. I'm the brute strength and you're the secret weapon."

A line formed between her eyebrows and her lips drew together like a cinched purse. "Either we're in this together, Cooper, or we're not."

Without another word, she turned and ran up the stairs, leaving him to chase behind her.

"No-ri," he growled. But he followed.

Her point made, she finally slowed several steps up. "How are we going to find Cal?" she asked.

"It was part of the original plan. He'll have heard the alarms and knows to meet us at the control room we used last time." Cooper's mind produced a gut-punching image of Cal laid out on the floor like Rodgers had been, a pool of red oozing from his body. He closed his eyes, which only made the image clearer. "If he's able to, I mean."

Nori twisted to look at him, but didn't give up her position in the lead. "You think he got caught?" she asked. "Since we were here last time?"

He was about to answer when Nori whipped forward again, her back rigid. Adrenaline spiked through his veins as he peeked around her and caught sight of what she had seen. A CCC soldier ran down the stairs, pistol raised.

Cooper didn't move— couldn't— as the scene played out in painfully slow motion. The soldier took aim at Nori's chest as she fumbled with her gun. His movements felt like molasses, but he thrust forward, knocking Nori aside and taking the fire intended for her.

He was too late.

He searched Nori's face, frantic for answers. Her eyes were wild, her mouth open, but she didn't move. He scanned her body. No blood. Had she been shot or not?

No time to wonder further, Cooper lifted his gun at the gunman, but he wasn't there. Instead he lay propped against the wall, his head lolling unnaturally to the side.

Nori was speaking, he realized. Well, not speaking so much as mumbling "No, no, no," over and over again. Her eyes were huge and glazed and her tiny body shook all over.

"It's okay," he told her and took her into his arms. She turned her face from the dead soldier and into his shoulder with a shuddered breath. "It's all right," he said again. "You saved us. You did the right thing."

Nori nodded against him, but took several more breaths before pulling away.

"I'll be okay. I'm okay," she said after a while, but he had seen the disconnected look in her eyes before. She was in shock, which was good for now, but once it wore off…

"Let's keep going." Cooper helped her from the floor and pocketed the gun she dropped.

When she held out a hand for it, he took another long look at her face. There was no emotion there, only drive, and that was something he understood. Good. She would need the ability to turn emotions on and off if she was serious about a future with the Lumineers.

He handed the gun back without ceremony, but took the lead — and the stairs two at a time.

THE LAST TIME Cooper had been in the control room, he had helped Cal stuff bodies in a broom closet. There was no way they were still in there, but he could not help glancing at the door. His stomach soured when Nori looked, too.

The room was as cold and sterile as he remembered, though this time the lights were on. Cal was there, leaned back in a desk chair with an ankle crossed over a knee like he owned the place.

"About time, you two," he said. His grin was wide. Too wide. Cooper knew Cal Standridge well enough to know something else was going on.

Cooper lifted a hand to keep Nori back when the lights, the computer monitors — everything — flickered off and quickly back on. He thought little of the glitch until it happened again.

That's when Mathers slithered around the corner and into view. Three soldiers followed, the black barrels of their rifles pointed at Cooper's forehead.

Nori made a little squeak beside him, and he had a maniacal little thought he wished they *were* mice and could scurry beneath the door and out of this trap. Instead he stood straighter, lifting his chest and meeting Mathers' frigid stare.

Cal hadn't moved. What was he playing? Was he waiting for Cooper to save them all? That would be a first.

"Mr. Cooper, we meet again." Mathers' voice was a sliver of steel. "Your friend Standridge and I made a little wager," he said. He took a step forward, and Cooper took one back, angling himself in front of Nori.

"Standridge said there was no way you'd risk coming back here. Not when you so narrowly escaped last time." He scratched non-existent beard stubble. "But I thought you would."

Movement in Cal's hand caught Cooper's attention and he slanted eyes in his friend's direction then quickly back.

"Looks like I won." Mathers' grin belonged on a gargoyle guarding a gothic cathedral. "Why is that?" he asked. "Why'd you come back here? You don't honestly think you can take this place down? Surely you don't believe you can stop my army. Not really. Not when all your Settlement people lay bloodying my floors."

Cal was signaling again with his hands. Cooper couldn't be certain what his friend was trying to say, but he had a pretty good idea. Four against two. Well, and Nori. Not the worst odds they had ever played. And they still had their guns.

As if conjured by the thought, Mathers drew a black pistol from the holster at his hip and pressed it to Cal's temple. "Why don't you and the girl kick your guns over here, hmm?" Though worded like one, it was not a request.

Cooper turned and nodded to Nori, her face no longer

pale with shock but flushed, her cheeks pink and angry. She gripped the gun tightly, as if she would run away with it, but eventually laid it down. Cooper kicked it halfway to Mathers along with his own.

"Lock 'em up," Mathers said to the soldiers before turning a dead eye on Cal, "This weasel, too, until I can get to him."

It is a universal law of electricity that on the third flicker, the power stays off. When the lights surged a third time, the room went black.

In the complete absence of light, Cooper couldn't see Nori or Cal; couldn't see his own hand in front of his face. He patted his pockets; there was a flashlight somewhere.

The sickening *thwack* of metal to skull sent him crouching. Something— or someone— fell heavily to the ground. Male voices rose, and he reached behind him for Nori, but she was gone. Another thwack, a miserable groan, a weighted thud.

"Nori?"

She didn't answer.

Thwack. Thud. Thwack. Thud.

He reached into his pocket for a flashlight with clumsy fingers and by the time he clicked it on, four bodies lay unconscious on the floor.

When he found Nori's legs, he followed the beam of light to her face. Her eyes reflected blue-green in the light, a dead giveaway of her chemistry she could never outrun. She was smiling— s*miling*— a rifle in her hands, butt out.

"What did you do?" Cooper asked before shining the light in Cal's direction. His friend was bent over Mathers' body, which lay face-down as Cal tightened zip ties on his wrists.

"I knocked them out," she said. "Obviously."

"They won't stay out for long." Cal's voice was strained. "Cooper, cuff those guys."

He found zip ties on the soldiers' uniforms and bound them with their own restraints. Man, were they gonna be pissed when they woke.

"But…" Cooper shined his light at Nori, who threw an arm in front of her eyes. He pointed the beam at the floor. "How did you do all this?"

"I didn't knock them *all* out. Not Mathers, anyway." She looked up at Cal. "Was that you?"

"Oh yeah." Cal gave his trademark grin. "I've been wanting to do that for two years. I actually wish we could do the whole thing all over again."

"But…" That sick feeling was back in Cooper's stomach. "What if the lights had come back on, Nori? You could've been killed."

"But I wasn't," she said, and though he couldn't see her face, he imagined her eyes narrowing, her mouth turning up on one side in a smirk that said *he* was the ridiculous one.

"But you could've been," he said again, rubbing his temples to relieve some of the pressure behind his eyes.

"Don't take it personally, sister," Cal cut in. "He always plays too defensively."

39

CONTROL ROOM CHAOS

In the absence of flashing lights and blaring alarms, the halls of the CCC headquarters were eerily silent. Occasional gunfire still sounded, the crack and report amplified with no other sounds present. Despite a major loss of Settlement troops, Nori was comforted by the thought Kade must have been able to disable the electrical — even the room-sized generator.

Cooper and Cal followed close behind her, their narrow flashlight beams bouncing from hall to wall and back again. It had taken less time for Cooper to agree to let her lead this time. Hey, progress!

"Lindgren's lab is just ahead," Cal whispered. "Can you see it?"

"Yes," Cooper answered before Nori could, and she shot him a look.

"You really think he's in there with all this going on?" she asked. "Shouldn't he be somewhere, you know, manufacturing apocalypse."

"I told you he wants out," Cal said. "That he regrets what they've done."

"Well, it's convenient to ask for redemption *after* destroying the world, isn't it?"

She couldn't wait to lay eyes on Lindgren again. A vengeful fire burned deep within her to watch the scientist responsible for killing her siblings and so many others die a slow and agonizing death. Burning would definitely be involved, she thought darkly.

"If he hadn't sinned," Cal said from behind her, "why would he need redemption?"

Nori whirled around so quickly Cal nearly ran into her. "They've killed millions of people and destroyed an entire planet," she seethed. "If what you say is true, this guy is almost solely responsible. You don't get to say 'sorry' and get off scot-free. That's not how this works."

"That's not what I'm saying." Cal had guns in both hands, and he raised them in a gesture meant to be soothing, but didn't come off that way. "I'm saying it's *because* he feels remorse for all that death and destruction he's helping us now." He shook his head. "Anyway, we can't kill him. We need him to tell the world what they've done here."

"But he deserves to die." She knew she was angry, but the statement surprised even her.

"Yes," Cal agreed. "And he'll surely burn in hell for his role in the scorches. But right now, I'll take the help. Right now, we need him."

Despite the nausea she had felt in the stairwell after shooting that soldier, Nori thought she was probably capable of taking out those involved with the sunscorches without long-term mental effects. Cal was right, though. It would have to wait.

When they opened the door to the lab, Lindgren turned toward them. For a murderer, Nori thought, he really was a coward. His face was covered in sweat, which he wiped on the sleeve of his lab coat after removing his glasses.

"I zhought you veren't coming," he said and replaced the glasses. "Ve can do nah-zing vis no electricity. How do you plan to get out?"

"Oh, we're not leaving," Cooper seethed. "Not yet."

"But you agreed to get me out." Lindgren started to approach Cooper, but stopped. Probably after getting a good look at his face.

"Yeah, if you help us destroy this place," Cooper said. "You haven't kept up your end of the bargain."

"That," Cal said, "is soon to be remedied. Let's go."

"Vere to?" Lindgren scoffed. "Out zere is suicide. Let zhem all kill each ozher, and zhen ve go."

It was without conscious thought Nori stomped toward the scientist, pulled back her fist, and punched him squarely in the nose. It hurt worse than she had expected and, hissing, she put knuckles to her mouth as Lindgren bent to his knees and squealed.

Cooper jerked him up by the arm and shook him. "Shut up," he warned Lindgren as they left the lab in search of the primary control room, "Stay quiet, or I'll kill you myself."

"Lights off," Cal whispered and toggled his headlamp.

"How vill ve see anysing?" Lindgren grumbled. "You'll get us all killed."

"Nori," Cal said and turned to her. "We need to go up three floors and to the western-most part of the facility."

His faith in her abilities bolstered her confidence, and she nodded first to Cal, then Cooper, then lead the way.

"Zhe girl had Lumin?" Lindgren's tone held a reverence

that gave Nori chills, and not in a good way. She could imagine his eyes alight, eager to get his hands on her, part of the Great Experiment.

"I told you to shut up" Cooper said and jerked the man's arm so hard his teeth clacked.

No one uttered a word as they crept past open doors and hallways. A lucky thing, too, because they heard voices bouncing down the hallway three flights of stairs and a dark corridor later. Both beams of light and the voices stopped at the end of the hall.

"Commander Mills and primary control are just around the corner," Cal said, his voice so low Nori could barely hear it. "Probably three guards outside the door." He moved his head back and forth. "Maybe four. Anyway, we've got to get past them to get to Mills."

"Nori," Cooper said, "you and Lindgren stay here until our signal." He eyed her as if daring her to argue. "Then we'll go in together."

She shrugged. She had taken the last guards out. Cooper and Cal could do these if it made them feel better.

The two slipped around the corner, and in no time called for her to follow. Careful not to step on a random limb, she tiptoed past the downed soldiers, Lindgren helpless in the dark and hot on her heels.

<hr>

How did these idiots ever manage to destroy the world, Nori wondered as three headlamps swung in her direction.

There were no guards besides those posted outside the door, leaving the men in the primary control room on their own. They had gone unchallenged for so long they had let down their defenses. They weren't prepared in the least to protect themselves. Despite years of preparation and training, when the time came to go live, they weren't ready. Hubris, plain and simple. It would be their downfall.

He and Cal had guns trained on the men from the moment they swept into the room. Three or four battery-powered lanterns were placed around the space, and Cooper saw when one of them finally snapped out of it and went for a weapon.

"Hands where we can see them," Cooper's authoritative voice boomed as he stomped forward. "Lindgren," he said, "go get their weapons and headlamps."

The scientist blanched and opened and closed his mouth like a fish out of water. Ultimately, though, he did as Cooper instructed and crept toward each of his former colleagues like he was the one under fire. He collected everything and dumped it at Cooper's feet.

Besides the lanterns, a battery-powered clock above the control panels was the only other light in the room, its large red digital numbers casting a strange glow in the near-darkness.

"All right," Cooper said, "which one of you is Mills?"

When no one answered right away, Cal motioned toward an imposing man in the back. He had passed retirement age a decade before, but apparently no one had dared tell him. Nori could certainly see why. He emitted a vibe that was at the same time charming and menacing, like a serial killer in uniform. The man met each of their gazes, and when he turned his attention to Nori, a cold shiver ran the length of her body.

"I'm Commander Mills," he said. "Put those guns down and go back to your sandbox, and I might let you live."

"You're in no place to make demands, old man," Cooper

said, and Mills' stern face hardened to granite. "We're driving this bus now." Cooper kicked a rolling chair toward him and stared down the other two officials. "Have a seat."

"You little turd," Mills spat. "I'll have a seat when I'm dead and cold."

"I can help you with that," was Cooper's smooth reply.

Nori sucked in a breath. Cooper wouldn't really shoot him here. Would he? Yeah, she thought, he probably would. She waited for her stomach to roil at the thought, but nausea never arrived. And not only didn't she feel nauseous, she felt a complete lack of guilt about not feeling nauseous. If she wasn't so busy being inhumane, she might appreciate the amoral meta of it all.

"Oh, wait," Mills said, rolling his eyes. "Let me guess. We can do this the easy way or the hard way."

Cooper shrugged. "I like it. Which do you choose?"

"My choice is for you to go straight to hell." Mills' smile was acerbic. "You all can. We've been building this world longer than you've been alive," he said. "You think you punks can sneak in here and stop an entire mountain of trained military?"

He leaned back onto one of the darkened control panels, his face full of condescension. "Naive, bush league brats."

"Yeah?" Cal said, and closed in on him, "well this 'bush league brat' has been living under your nose for the last two years. Stealing your secrets, learning your plans, and," he leaned into Commander Mills and whispered conspiratorially, "sneaking out your single malt scotch."

"You little prick," Mills surged forward and grabbed Cal by the collar. "I'll send you to the chair for this."

"I don't think you will," Cal said, then threw in "Commander."

The distinct sound of military-issue boots double-timing toward them stopped all the posturing. Commander Mills smiled and moved a hand from the radio at his waist.

"You sneaky old— ," Cal began. "I'm gonna make sure you go down with this place."

"Enough," Cooper's tone was all business as he motioned toward the back of the room. "Mills, you and the others, against the wall."

When Mills scoffed, Cooper's voice thundered through the room. "Move!"

Nori held her rifle to her shoulder and joined Cooper and Cal, who faced the door ready for the aid Mills had silently requested.

There was no time to think before a horde of soldiers burst into the room. Lights were attached to the ends of their rifles, and Nori turned her head, temporarily blinded. Cooper dove for cover and jerked her down with him.

Braced against a metal file cabinet, she blinked and swallowed, desperate to clear her vision.

"You all right?" Cooper asked between breaths, but didn't wait for her answer before standing to shoot at the invaders.

"Yeah," she nodded, more to herself than him. "I'm okay."

"Too many," Cooper said, then, "What the— "

The air pressure shifted, like a door had opened. Nori peeked around the file cabinet to get a look at what had caught Cooper's attention.

Settlement troops. She did a mental fist pump and ducked back to safety.

"Stay here," Cooper commanded before rising to a crouch and rushing toward the fray.

She had just enough time to think *yeah right* before someone yelled "That's it. We got 'em."

That's when Nori saw him.

Commander Mills dove for Cooper from behind, a dagger in his left hand. With a grip on Cooper's right shoulder, Mills slipped the blade beneath his shoulder blade. Cooper went down with an "ooph."

Panic and horror sent her body shaking and she fell to her knees beside him. Her eyes locked on Cooper and she barely noticed Cal, who had tackled Mills, and Gisa, who had entered the room and was screaming at the top of her lungs.

Cooper's eyes were wide, his body stiff, but he was conscious. He was alive. Nori had a fraction of a second to feel relief before Gisa hit the floor beside her and frantically repeated, "no, no, no, no." She watched as the woman lifted Cooper's head and lay it in her lap, bending over him as her body wracked with sobs. Cooper and Gisa were close, Nori knew that. Her brain was a panicked and staticky mess, but the reaction was beyond bizarre for a soldier and his superior.

Someone was squeezing Nori's shoulder. She looked up, expecting Cal after he got Mills back under control, but she found Kade instead.

"Kade." The name left her lips in a child's voice. She was tiny and helpless and glad to see her friend but scared to death she had lost Sam Cooper.

"Mom?" A wholly unexpected word, Nori's head snapped back to Cooper, who was squinting up at Gisa.

"Where's Mills?" he asked and attempted to raise up. He didn't get far before throwing a hand to his back as his knees buckled. Nori rushed to help him lean against the control desk. "I can't decide what hurts worse," he said and sucked air through his teeth, "my head or my back."

"Well, I can't decide how you're not dead," Cal called from across the room.

"He missed," Cooper started to laugh, but groaned instead. "I mean, he stuck me pretty good." He pulled his hand away and it was covered in blood. "But he missed my heart."

"Oh, thank God," Gisa said. "Thank God."

Nori looked from Cooper to Gisa and back again. She raised eyebrows at him. "Care to explain?"

Besides the obvious pain, Cooper looked both embarrassed and contrite.

"Ah. Did I never tell you Gisa's was my mother?" He looked away conspicuously. "I thought I did."

"Pretty sure I'd remember that," she answered.

Cooper cleared his throat, and silence stretched for so long Cal changed the subject.

"Lindgren," Cal said. "It's time."

The scientist sat meekly in a corner of the room, sunk in a chair as if everyone would forget he was there if he just made himself small enough.

"Time for vhat?" he asked.

"To disable the combustion device," Cal said. "To stop the scorches once and for all."

The subject was probably the one thing that could detract Nori from the genealogical bombshell Cooper had just dropped.

Commander Mills' laugh began low and slow, but worked into a full-on maniacal cackle. Nori, Cooper, Kade, Gisa— everyone— turned toward him.

"What are you laughing about?" Cooper growled.

"Can't disable… without power," Mills said between frenzied howls.

Nori's heart sank with the realization he was right. It didn't stay down for long. Gisa's battle cry was powerful and practiced. She gave it just before she attacked Mills, who was tied to a rolling desk chair. She wrapped her hands around the man's neck, and he finally stopped laughing. His face turned red for a different reason.

Cooper lunged for them, but Cal got there first, pulling Gisa off of Mills.

"Ma'am," Cal was saying. "Ma'am. *Gisa*." She finally looked up. "We can't kill him. Not yet."

She fought Cal too, but finally closed her eyes and nodded. "No, you're right," she said, straightening her jacket and smoothing her bun.

"Excuse me," Kade said, addressing no one in particular. "I think I can fix it."

"What?" Nori asked at the same time as several others.

"I can fix it," Kade repeated. "I can turn it back on."

"The power?" Cooper asked.

"Yes. I can turn it on the same way I turned it off." Kade lifted his thick shoulders. "I just have to go back down to electrical. Rewire some things I tore apart."

Nori snuck a look at Mills, who had gone pale. His jaws flexed and she dared to hope again.

40

TERMINAL COMBUSTION

Not much had been said since Kade left to rewire the electrical. The room was thick with tension. Everyone was on high-alert, wary of more CCC soldiers— or for the whole thing to blow up in their faces.

"I found these butterfly bandages in the first aid kit," Nori said. She was wound impossibly tight, but staying busy helped keep her from unraveling. "They'll work for now," she said, "but you really need stitches."

"Doubt that'll happen anytime soon." Cooper grabbed her hands before she had a chance to lift up his shirt. He ran his thumbs across the back of her hands, a familiar touch that said much when they were surrounded by people and danger and world-destroying tech.

For Nori, seeing and touching the knife wound on Cooper's back, a real-life reminder of mortality, was a punch to the gut. She pulled her hands from his and breathed through the anxiety that sent her heart pounding. She worked on his wound, quelling her distress before he noticed. Her hands shook as she placed the final bandage across the angry red slash beneath his shoulder blade.

"All done." She patted his waist and left her hand there, touching her forehead to his bare back.

"Thank you." Cooper tried to hide a grimace as he turned. "Hey." He scooted toward her. "What's wrong?"

Nori ducked to hide tears pooling in her eyes, but he lifted her face. He must've seen how close she was to losing it because his eyes went wide as he pulled her into his body.

"I thought I was going to lose you," she said in a rush. "I thought that was it." She shook her head against his shoulder. "And God, Cooper, I wasn't sure I could leave this mountain without you."

"I'm fine," he said. "I'll be fine. We all will. You'll see." He pushed her back and found her gaze again. His green-gold eyes were hardened and sure. "We're so close, Nor. So close to stopping them."

She nodded as she ran a hand under her nose. "I know. I know that."

When the lights flickered, a heavy charge buzzed through the room and Cooper smiled. "See?"

The overhead lights flashed on first, followed by the slower powering-up of computers and control panels. Nori squinted. The room was too bright, too much, as the white overhead fought for attention with red and green at the controls.

"Lindgren, you're up," Cal called as if the scientist was next at-bat in a dugout.

He reluctantly took a chair in front of a computer and worked through several screens as everyone in the room watched.

"Now I need Mills' security key," he announced when a rectangular box popped onto the monitor.

"I thought you had that?" Cal said.

"I have mine." He knocked on his head. "In heyah. But Mills gets a new von efry day."

Mills, Nori noted with some suspicion, had not been objecting in a manner the situation called for. He sat silent. Smug, even, as everyone around him worked to save the world.

"Is that true?" Cooper asked, sitting up and pulling his shirt down over the fresh bandage. He marched to Mills dramatically and rifled through his pockets, ultimately pulling out an electronic keychain.

"This it?" he asked Lindgren, who nodded.

Cooper pressed a button, then looked between Mills and Lindgren. "It's not working."

"Fingaprint," Lindgren said, pointing to Mills.

Cooper seemed more than happy to man-handle the Commander, and his wide smile after twisting the man's finger onto the tiny keypad said it had worked.

Lindgren's hands were poised above the keyboard when Cooper called out the series of numbers and letters. But after several keystrokes and frustrated growls, he pushed the keyboard away. "It's not vherking."

"What do you mean, "not working?"" Cooper asked, his voice hard. "We checked the code twice. I watched you enter it."

Nori looked again to Commander Mills, who had sat as still as a monk while the others argued. He was far too at ease.

"What did you do?" Nori asked the Commander, whose steely grin returned. "What did you do?" she said louder.

"It can't be done," Mills replied. "You can't stop it. I made sure of *that* when I saw that bunch of hippies sneaking around outside."

Cooper was suddenly nose to nose with Commander Mills. "What do you mean?" Cooper demanded. "What can't be done?"

"Terminal combustion can't be disabled," Mills said haughtily. "I put the security feature into place hours ago. It's locked on go."

Nori followed Mills' gaze to the digital clock above the bank of controls. The one she had noticed earlier. When she comprehended what was happening, her heart left her chest, bludgeoned by each rung of an iron ladder as it fell to the basement of the military bunker. She wasn't looking at a battery-operated clock. The numbers were falling. It was a timer, and when it zeroed out the whole world was out of time.

"Cooper," Nori attempted to say, but had to clear her throat. "Cooper? Guys?" She pointed to the angry red numbers. "It's a countdown."

If the situation wasn't so very serious, it would have been comical. As if synchronized, everyone in the room froze and turned toward the counter. In unison, their eyes locked on the falling numbers and their mouths fell open.

"Is that... days?" Cal asked.

"Hours," Cooper croaked. "Less than two hours."

And in another heartbeat the stunned and synchronized silence was over, everyone speaking at once. Well, everyone but Cooper, whose gaze remained on the timer as seconds flashed by and disappeared.

"I'm really going to kill you this time," Gisa seethed, her hands twitching at her sides.

"Go ahead," Mills shrugged. "What's done is done. I'll die

happy knowing I've taken you bleeding hearts out along with the remaining pieces of trash who're picking the bones of my world clean."

The only thing keeping every one of them from pistol whipping Commander Orval Mills, Nori thought, was the fact Gisa Meier attempted it first. She lunged for Mills, gripping her gun's barrel behind her head as she readied to swing.

Cooper was quicker and caught Gisa's arm before she made it all the way down. "Wait," he said. "Just wait, Mother. Let us think."

Gisa's face contorted in rage and she fought Cooper to get at Mills again before settling down and jerking her arm away. She backed away from them both, sniffing to regain some composure.

Then, without warning, she bent forward and spat directly into Mills' face. If the crazed look in the man's eyes was any indicator, the insult did far more damage than the hard end of a gun would've. He wiped his face with a sleeve but kept a murderous gaze on the Settlement leader, whose chin pushed high.

"And that's 'Gisa' to you," she said, whipping her head in Cooper's direction.

Not one single emotion crossed Cooper's face as he nodded his understanding. Not even in his eyes. Nori's heart broke for him, because she understood a little better the complicated man she had grown to love.

When Cooper caught her looking, she tried to clear her face of pity. He saw it before she could, but his expression didn't harden.

"There's only one option left." Cooper spoke to Nori alone. She knew what he was thinking, and nodded her agreement. "Back to Plan A."

"I vill not participate in zhis." Lindgren folded his arms across his chest and leaned back in the chair. "No. Absolutely not."

"You'll kill us all, you damned idiots." The red of Commander Mills' face had spread to his ears. "And you won't change a thing."

"Cooper, are you sure this is the only way?" Gisa asked. "Surely there's something else we can do."

"Such as?" Cooper barely glanced at her, all-business just like she requested.

"Well, I don't know," she said. "That's what I'm relying on you all for."

"Then let us do our job." Cooper's tone was too sharp, and he closed his eyes for the span of a breath. When he opened them again, some of the fury was gone. "We've tried everything else we know to do."

"All right," Gisa said, not a hair in her light brown chignon out of place, "but we all have to agree. If we're risking suicide, it must be unanimous."

"What has to be unanimous?" Kade asked, maneuvering around several of the Settlement soldiers that had arrived with Gisa, standing just inside the control room door.

The vice of worry around Nori's heart loosened at the sight of her friend. He winked at her and crept into the room — inasmuch as a six-and-a-half-foot cage fighter can creep.

"Mr. Kade," Gisa said, her stern face lifting for a fraction of a second. "Excellent job on the electrical."

He ducked his dark head and uttered a mumbled, "Thank you."

With a welcoming slap on the back, Cooper filled Kade in

on the situation, his talent for getting to the crux of a problem particularly on-point. "Commander Mills has locked the terminal combustion, the final sun scorch, into schedule," he said. "We'll have to set this whole place to self-destruct to stop it."

"Oh that." Kade's light tone was heavy with irony. "I'm in."

"Me too," Nori said more to Cooper than anyone else.

"Food here sucks anyway," Cal said. "Let's do this."

All eyes turned to Gisa, who looked to her troops still stationed by the door, then nodded professionally to Cooper. "It's unanimous. Tell us your plan."

***

"Zhere has to be anozher vay." Lindgren leaned back in his chair, his bottom lip protruding like a petulant child.

"You've tried for an hour to cancel Mills' order." Cooper paced behind Lindgren, hands in his own hair. "You can't do it. None of us can. It didn't cancel out even when we shut down electrical."

"This is it, Lindgren," Cal said. "This is the only way."

"I von't do it." Lindgren shook his head. "I von't risk my life for zhis."

Before Nori could blink, Cal was in the scientist's face, a gun to the side of his head. "Your life *is* at risk," Cal seethed. "If you don't give us that number sequence, I'll take you out right now."

It was a bluff, and everyone knew it. Without Lindgren the terminal combustion would proceed on schedule. He literally held the security key to their success.

Nori had endured far too many hours in the same tense

room with the same stressed and angry people. Cal and Cooper had gagged Mills and the other officers early on, their objections so angry and loud she couldn't think.

Over and over again, Nori, Cooper, Gisa and Cal's pleas had met with Lindgren's refusal. Anger and threats weren't working. Lindgren had shut down like a robot off-grid and they were getting nowhere. Why had he agreed to help them in the first place if he was holding out now? Didn't he want out of the CCC? It wasn't like there was a place for him after the terminal combustion. Mills, the other officers, everyone knew Lindgren had betrayed them. He would be forced out— or worse— anyway. Hadn't Cal said Lindgren regretted the actions of his past?

Nori found a spare desk chair, pulled it beside the scientist, and took a seat.

"I was five when the first sunscorch hit," Nori said softly. "I remember bits and pieces, just flashes of memories like flickers of a movie in my head." She swallowed and rubbed her palms on her pants. "My father made a sound... I had never heard him make it, and I'll never forget it. It was like his voice was ripped from his throat." She swallowed and went on. "Then, a flash of light. A wave of stifling heat. The smell of melting plastic and burned hair. Confusion all around. My mother's screams. And the contrast of my brother's soft, pudgy legs to the concrete he lay crumpled on."

Lindgren's gaze left the timer and focused on the hands clenched in his lap. Nori spoke only to Lindgren, but the others in the room had gone still and silent.

"The baby," Nori purposely looked at Lindgren as she said her name, "Bevan, died that day in my mother's arms. Mom didn't know what was happening. None of us did. She instinctively bent her body over the baby's, but it didn't matter. She couldn't save her.

"Of course, I saw all of this through a window," Nori said. Her inhale was deep and shaky, and her voice was, too.

"I'd gone back into the restaurant for my raincoat. That's ironic, isn't it? I'd always been sensitive to the sun, wearing that raincoat every time I went outside, and it's what saved me when you monsters burned up the atmosphere and killed my siblings. You gave me a life sentence, but you also commuted it."

Nori shook her head to get back on track. "There were lots of babies lost that day," she said. "Lot of adults, too. After hearing Commander Mills talk, I imagine it's no coincidence the majority of them had little shelter. That they were poor. And brown."

Even bound and gagged, Mills got his message across. *Damn straight*, he said by way of a contemptuous nod.

Nori's temper flared at the man's undisguised disdain. For a moment, she thought to resume Gisa's grip on his fleshy white neck. But, no. She closed her eyes and flexed her hands to release some of their tension. She had a job to do. When she opened them again, she focused solely on Lindgren.

"Haven't you done enough damage?" she asked him. "Haven't you destroyed enough? Haven't you killed enough *children*?"

Her voice cracked on the last word, but she went on.

"Do you believe in God, Mr. Lindgren?" she asked.

A frown. A shake of the head. He didn't.

"A higher power, white light, Karma— something?"

Though he didn't answer, his eyes shifted down and to the right. He believed in *something*, and Nori seized it.

"Don't you see?" she said, scooting to the front of her

chair. "This may be the one way you can save your soul." Nori laid her hand on his, and he looked up, meeting her gaze for the first time since she had begun her story. "Please," she begged him. "Please help us save the people who are left."

Nori held her breath while the battle between good and evil played out in Hugo Lindgren's conscience.

She glanced at Cooper, who nodded his fierce approval. There was something else in Cooper's eyes, too, she noticed: amazement. A thrill threatened to skip across her shoulder blades, but she tamped it down. She would take pleasure in nothing until the terminal combustion was derailed.

It was clear the moment Lindgren came to a decision. His posture morphed into something proud, determined. He nodded once and attacked a computer keyboard.

"*Lindgren!*" Mills' words were clear even through the gag. There was no mistaking his furious tone. "*Don't you dare!*" Nori thought the Commander said. A vein bulged across his forehead. He kicked at his bindings, but they stayed put.

Lindgren ignored Mills completely and entered a series of keystrokes with dramatic flair. After a final, embellished click, he turned to Nori.

"It is done," he said.

41

GREAT ESCAPE

The ability to think during the sensory overload of a forced evacuation, Nori thought, was the true test for survival of the fittest. Red bulbs she hadn't noticed before flared to life, casting the room in an angry, urgent hue. The lights, along with the deafening alarm that blared every three seconds, prodded an instinctual drive to exit the facility as soon as possible. Exactly as it was intended to do.

Mills was screaming through his gag again, but no one paid attention.

"How long do we have?" asked Cooper.

"I set zhe self destruct before zhe terminal combustion. Ozherwise it does no good." Lindgren's eyes were shifty, but his voice was firm.

"How. Long." Cooper ground out.

As if answering him, an automated female voice drifted through the loudspeakers in an unnaturally-calm tone.

"Your attention, please. This facility is preparing to self-destruct. Please locate the nearest exit and follow predetermined escape routes. You have *twenty* minutes."

Nori—and everyone else—had frozen in place to hear the message. Once it was complete, though, the room exploded in an uproar of very foul, end-of-the-world-type language.

"Can we make it in twenty minutes?" Cooper asked.

"We can," Cal said. "We need to leave now, though."

"Lead the way," Cooper urged him.

"What about them?" Cal jerked a thumb toward Mills and the other officers, all bound together in their corner, all wide-eyed and rigid.

"Leave them," was Gisa's order, and no one argued.

Nori felt a twinge of guilt as she imagined their imminent death, the skin of their faces sliding off of bone like the Indiana Jones movie she had seen a lifetime ago with Cooper and Kade. Then she remembered their role in the calculated genocide of millions of people, and the guilt lessened to something more manageable.

"And Lindgren?" Cooper asked.

"We had a deal," Cal said, the pinch of his face indicating he would rather not have to speak his next words. "He kept his end. I'll keep mine."

"He should fry for his role in the scorches," Gisa said. "Deal or no deal. We'll leave him with the rest of them."

"No," Cal and Cooper said at the same time.

Gisa's head snapped back and she opened her mouth to argue, but she closed it and breathed through her nose. "He will go his own way, then," she said. "Cal, show us ours."

CAL PUNCHED ANGRILY at the button outside the elevator, but it was stuck somewhere between the seventh and eighth floors.

"We'll take the stairs," he said.

"Can we make thirteen floors in twenty minutes?" Cooper checked his watch, the brass face reflecting an ominous orange in the alarm lights.

"We'll have to be a lot faster than that," Cal answered. "We'll need to be far from the facility to live through the explosion."

"We should set a meet-up location," Kade said. "In case we get separated."

"Zhat is my cue," Lindgren said.

Nori didn't turn when he spoke, the thought of watching a mass murderer walk away too much to bear. She had picked up her gun as they left the control room and found herself tracing the trigger cage with her finger. It would be so easy, she thought. So easy to turn her body, and the gun, and put the slightest of pressure on the trigger. No one would care. No one would miss him. He certainly deserved it, and probably more.

Nori looked up when Cooper cleared his throat. He shook his head slowly, his gaze intent. Don't do it, his eyes said. You can't do that.

He was right, of course. But temptation was still there, and it was strong.

"Your attention, please. This facility is preparing to self-destruct. Please locate the nearest exit and follow predetermined escape routes. You have *fifteen* minutes."

"Already?" Nori said at the same time Kade threw out a string of curse words.

"Stairs. Now," Cal ordered.

He didn't have to repeat himself. Nori, Kade, Cooper, Gisa, and the soldiers sprinted behind him toward the end of the hall, where he threw open a metal stairwell door. Lindgren was nowhere to be found, and good riddance.

Nori had always been a strong runner, but Cooper usually gave her some competition. As the group raced up the stairs, he fell farther and farther behind. Somewhere around the ninth floor, she slowed.

"Is it the knife wound?" Nori asked him.

"I'm fine," Cooper said, though his voice was strained. "I'm right behind you."

"Stop for a minute and let me see," she said, stopping at the next landing.

"I'm *fine*, Nori," Cooper said and ran past her on the stairs.

She didn't argue, but quickly noticed the spot on his back.

"You're covered in blood. It's running down your leg, for God's sake."

He didn't turn, didn't answer, and she didn't bother him again. If he passed out from blood loss, well, he was going to be sorry. Actually, it was Kade who'd be sorry since he was the only one who could lift him.

"Eighth floor," someone, probably Cal, called from above, and Nori stopped climbing.

Eighth floor. The jail cells. Would someone open them under a self-destruct warning? She knew the answer. Not if idiots like Iberville were in charge of it. Prisoners were probably locked inside a death trap. No one would help them.

No one but her.

"Cooper," Nori called up the stairwell, but he didn't stop. "Cooper," she said louder.

He finally stopped, his head bowed as he gripped the railing. "What?" he said, his tone way past impatient.

"The people in the brig..." she said. "I have to let them out."

"I'm sure there's an automatic release or something when the place is set to blow itself up."

"It's all locked by key," she argued. "You know that."

"There are going to be casualties, Nori. We don't have time to save them."

"I have to, Cooper," she said and jerked the door to the eighth floor open. "Go ahead," she called as she stepped through the door frame. "I'll meet you at the rendezvous point." She didn't wait for his answer, but ran toward the cells and let the door close behind her.

It was a lot easier to navigate the hall when she wasn't being forcefully dragged. And thank God for that because the flashing lights and angry alarm made every inch of her body want to run the other way. "Get. Out." her brain demanded over and over, but she couldn't. Not knowing there were people inside. Maybe even people like her, who had been imprisoned but done no harm.

What she needed were keys. The halls were empty; whoever was on duty had obviously evacuated. She craned her neck and scanned the hall. There had to be an office somewhere.

"I bet you've waited your whole life to say 'rendezvous point.'" Though Nori's head was bent as she searched the tiny brig office for keys, she would know Cooper's voice anywhere.

"You should've gone ahead," she said, her hands shaking as she searched through drawers stuffed with paperwork. "This was my idea. No reason for you to risk your life, too."

"So, we're not a team?" Cooper asked.

She couldn't help but smile at her own words when he threw them back at her.

"Found 'em!" She snatched the keys from the desk and

raced down the narrow hallway beating on doors and hoping for an answer. "Hello?" she yelled. "Is anyone down here?"

"This one," Cooper yelled, peeking into the small, tall window of a cell Nori had already passed. She tossed him the keys.

The man who emerged was in his seventies, at least, his hair long and partially covering a dirty face marked with deep lines. His narrow back was hunched over thin legs that carried him despite a heavy limp.

"Place is going to blow," Cooper told the man. "Better make a run for it."

When the man glanced in Nori's direction, her breath caught in her throat. Something about his eyes scared her. They were close together and mean, and she had a sudden, panicked feeling of having made the wrong choice. She shook her head and looked away. Who lived and died was not her choice to make.

While Nori second-guessed her decision, Cooper had moved on to unlock another door, repeating his advice to a soldier still in uniform. He nodded thanks and raced in the other direction, and she breathed a little easier when the old man took off, too.

"No more," Cooper said, shaking his head and working to catch his breath.

Their gazes met, and they said at the same time, "Women's wing."

Only one answered their calls.

"Nori?" the voice inside the cell called back. "Nori, is that you? In here!"

"Indigo?" Nori raced to the door, her hands shaking as she manipulated the keys. "What are you doing back here?"

The woman emerged with much less fanfare than she had

the last time Nori stood outside her cell. There were both old and new bruises on her face, and one arm bent unnaturally in the middle.

"I could say the same to you." Indigo laughed, but then groaned. "Instead, I'll say thank you. Again." When the woman's eyes met hers, Nori saw a flash of pride. "Looks like you kept your head down," she said.

"And fists up," Nori finished with a grin. "Where's your husband? We've already checked the cells on this floor."

Indigo's battered face melted, and a look of profound grief dulled her eyes. "Gone," she said.

"I'm... so sorry," Nori said, then, with no time to lose, "You're coming with us."

Cooper jerked in surprise, but didn't say anything.

When the hollow female voice came over the loudspeaker again, Nori's body locked up.

"Your attention, please. This facility is preparing to self-destruct. Please locate the nearest exit and follow predetermined escape routes." An interminable pause. "You have *ten* minutes."

"Outta time," Nori yelled as she ran toward the stairwell. She didn't have to turn to know both Cooper and Indigo were hot on her heels.

Two floors up, she stopped so quickly she had to throw her hands out to stay upright. Kade was hurdling around the corner of the stairwell toward her and nearly bowled all three of them back down.

"Where have you been?" he yelled, breathless. "I turned around and you two were gone, and—" His mouth snapped shut almost comically. "Who is that?"

"No time," Nori said, forging past Kade and up the stairs again.

"If we don't make it out of here, Nori Chisholm," Kade said from behind her. "I'm going to murder you."

"Get in line," she thought she heard Cooper murmur darkly.

But four floors up, Cooper began to slow again. Nori trotted back down to where he stood staring straight ahead, seeing nothing.

When his knees buckled, she rushed to catch him, but he recovered his balance and leaned into the handrail. While Cooper pressed his forehead into the concrete wall, she lifted his shirt. The wound gaped vulgarly, rivulets of blood seeping from its mouth.

"Can you go on?" Nori asked, but he didn't answer.

"Come on, you two," Kade yelled from above. "What's the problem?"

"Cooper was stabbed today, in case you've forgotten," Nori yelled angrily back.

Kade was on the landing with them in a matter of seconds, ducking under Cooper's shoulder and lifting the right side of his body.

"Do your best, man," Kade said. "I've got you."

Their movements were awkward, but movement was the most important thing.

How far ahead was Gisa, Nori wondered. Had she made it to the top floor? Did she know her son was struggling to make it out alive? It was obvious she cared, but after the odd display in the control room, Nori doubted the woman had ever spared much maternal affection.

Nori stayed behind Cooper and Kade, more for moral support than anything else. What chance did she stand against their bulk, after all. Indigo brought up the rear, the flexing muscles of her thighs visible in ragged shorts.

Two more floors. They were going to make it.

"Your attention, please. This facility is preparing to self-destruct. Please locate the nearest exit and follow predetermined escape routes. You have *eight* minutes."

Five seconds after Nori passed the door marked "2," it swung open. Fleshy lips fell open in shock. *Iberville.*

A thousand thoughts flashed through her head. Kick him in the gut? Shoot him? Let him go? Her next move was decided for her when he unsnapped the holster at his side and raised a pistol in her direction.

He never saw Indigo coming. She launched herself at him, sending them both tumbling down the stairs. Iberville gave a fat grunt and Indigo let out a primal scream that made the hairs on Nori's arms stand up.

There was a gunshot. Then no more sound.

"Indigo?" Nori called.

No answer.

She leaned over the rail and looked down the stairwell. Both Indigo and Iberville lay sprawled on the third floor landing. Neither of them moved.

"Indigo?" Nori called louder. "You okay?"

Full-blown panic simmered just below her esophagus. She did not have time for this! Still, she raced down the flight to help her new friend. But when she got close enough, she froze. Indigo's eyes were open and blood seeped from her middle. Iberville's neck lay at an odd angle, pistol at his fingertips.

"Nori?" Kade called from above. "What's going on?"

Bending to close the lids of the Indigo's chestnut eyes, Nori closed her own and said a quick prayer for the woman who'd briefly but powerfully affected her life.

There was no time to linger. As if the obnoxious lights and

alarm weren't reminder enough, half-eaten food and discarded belongings littered the stairs and halls. There was evidence at every turn of people dropping everything to find the nearest exit. Something she needed to do, too.

"Your attention, please. This facility is preparing to self-destruct. Please locate the nearest exit and follow predetermined escape routes. You have *five* minutes."

"Nori?" Cooper's voice bounced down the stairwell, faint but urgent.

"I'm all right," she said. "I'm coming."

When she caught up to Cooper and Kade, they had reunited with the rest of the crew on the top floor of the facility. Gisa and a few Settlement soldiers were skidding down the hall opening and closing doors. What were they looking for?

"Your attention, please. This facility is preparing to self-destruct. Please locate the nearest exit and follow predetermined escape routes. You have *four* minutes."

Nori wanted to scream. She wanted to cry. She wanted out of the godforsaken place.

"Here it is!" Cal slid to a halt in front of them. Instead of a stairwell, there was a ladder leading up to a round turnstile door.

"A ladder?" Cooper groused and cursed.

"Leads out," Cal's breaths were hard and fast. "Or it's supposed to."

"You don't know?" Gisa's sharp tone shaved three inches from Cal's height.

"I know the residents' escape plan," he said. "Ours is different. They all evacuated into tunnels, but we're going to the Surface. This leads out of the mountain."

Nori couldn't breathe. "Is it daylight?" she asked, then louder, "Is it light outside? Does anyone know?"

"Kade, help me with this," Cal begged, his words guttural as he pushed up on the thick metal.

Kade leaned Cooper against the wall and climbed the ladder. Nori stood beneath them, chewing at the skin of her thumb as Kade squeezed in beside Cal.

She was lightheaded, and struggled to think. If she stayed in the bunker she would be blown to bits. It'd be quick, though. Not like if sunlight got her when Kade and Cal finally pushed open the door. Agony and infection from exposure was the very last way she would choose to die. Honestly, she would prefer to go like Indigo, unleashing her wrath on an abuser. Maybe she could find Lindgren if she left now.

"On three," Cal grunted. "One. Two. Three."

The rusted metal door creaked and groaned, but it finally broke free.

Nori performed a silent benediction, glancing longingly at Cooper. She would've liked more time with him. To show him the tenderness and acceptance that came with love he had probably never received. To wander the wilds of the Subterranean. To live the life they'd only just begun to plan together. And she would've liked to be a Lumineer, to be on the frontline, the only thing standing between purpose and darkness.

She would've liked to see her father again.

Sadness was suddenly overwhelming, and she struggled to shake it. She opened her eyes, feeling bleak and empty and scared, but prepared for whatever lay on the other side of that door.

Cooper stood in front of her, his hands gripping her shoulders as he shook her. "Nori," he was screaming, "we have to go."

She blinked. Glanced at the opening. Blinked again. Then grinned at Cooper, whose eyes were crazed as he tried to reach her.

She bolted for the dark opening. "What are you waiting for," she called behind her. "Let's go!"

THIRTY CAR GARAGE

How Cal Standridge, a notoriously bad driver, ended up behind the wheel Cooper had no idea. The double-cab military truck pitched and jerked with every grind of the gearshift. Cal's clutch work was primitive and unpracticed.

"Oh, whine a little louder," Cal said, the roll of his eyes visible in the rear view mirror. "I don't think your mom heard you."

Cooper gritted his teeth against the pain that speared through his back each time the truck took a corner. "When this is all over and I find you alone," Cooper said, "you're gonna wish your momma was there to save you."

"The way you're complaining," Cal shot back, "I doubt you make it out of here alive."

His and Cal's ribbing, tossing insults back and forth and bringing mommas into it, was an old habit, a way to distract themselves from the very real threats of danger. But nobody spoke after Cal's last comment, the protracted silence saying loud and clear what they were all thinking: it was likely *none* of them would make it out alive.

After helping pull Nori through the escape hatch, Cooper and what remained of their crew sprinted behind Cal until the new tunnel opened to an enormous underground garage.

There had only been one vehicle left in a space that could've housed fifty such military monsters. The one they appropriated had two flat tires— and a dead man beside it. He wasn't one of theirs, and no one spared the time to investigate what happened to him, though it wasn't hard to imagine. Guess Cal was wrong about everyone escaping through tunnels.

It was tough, but Cooper had made it into the back seat of the truck. Kade had shoved both him and Nori inside before climbing in behind them. Gisa rode shotgun, and what was left of the troops hopped in the covered truck bed.

Nori had scooted in close to him at first, fretting about things he had no control of, like the amount of his blood running onto the bench seat. He swatted her hands—and her concern—away. Getting out of the mountain alive was their priority. He would worry about the hole in his back if they were still breathing in two minutes.

He did worry about something else. Had Meg survived? Had she found a way out? His chest was so tight when he thought about his sister he could barely breathe.

Was Gisa even thinking about Meg?

He watched her in the front seat, the muscles of her arms flexing as she gripped the handle above her head. Even as the truck skidded wildly around corners, her back was straight. No indication she feared death.

"Turn there," Gisa ordered, pointing to a tunnel marked "exit." Never mind that Cal had already begun turning the wheel.

Whether it was the blood loss or the flashing lights that

gave Cooper the headache, he didn't know. He couldn't think past one driving thought pounding his brain with each beat of his pulse: get out of here before it blows.

"Faster, Cal," Cooper urged, gripping the seat in front of him. "You've got to go faster."

Cal caught his gaze in the rear-view mirror, the hazel of his eyes replaced mostly with white. Cooper felt a half-second's regret for putting more pressure on the man now responsible for all their lives.

"I'm trying," Cal said from the edge of the seat, his knuckles white on the steering wheel. "My God, don't you know I'm trying?"

Cooper nodded and gripped Nori's hand, leaning back to stare at the roof of the truck. Any second. Surely the place would implode any second.

But after an impossibly-tense eternity, Cal made a hard right turn and drove them out of the mountainside.

Cooper looked to Nori, the outline of her body bouncing in time to the ruined tires' rotations. He couldn't see her face, but imagined she was as relieved, as cautiously optimistic as he was. They might just make it.

Wait. He couldn't see her face because it was dark out. Thank God, he realized, rubbing at the pain in his chest. What would've happened if it'd been light? Cooper squeezed her hand again, silently vowing to take better care of her in the future. If they got through this, and there were no more scorches to deter, protecting Nori would be his new obsession.

The military truck's headlights illuminated blacktop that stretched toward another mountain peak. Cal nailed the gas pedal, throwing Cooper roughly back, but he did not let another moan escape.

He grinned at Cal and patted him roughly on the back.

"We're gonna make it," he said. "Guys, we're gonna make it out alive." The cab was eerily silent as everyone dared take a breath. Dared to hope.

The vibrations came first, a jarring tremor that pitched into a full-blown convulsion. Nori threw a hand out, probably in reflex, smacking Cooper in the neck. He clasped her hand to his chest and held on.

Sound came next, the long, low rumbles like a thunderstorm creeping behind them.

Then the explosion. Or rather, implosion.

It wasn't a fiery eruption that launched boulders a half-mile. It was the final dusty cough of an expiring giant buried deep in the Earth's core.

Cooper stuck his head from the window and looked back, but there was nothing to see. Nothing. Where a mountain once stood, there was only dust clouds and the cragged edges of a crater.

43

NEXT FOR NORI

The problem with war is once it's over there are no battles left to fight. Victors, and those losers fortunate enough to walk away, must find something else to do with their lives.

Nori stood on a rock cliff newly formed by the implosion. Still dark out, she closed her eyes, cherishing the final moments before she would be forced to return to Subterranean life where it was always a little too damp, a little too stale.

Even with her eyes closed, she knew the moment Cooper closed in behind her.

"You gonna miss this place?" he asked.

Nori smiled as she leaned back into his arms. "Definitely not."

"Have you thought any more about Chicago?"

She had known the conversation was coming, but that didn't make her any better prepared. Becoming a Lumineer was her future. She knew it in her soul, just as she knew she belonged with Cooper.

But her father was grieving and alone. And in truth, Nori hadn't given *herself* time to grieve. She had been fighting for her own life since she learned of her mother's death.

She pulled Cooper's arms tighter around her before revealing the decision she had made.

"I'm going back home to my dad's, to the 25th Parallel." She turned in Cooper's arms and looked up at him. "He needs me right now," she said, taking a breath and pushing back her emotions. "And I need him."

Cooper leaned forward and his lips brushed her forehead, her hair, her cheeks. "I know," he said. "I know."

She could hardly breathe he squeezed her so tightly but she didn't want him to let go.

"Nor?" he asked.

"Hm?" she mumbled into his chest.

"Do you need me?"

Nori couldn't remember a single time Sam Cooper had ever seemed insecure. She thought she had caught a glimpse of doubt once or twice before, but then he said something clever, or kissed her, and the moment was gone.

But when she leaned back to search his face, she found a tightness around his mouth, a question in his eyes. He honestly had no idea how much she needed him, how her life could never be the same without him. How she refused to even try.

"It's you I need most of all, Cooper." Nori stood on her toes to kiss his lips, which had parted at her words. His warm breath skated across her cheek in a sigh. Then neither of them worried about breathing at all.

44

SUBTERFUGE AND SUSPICION

Nori jerked awake at the shake of her shoulder.

"It's just me," Kade said and squatted beside her, his whisper urgent and his gaze focused beyond her to the entrance of the cathedral cavern.

"What is it?" Nori asked. Her throat was dry and scratchy from sleeping near a campfire that had long since reduced to embers.

"Something's going on," Kade said. "A group has just arrived."

"Can you tell who it is?" she asked at the same time Cooper peeled away from her back and raised onto one arm.

How long had they been asleep, she wondered. Much of the encampment was silent. Settlement soldiers lay crumpled across the cavern floor, exhausted from a battle hard-won.

"Is that Franks?" Cooper asked, his lip curled as if even the name put a bad taste in his mouth.

Zenon Franks was half-way through his story by the time Nori, Cooper and Kade made their way into the small crowd that had gathered at his arrival. The man seemed more than happy, though, to rehash some of the dicier bits once his audience had grown.

"That's when I pointed my rifle at the grenade," Franks said. "I was sweatin' at that point, I admit. But I said to him, I said, 'You go near that trigger again, I'll blow us both up. Try me if you think I'm kidding.'"

Franks elbowed a very tall, very serious-looking man beside him. Norton, Nori thought his name was.

"And these CCC soldiers kept you at bay for the entire battle?" Cooper cut in, his voice undetectable poison in sweet wine.

"Hell yes," Franks said. "Picked off a quarter of my men as we tried to advance."

"Why didn't you send someone for back-up? Why didn't you radio us?" Gisa asked the questions this time.

"I sent a runner, but he must've been intercepted." Franks lifted his arms in a helpless gesture. "And no one answered the call when I radioed."

A soldier Nori didn't know darted his eyes at the back of Franks' head then quickly away. Norton remained stoic, his eyes straight ahead.

"So how was it you were able to enter the facility just minutes before the explosion?" Cooper asked. "What happened to the stand-off?"

"They turned and ran!" Franks answered. "Or so we thought. After hearing now what went down, my guess is they got word of the self-destruct order and high-tailed it out of there. We followed them inside only to learn the place was about to blow."

"So you turned and ran, too." Cooper's cold look could've frozen time.

Franks' gaze snapped to Cooper's, and the two had a

stand-off of their own.

"I made a strategic decision that saved the lives of my remaining men, Mr. Cooper," Franks said, and Nori could almost swear she saw steam spewing from his ears. "As commander of this force, I don't have the liberty of being a lone wolf, of making deals with the devil and playing pretend with the enemy."

"Second," Gisa said, cutting off what Nori knew would've been a heated response from Cooper.

"What?" Franks barked, snapping an irritated gaze to Gisa.

"You're second in command of this force," Gisa said.

"Of course," Franks ground out. "Everyone knows that."

Gisa's lips were a hard, thin line and she lifted her head just once, leaving her response unsaid. But the words came easily to Nori's mind. Sometimes Gisa wondered if *he* knew it.

The crowd dispersed. Some went back to their beds and some warmed by fires. It was only an hour or so later when Meg and Jake limped into the cathedral cavern, too. Cooper's relief was visible, as if he was only then able to take a full breath. He rushed to his sister, covering the top half of her body in an embrace.

Jake made a sharp grimace, then braced himself against the wall and slid down to the rock floor. There was a deep gash across one cheek, he held his arm strangely close to his side, and his pants were ripped and covered in blood.

"Medic!" Nori shouted, and a flurry of activity quickly surrounded them.

Cooper hadn't moved far from Meg during the ordeal, and, with a start, looked from her to Jake. "Where's Newt?" he asked.

Meg shook her head as she swiped a tear from her cheek.

"He'll turn up!" Jake yelled obstinately from the floor, jerking from the man trying to clean his wounds. "He'll turn up," he said again.

Nori hoped Jake was right about his twin, though she couldn't help thinking he was buried somewhere beneath the mountain like so many others.

NO CONTEST

Cooper took one last look at the men and women who had made it back to the cathedral cavern. Parting with what was left of the Settlement forces was bittersweet. They were battered and bruised, but alive. He couldn't help but think of Rodgers and Newt and so many others who would never leave the decimated mountain bunker. The Settlement had suffered substantial losses, but the world had won. There would be no more sunscorches.

Whether Lindgren had survived, and what was next for him and the others who escaped was anyone's guess. There were certainly other military bunkers. The closest was Cheyenne Mountain in Colorado, which was not close at all. How many had heeded the self-destruct warning and gotten away? Were they somewhere regrouping, plotting world destruction and domination yet again?

No. Cooper shook his head. Destroying the CCC headquarters had crippled the operation. There might be survivors, but they weren't going to be a threat anytime soon. And never again if he had anything to do with it.

Cinching his motorcycle's saddlebag, Cooper prepared to leave and searched the crowd for Gisa. She had certainly kept her distance since they returned to the cavern. When he stood the bike and readied to mount, he finally spotted her. Her sleek bun had not a hair out of place as she held her hand high in a cold farewell.

Cooper ignored the gesture, resting the bike and stalking toward her. Her eyes went wide, but he paid her stiff posture no mind and ran his arms around her thin shoulders. From now on, he was hugging his mother whether she admitted she wanted the affection or not.

As for she and Franks, a storm had been brewing for years and it looked like rain was on the horizon. Cooper suspected she had a battle to face when she reached the Settlement, but she would not be alone. She had Meg and Cal and so many others.

But Cooper couldn't be there for her. Not yet. His priority lay elsewhere.

"You ready?" Nori asked. She slid a leg over his bike and settled at the front of the seat. When she patted the seat behind her, he arched an eyebrow.

"I'll take first shift driving," she said and winked. "We're a team, remember?"

Cooper shook his head, then saluted the woman he loved.

ACKNOWLEDGMENTS

I'm not afraid to admit 2018 was a tough year. Both *Sunscorched* and *Terminal Combustion* were released after months (years?) of work. This, on top of family commitments which are, to put it mildly, freaking extensive.

But we all have work and responsibilities— and lives, don't we? I hope your friends and family are as generous with their support as mine have been, for without them, I could not pursue my dream. I could not produce these books.

Without a husband who does far more than his fair share of things at home, and pushes me out the door for long weekends alone to create, I could not build worlds. Without a dear friend who buys me chocolate, pitches in with my family, and makes sure I don't go nuts, I could not stay on track.

To the best readers in the world:

Thank you for supporting me and my writing. Thanks for your encouragement, thank you for your kind notes and generous reviews. Thank you for recommending this series to your friends.

To Brock, E., L.B., and H., who are the joy and loves of

my life! Thank you for understanding tight deadlines and long nights, and never making me feel guilty about them.

To Bebe and Gary, Marianne, Papaw, Angela, Erica, Skyler, Peyton, Brinda, Kathleen, Kelly, Rachel, Kat, Marissa and Dave D. for support and encouragement. To Beau, for answering my many military questions.

To Brooke L., who's become an invaluable resource and friend.

To Peter Seftleben for thoughtful and meticulous editing and advice.

To Cassie Hess for lightening-fast proofreading.

To Cary Smith for exceptional cover art and a shocking amount of patience.

Thank you. Your support is so appreciated.

ABOUT THE AUTHOR

 Though she grew up on a working cattle ranch, it's fantasy and sci-fi that shine Jen Crane's saddle. Her novel Sunscorched received the 2017 Rosemary Award for excellence in young adult fiction.

Jen has a master's degree and solid work histories in government and non-profit administration. But just in the nick of time she pronounced life *too real* for nonfiction. She now creates endearing characters and alternate realms filled with adventure, magic, and love. She lives in the southern US with her family and too many pets.

Sign up for sneak peeks, news, and giveaways (*and a free six-chapter novella in the Subterranean world*) at

    bit.ly/JenCraneNewsletter

Follow Jen on social media @JenCraneBooks